Additional Acclaim for *The Night Country*

"Scary, sad, funny, and when it comes to young people at the end of their ropes and hopes, dead on the money. [*The Night Country*] takes you away to a strange and special place while reminding you of the places you've been—especially the spooky Halloween places. A gracefully written, mesmerizing read."
—Steven King, author of *Wolves of the Calla*

"O'Nan has . . . [an] extraordinary ability to enter the lives of a diverse spectrum of people."
—*St. Louis Post-Dispatch*

"O'Nan is wonderful at describing teenaged ritual."
—*The New York Times Book Review*

"[O'Nan] upholds his reputation in this rigorously contemporary tale of life and death, in which he renders small-town strip malls as eerie as any haunted castle."
—*The Seattle Times*

"Haunts the reader from page one . . . There's truth to be found on nearly every page of this book."
—*January Magazine*

"Leave it to author Stewart O'Nan to take this idea of a 'holiday book' and turn it into a really gorgeous portrait of small-town life and death."
—*The Capital Times*

"*The Night Country* burrows into the heart of suburbia with surgical skill . . . Never has elegiac writing been so simultaneously lovely and fun."
—*Trashotron.com*

THE NIGHT COUNTRY

STEWART O'NAN

PICADOR

FARRAR, STRAUS AND GIROUX **NEW YORK**

The author would like to acknowledge and thank Brett Eisenlohr, Drew Gallagher, and Timothy Ray for generously sharing their expertise.

www.picadorusa.com

Picador® is a U.S. registered trademark and is used by Farrar, Straus and Giroux under license from Pan Books Limited.

For information on Picador Reading Group Guides, as well as ordering, please contact the Trade Marketing department at St. Martin's Press.
Phone: 1-800-221-7945 extension 763
Fax: 212-677-7456
E-mail: trademarketing@stmartins.com

Designed by Gretchen Achilles

Library of Congress Cataloging-in-Publication Data

O'Nan, Stewart, 1961–
     The night country / Stewart O'Nan.
       p. cm.
     ISBN 0-312-42407-8
     EAN 978-0312-42407-7
     1. Traffic accident victims—Fiction. 2. City and town life—Fiction. 3. New England—Fiction. 4. Halloween—Fiction. 5. Teenagers—Fiction. I. Title: Night country. II. Title.

     PS3565.N316N54 2003
     813'.54—dc21

First published in the United States by Farrar, Straus and Giroux

First Picador Edition: October 2004

10 9 8 7 6 5 4 3 2 1

FOR RAY BRADBURY

Is it possible to feel love for a sidestreet without sidewalks? For parked cars and wooden houses?

THEODORE WEESNER

I hate myself and want to die.

KURT COBAIN

THE NIGHT COUNTRY

COME, DO YOU HEAR IT? The wind—murmuring in the eaves, scouring the bare trees. How it howls, almost musical, a harmony of old moans. The house seems to breathe, an invalid. Leave your scary movie marathon; this is better than TV. Leave the lights out. The blue glow follows you down the hall. Go to the window in the unused room, the cold seeping through the glass. The moon is risen, caught in nodding branches. The image holds you, black trunks backlit, one silver ray fallen across the deck, beckoning. It's a romance, this invitation to lunacy (lycanthropy, a dance with the vampire), elemental yet forbidden, tempting, something remembered in the blood.

Don't you ever wonder?

Don't you want to know?

Come then, come with us, out into the night. Come now, America the lovesick, America the timid, the blessed, the educated, come stalk the dark backroads and stand outside the bright houses, calm as murderers in the yard, quiet as deer. Come, you slumberers, you lumps, arise from your legion of sleep and fly over the wild woods. Come, all you dreamers, all you zombies, all you monsters. What are you doing anyway, paying the bills, washing the dishes, waiting for the doorbell? Come on, take your keys, leave the bowl of candy on the porch, put on the suffocating mask of someone else and breathe. Be someone you don't love so much, for once. Listen: like the children, we only have one night.

It'll be fun, trust me. We're not going to get caught. It's a game anyway, a masquerade. This is the suburbs; nothing happens here.

So come, friends, strangers, lovers, neighbors. Come out of your den with the big-screen TV, come out of your warm house and into the cool night. Smell the wet leaves crushed to mush on the driveway, a stale mix of dust and coriander in the wind. It's the best time of year up here, the only season you want from us, our pastoral past—witch hunts and woodsmoke, the quaintly named dead in mossy churchyards. Never mind that it's all gone, the white picket fences easy-to-clean vinyl, the friendship quilts stitched in the Dominican, this is still a new England, garden-green, veined with black rivers and massacres.

Keep coming, past the last square of sidewalk, past the new developments and their sparse lawns, past the stripmalls with the Friendly's and the Chili's and the Gap, the CVS and the Starbucks and the Blockbuster, the KFC and the Chinese, their signs dying comets in the night, traffic signals blinking. Come back through Stagecoach Lane and Blueberry Way and Old Mill Place, solving the labyrinth of raised ranches where the last kids (too old but not wanting to grow up just yet) spill from minivans like commandos, charging across lawns for the front door, their bags rattling. The candy is serious here, full-sized Hershey bars and double Reese's Cups. No, there's no time to stop, no need. That's in the past, the happy childhood we all should have had, did have, half missed, didn't appreciate. Keep your mask on. Say something now, it would give us all away. We're past that, the grinning pumpkins left behind, the stoops and warm windows, the reaching streetlights. Out here there's nothing but muddy creeks and marshland, stone fences guarding back pasture gone wild. Here you can still get lost if you want to.

So come ride with us, driving the night in circles, the trees startled in our headlights. What, you don't recognize the road, the blind curves and crumbled cutbanks twisting so we lean into each other, intimate, even cozy, laughing as we crush the one on the end against the locked door? Remember the incense of cigarettes, the little attendant rituals. Make your fingers a scissors and bum one, it's okay, just don't pocket my lighter. The music's too loud to talk and there's no reason, we're happy trapped in ourselves and the night, this illusion of endlessness—high school, the freedom of wheels. Be seventeen again and ready for the world to love you. Feel the speed through the floor, the air lipping the windows. We're cutting corners, bowing the yellow line, floating over bumps. A deer and that would be the end of us, yet the driver only goes faster, the woods dark as space, still wilderness.

Look around now. Do you remember any of us? Your face has changed; ours are the same, frozen in yearbook photos in the local papers, nudged up against the schoolboard news, the football scores, the library booksale. One week we're history, martyred gods, then forgotten. Our names, you can't even make a guess (it's those kids that died), but you remember what happened. So you know where we're going.

Have you seen it? Not just driven by, but have you stopped and gotten out and looked at the tattered bows and ribbons, the sagging mylar balloons and greening pictures sealed in freezer bags, the plastic crosses and browning flowers, the notes written in girlish script, illegible now, pledging to remember us forever? Have you searched the trunk for scars, amazed at nature, since there's not a mark on it?

Of course not. Even if you were from around here you'd be used to it, maybe even annoyed at the cards and flowers, the shameless sentimentality of teenagers. Don't worry, they'll graduate and move away, and then our younger brothers and sisters, off to college and jobs and marriage, leaving our parents, a mother who dedicates herself to a larger cause, a father who turns inward and strange. One wraps herself in bitterness, another discovers religion. Do they change into gaudy polyester snowbirds or let the house fall down around them? Whatever. Everyone forgets— you have to, isn't that true? Isn't that proof that time is merciful, and not the opposite?

Don't answer. You'll have time to think about it later—an entire night, an eternity. Halloween comes once a year.

Can you breathe inside that thing? It's not too hot, is it?

But look, we're almost there, where the curve bears down on the crossroads. There's no other car, no bad luck, just the tree, the slick of wet leaves on the road, the romance of speed. It's the time of year that kills us, a lack of friction combined with a sideways vector, loose and centrifugal. The police will reconstruct it, pacing off the distances with a limp measuring tape (there's my lighter by the red X), taking statements from the people on-scene, photocopying the long report for the courts and insurance companies. Someone you love has read it or not read it, the contents life-changing and unimportant, checks deposited, money spent.

From the backseat you can't see the tree, or only at the last minute, if you happen to be backseat driving, chickenshit ("Slow *down*"). There's a second in which we realize we're not going to make the curve—all of us, even the most hopeful. The sound of the road, so constant, disappears, vacuumed into black silence. Light comes back from the trunk, as if the tree has flashed its brights, warning us off at the last second. It *is* a game of chicken.

"Oh *shit*," Danielle says; you feel it because she's on your lap, your arms wrapped around her ribs, her perfumed thinness.

"Toe, you fuck"—Kyle, right beside you. (Who? Toe, Kyle, Danielle. See, you've already forgotten. What's my name? What's yours?)

It's a trick (not a treat), but the tree seems to leap out, seems to drive right at us, wide as a semi. Scream if you want to. After the first few times you'll realize it's useless. You'll remember us, and remember to say good-bye. You'll grow as sentimental as our friends and make this night and this drive stand for our lives, the five of us inseparable. So keep your eyes open. Don't cover your face as we leave the road and shoot through the high weeds (sifted by the grille like wheat meeting a thresher). Remember what happens, how it sounds and smells and tastes. Enjoy the ride.

Didn't I tell you? There's a reason we call on you, why this night comes again and again, bad dream within a dream. You think it's torture but you know it's justice. You know the reason. You're the lucky one, remember? You live.

BROOKS'S WATCH GOES OFF IN THE DARK CAR, military, the way he's set it since basic, another inelastic habit, and tomorrow starts at zero, a clean slate. There is no midnight, just a digital tick at 23:59:59 that crosses off yesterday, says he's got seven more hours before he can go home to no one (just us, sitting in his kitchen, flitting through the woods). The dogs bark, even with the kitchen light on (and you know we love to tease them), but where they're at it's not a problem. All the way to the front door he'll hear them warning him to leave, just get back in the truck and drive, and don't think he hasn't thought about it. If it wasn't for Gram, Brooks thinks he would—leave it all to the realtor—but that might be a lie. He's lived here his entire life, a real townie; he wouldn't know where to go. (He's going nowhere. We've seen him hang up his gun in slow motion, deliberate as a horror flick, and only Toe's twisted enough to make the holster swing, a cheesy temptation. Don't think about us too much, Brooksie.)

His watch goes off, cheap Korean double-beep, and wherever he is around town—cruising the shadowed docks of the Stop'n'Shop, cherrypicking in Battiston's parking lot for fathers trying to get their videos back on time—he can see the fastest route to the tree, like a diagram, the map on the wall at dispatch lit up, Old Farms branching off Country Club, taking him there too late, always too late.

So no one has to tell Brooks it's the anniversary. There's one every night—*bee-beep*—and he's been dreading it since mid-September, watching the leaves drop, the wind dragging them scratching over the roads, massing drifts in the lee of his truck, maple seed whirlybirds lining the wipers. Weekends he skips his wake-up shower and rakes himself into a dizzy sweat. He knows he can't stop the fall, the painfully clear days, the frost on the grass; it's just the rotation of the earth, its senseless spin around the sun—out of control, no brakes. He's lucky there were no tasteless jokes at the station, no cardboard skeletons squirted with runny vampire blood and shoved in his locker (maybe there are, maybe right now Ravitch is scheming at his console, deciding how far he can go with him; it's a night for phony phone calls).

Tonight it's Battiston's, old faithful, running radar, his cruiser tucked behind the landscaped hump, the darkened cleaners at his back with its still carousel of plastic hanging bags—stiff tuxedos and Cinderella gowns for the fall formal. Last Friday's movies are due. Brooks waits in the dark, the tiny red light shuttling over the face of the scanner, searching for voices. He put too much sugar in his coffee and it's making him twitch. He wants something routine, something dumb, just something to chew on, like the plastic stirrer he realizes he's chomping flat, another bad habit. He stops and folds it into the ashtray among the gum wrappers.

He hates midnights; days there are errands to run, favors to do for the chief. He never thought he'd miss them.

Across 44, a silver Mercedes SUV slips into Webster Bank's drive-thru. Brooks files away the state plates. The rest of the plaza's bare, nothing but parking spots—white lines and oil stains, the high lights burning without purpose.

Today's the day, tonight's the night. What does it mean, if anything? Every season has its tragedies, and how can you take back something that's done? It's the argument he used to have with Melissa. Now that she's gone he takes both sides and fights by himself. (We don't have to do anything, just sit and listen in; Danielle says it's cruel, and that starts a different argument.)

He wants a call to stop him from thinking and checks the green screen, the cursor tinting his hands like Frankenstein. He has reason to be hopeful; it's still Cabbage Night, home of soaped windows and pegged eggs and toilet paper orchards, the free delivery of sizzling dog doo, and that staple of Avon, mailbox baseball. Just the aftermath, that's all he wants, one of our fathers pissed-off in his slippers, asking what Brooks is going to do about it—some unhappy taxpayer used to pushing his secretary's buttons. "First I need to take your information," he'll say, letting whatever kids did it get away clean, no muss no fuss, all the while the cherry strobing over the housefront, telling the neighbors everything's under control. "And you said you didn't see a car, just heard the mailbox and that was it?"

This is your big hero. Because there has to be a hero, right, someone to root for? Sorry, he's all we've got, him and Tim, and Tim can't be the hero, can he? (Toe thinks what Tim is going to do is heroic, or at least supercool, but Toe, of course, is a psycho. Danielle thinks it's stupid, that's all she'll say; she's still mad at him. Me—hi, I'm Marco—I'm in the middle. I'm the quiet one.

You'll see, nobody listens to me.) I don't even know if we're going to try to do Kyle, he's so messed up. You'll see, he's a good guy, Brooksie, a little whacked after everything but who isn't. It's not a perfect world. It's not a perfect story, just something random that happened to us, bad luck. Of course you can't tell that to Brooks. He's the kind of guy who needs reasons for everything, who needs everything to make sense.

A call, a false alarm, a fire, a barking dog, a heart attack, backup on a car stop, a domestic, a prank, a prowler, but there's nothing coming in, no one screaming down 44 for the Blockbuster. He runs the Mercedes' plates for the hell of it, using two fingers. Enter, send. The screen goes black, the faded light trapped in his eyeballs, then flashes on again.

Registered to a local: Ronald Seung, 25 Candlewood Terrace—no wants or warrants. What did he expect?

He knows he has to relax. Midnights you have to just let time go by. Five minutes into the longest day of his life (by a mile; this one he's taking to the grave), Brooks is clockwatching. He thinks of closing his eyes right there and cooping—ten minutes, that's all he wants. He had to wake up early and clear out of the house so Charity the realtor could show it empty, and now that missing sleep is catching up with him. He's never going to sell the place with the roof looking like that, but he doesn't have the money to fix it; he's going to take a hit on it one way or the other. He dreams of Florida and fishing for tarpon, walking the dogs on a white beach, throwing bony driftwood sticks for them to fight over, but it's just a dream, a cheesy ending to a movie. He's got six years till he can take retirement—seven, really—and Ginger's already ten, Skip's eight; they won't make it. (He won't think about Gram in her cubicle of a room at Golden Horizons, the picture of him with the red cowboy hat and silver pistols on the wall, very cute.) He'll rent a townhouse over at Towerview and shove most of his stuff in storage—if they take dogs. If not, there's always that place in Canton Charity recommended; it's cheaper anyway. But he's always lived in Avon, it's his town. How many people can say they're natives? It seems like everything's being taken away from him. (Tell us how that feels.)

He's trying to think of the name of that place down by the Farmington line when a white Cabriolet flashes past, clocking a 53 on the Stalker. It blows through the blinking yellow in front of the Blockbuster, too fast for him to get the tag, that smoked plastic over it that should be illegal.

No brakes, they don't even see him. Or if they do, they're not stopping.

And here's where we come in, where we tap old Brooksie on the shoulder and he thinks it could be us, it could be last Halloween, before he got the medal and then the story came out in the paper and everything turned to shit. Maybe this is a test, a second chance, to see if he's learned his lesson. A blink, a thought bombing like an electron across the dark screen of his brain, that's how fast it is—a picture of Toe's mom's old Camry with the door torn off and one turn signal blinking—tink, tink, tink. If he does nothing, nothing bad can happen. But reflex is quicker than thought, and his hands have memories of their own.

For a second he forgets his lights and surges out invisible, only realizes he's driving blind when he outruns the glow of the plaza and can't read his speed. He twists the stem and guns the Crown Vic, the goose of his foot sending the front end drifting. He lets up and gets it under control, muscles out into the left lane so no one can pull in on him.

He's got them in visual, far down the long hill, flying by the

commuter lot by the new Wal-Mart (impressive, a definite improvement on the Caldor's with its shoddy offbrands and slow-
motion cashiers), by the drive-thru dry cleaners that used to be a
Fleet Bank, by the Foreign Auto Experts with their lot full of
deathtrap Fiats. Nothing's open this late, and the lights are blinking yellow, a free shot all the way to Old Farms (come on,
Brooksie, it's Halloween, you didn't forget us, did you?). After that there's only Route 10 before the long climb up Avon
Mountain to the town line. He decides to hang back, not pop on
his takedown lights—a tactic he learned at his mandatory classes,
and completely against his instincts, but comforting now, knowing he can just escort the Cabriolet out of town and let West
Hartford deal with them.

Why doesn't he call it in? All he'd have to do is hit the button and say he's got a 10-36—vehicle evading a stop—and his
supervisor would be right on to advise him. But then he'd be at
the mercy of the new pursuit policy. (Thank you, thank you very
much. Nice of you to remember us.)

He loses them at the dip past the bagel place and picks them
up again beside Stub Pond, blazing the straightaway. His instinct
is to punch the Vic, torque it and let that interceptor V-8 catch
him up, but he feels us, noisy as little kids in the backseat, and the
heat of the chase dissipates. It feels wrong, a trick, as if there's no
right answer. The Cabriolet brakes to make the ess curve ahead,
and he loses visual again, the taillights eclipsed. They're coming
right by the station; Ravitch could be sneaking a smoke with the
side door open, watching, wondering what he's up to. He eases
out of the curve and into the splash of orange lights leading to
town center, just in time to see the Cabby cut the right onto Old
Farms Road (don't roll it, he prays).

I swear to God it's not us, but Brooks is having flashbacks. (Toe laughs and Danielle tells him to shut up. Nothing's funny to her; you wouldn't believe it, she's turned into such a bitch.)

He slows. There's no one at the intersection, the old colonial heart of Avon. On his left the Congregational church rises white and commanding, its steeple floodlit, throwing the graveyard in back in shadow; on his right shines O'Neill Chevrolet, its carpeted showroom the ghost of the IGA his mother shopped at when he was a boy, the aisles a mint green linoleum from before he was born, the corners chipping to show the prehistoric floor underneath.

Brooks has infinite choices at this point (the past, the present, the future—the dude is like Mr. Magoo's Scrooge and we're his spirits: "Tell me, Spirit, are these things that might be or things that must be?") He still hasn't called the 36 in. He could go straight and cruise 44 up the mountain to the town line, come back and set up behind the WELCOME TO AVON sign by the golf course, screened by the trees. He could wait and take a left, sweep the lots at the post office and Sperry Park with his spot (there's a kid working over the concession stand with a box of chalk and a tube of superglue who's glad he doesn't). He could even slip into O'Neill's, shark it among the rows of pricey new Luminas and Malibus, do a three-pointer and leave the nose of the Vic sticking out to make people brake. But he's Brooks (maybe it's the Marine in him, the boot recruit who busted his ass, scared shitless of washing out), and for him there's no decision.

He turns right onto Old Farms Road, hoping to pick up their trail. Nothing, just a couple of porchlights burning, red reflectors on metal stems. Bedsheet ghosts swing from trees, stuffed scarecrows sprawl in lawnchairs. There's sidewalk here from when the town was a town. Brooks thinks he's lucky: tomorrow—today, tonight—it'll be packed with kids in costume, parents walking their toddlers. He's taking an extra shift, grateful for a shot at that doubletime. He needs to eat up those hours somehow.

There they are, far ahead, passing through the high streetlight by Arch Road with their lights off, blowing their chance to turn under the railroad overpass. (Toe's got to give them props; he didn't even think of that old trick.) Probably kids, Brooks thinks, and has to stop himself from racing straight after them. In class the hardass statie teaching them showed slides of cars accordioned into phone poles and torn in half, pancaked by semis, some of them cruisers, all of them the result of misdemeanor pursuits. Brooks half expected us in all our ugly, bloody glory, the Camry and the famous tree. "Can any of you tell me what speed defines a high-speed chase as high-speed?" the statie asked, and none of them were brave or dumb enough to answer. "A high-speed chase," he lectured, pacing between their chairs like a DI, "is defined as any chase in excess of the prevailing speed limit."

The speed here is 40, but with the new surface people do 50, no trouble. Brooks is pushing 60. He doesn't want to spook the Cabby and backs off to 45. The road curves and the streetlights give way to trees, a rocky hillside, a tacky apartment complex perched on top. Brooks leans over the wheel but doesn't see the car; he wonders how they're seeing anything. Leaves somersault into his path and scatter beneath him.

There's only one more road before the woods, Country Club, and when he gets there there's no trace of them. The turn up Country Club is switchbacked, rollover sharp, and while he knows some good hiding places off it, people always choose the woods—like we did. (Like Toe did, Danielle says. Oh right, Toe says, like you would have gone up Country Club.) And Toe's not completely wrong. It makes sense; the woods is a place to get lost. It's part of the old Scoville estate, its buildings slate-roofed fake Tudors, even the winding drive landscaped to make you think of England, fog in the dips—real werewolf country. We all would have picked it.

You've got to love Brooks. He's not sure the Cabby is real, or what he's trying to prove, but he knows quitting isn't right. (Toe can knock the holster off its peg in the closet and he still won't get the message.) He feels responsible, so he glides right by Country Club, past the redone carriage house and between the old brick pillars with their smashed gaslamps, his headlights shivering over the balding road.

And he can't fly through here, it's so twisty. He's seen what these curves can do and keeps the needle on 30. He feels like he's creeping. He knows he's not going to catch the Cabby, that it was just a trick (because he's paranoid now, feels eyes staring from behind trees). With every bend he thinks he's going to see us again, this year's model, the Cabby off the road on its flimsy roof, branches white in its headlights, the radio going, a tire still spinning like in the movies.

But it's not the right night yet, he thinks, clinging to it like a rule. (See, and nobody told him. He knows the whole deal, it's like he has ESP.)

Should we send a squirrel scurrying across the road, the white ruff of a doe's belly floating out in front of him?

He doesn't need it. Part of him knows what he's doing here, why, first thing after midnight, he's rolling up on the one place he really shouldn't be. If our parents could see him, or the chief, he'd be fired, out on his ass, and forget about ever getting Melissa back.

The thought makes him slow, sobered. The Cabby's long gone as he turns into the curve and climbs the rise where we went airborne. The Vic's nose lifts and dips, levels out, and there, dead center in his headlights, stands the tree with its moldy litter of remembrances half-buried beneath the leaves. Our tree. Tim's. His.

Brooks stops. It's not an admission of guilt. It's not the first time since the accident that he's seen the tree. Avon's not that large; there are only so many ways around town. He's even taken the curve too fast, going to some Code 3, lights wheeling, but the Vic is heavy and his tires are new. He's a driver, Brooks; he's not going to die in a car. (I'm not saying anything, Toe. Just shut up and let me tell it, okay?)

Brooks sits there with his foot on the brake, a cloud of his own windblown exhaust rising in his lights. If he got out to squat and clear the leaves away from the browned flowers and soggy teddy bears, we'd be on him like vampires; they'd find his car drained in the morning, the door open, the key still in the on position. So he doesn't. Instead he turns on his takedown brights, two blinding white spots on the rack designed to give him a sneak peek inside a car stop (drivers reaching for Glocks or bottles, trying to change places with passengers just as drunk), and with a flick the night jumps back, trees behind trees, very *Blair Witch*.

The light tricks him, shows him motion where there isn't any, a white shift in the dark that's really on the liquid skin of his eye. It's not Kyle lost and wandering between the trees, but for an instant the memory joins with the illusion and fools Brooks, and he sees the boy staggering deep in the woods, grunting and unable to say anything, his face a smashed mask.

Because Brooks is primed tonight—spooked, you might say. He wouldn't be surprised to find us standing there all bloody, or just Danielle lying facedown. He remembers Danielle more than us (we're not jealous, it's just a fact). He spent more time with her, taking her picture, taking his measurements. She was the mystery, the physics problem he needed to solve, here's the body, here's the car. We were sitting there like dummies shoved under the dash, boring, he'd seen us a dozen times before, but Danielle was out, facing away, like she was trying to escape. Kyle, because he was alive, was terrifying; Danielle was interesting, a specimen. In the last year, Brooks has tried to understand how he became a person who could think that way, but it's unmistakable: he has— he is. Melissa's right.

"232," Ravitch says. It's his name, but Brooks doesn't respond. The brights remind him of later that night, after he'd taken Tim to the station, the fire department setting up their worklights so they could search the scene. He'd just picked up a Bud can (not ours) with the tip of a pencil when he saw what he thought was a piece of jewelry tucked under a leaf, a flicker of gold.

(Shut up, Marco, Danielle says. You're so mean. I can't believe you're going to tell them that.

I was just going to say it was an earring.

Bullshit, Danielle says, and punches me hard in the arm. And here I'm trying to tell it nicely.)

"232, this is dispatch."

Brooks remembers bending down to see what it was, careful not to disturb the sheaf of leaves. A dangly earring, the kind

Melissa liked, see-through purple beads on fine gold wire. He waved Saintangelo over to get a picture of it. The flash silvered their legs—twice, three times—then Saintangelo went back to work on us.

"232, please copy."

Brooks paid out his measuring tape, found out how far it was from the car, how far from Danielle, jotting the numbers down on his clipboard, another clue. In his mind he was diagramming triangles, connecting the dots, turning us into a puzzle, something he could do on his computer that weekend. When he was sure he'd gotten his documentation, he knelt down with a glassine envelope and a pair of tweezers and gently uncovered the earring. It was still attached.

(I don't believe you, Marco. You are such an asshole.)

His first thought—and God knows why he told this to Melissa—was that he'd seen worse.

"232, 232."

Brooks takes his time punching the button. "232, go ahead."

"The hell you been?" Ravich asks, but doesn't really want to know. "Listen, can you take a 10-65 at Riverdale? Stones and Sterling."

An alarm, not far. (Riverdale Farms is a quaint little shopping village they made out of a bunch of old tobacco barns moved there on flatbeds; it's a place our mothers used to go to buy scarves and have lunch, swapping gossip over sushi or nouveau Italian.)

"Got it," Brooks says, already shifting into reverse. He should be glad Ravitch has something for him, but now that he's here, it's tough to leave. Because he's not dumb, Brooksie. He knows it isn't over. It's not just the past that nags at him, he's got a feeling about today—tomorrow, tonight. ("Mercy, Spirit, show me no more!" It's here we remind him of Tim, flash the memory of him calling to Brooks from the backseat, the door crinkled like tinfoil, crushed shut.)

He cuts a three-pointer, his lights flying sideways through the trees, ghostly. Driving back toward town, he wonders what happened to the Cabriolet—no hallucination, just a coincidence. Kids. He believes what he needs to. And it's true, at least partly; we didn't bring him here, we just helped. He's the one who called us, not the other way around. (Wouldn't that be cool? Toe says. If we could just show up whenever?)

Brooks follows the road out, rolls the big Vic through the curves. He needs to get there before his back-up and gives it a little juice. Now's the time to give him the squirrel, send one shooting beneath his tires, thump-thump. Toe's up for it, he's even picked one out, but Danielle stops him.

I swear you guys are like obsessed.

Hey Marco, Toe says. Let's make the streetlight blink.

Why?

Because it's scary.

It is *not* scary, Danielle says. Kyle is scary. *Tim* is scary.

Tim is cool, Toe says, and while they're arguing, Brooks slides between the pillars, returns to the world of the living.

Look.

Shit, Toe says, and makes the light blink—too late, the cruiser's already beyond it. He wants us to follow, to haunt Brooks all night long, go home with him, but it's early, and compared to Tim, Brooks is easy.

Let him go, Danielle says, and she's right. We've got all day. With Brooks it's just a matter of time. Because he's like Tim (We love you, Tim)—he remembers. Or is it that he can't forget? Whatever. It's not so much ESP as Brooks being predictable, and he understands this, he can see why Melissa had to leave. Like us, he's stuck. Even as he's driving away, he knows he'll be back.

There's one empty shopping cart way out in the middle of the lot, right under a light. Kyle doesn't know how he missed it—all the cars are gone. It's almost time to go home. At home there's hot chocolate. He hopes there are marshmallows. His mother was supposed to buy some, but what if she forgot? (She didn't. She bought them yesterday, Sta-Pufs, his favorite, making a point of showing Kyle the new bag as she put it away because that's all he talked about the whole weekend. There's no way to explain it. Imagine diving off a five-story building and landing on your face. Now imagine getting better.

Tim's easier; he's just nuts.

Tim rules, Toe says. Don't be bustin' on Tim.

It starts the usual argument, but one look from Danielle and we both shut up.)

Tim's velcroing the strap around the handle of the lead cart so he can push the whole clashing train through the door when he sees the stray. With Kyle, nothing surprises him anymore. Sometimes he gets impatient with him and then hates himself. It's just Kyle—or it's not really Kyle anymore, not the real Kyle, whichever. The world isn't the world, but everything's supposed to be okay.

"C'mon, bud, don't stop now. Gotta catch 'em all."

"Okay, Tim," Kyle says, and smiles at the Pokémon joke, the unexpected connection pleasant, like doing a puzzle right. He does puzzles at the rehab. There's a table where he does them with the other kids. One time a girl his age threw a block that made his nose bleed. Kyle doesn't remember her name. His mother's name is Nancy, Nancy Sorenson, 675-0257. (We've visited her, stopped at the light on Country Club, lost in thought, the radio babbling away unheard, then calmly turned off. At night she hears his springs squeaking; in the morning, after she gets him on the van, she does his sheets, stands in the bleached light of the basement windows, thinking she can't take care of him forever, that in time it will destroy her. Has.)

"Hey, chief."

"What?" Kyle looks at Tim, waiting with a face like he might have messed up.

"Forget something?"

It's only when Tim points that Kyle understands. Who left the cart there, was it him? He does stupid stuff like that and then doesn't remember it. They're supposed to get all the carts so they can go home.

Tim watches him walk across the parking lot, deliberate, his posture perfect, robot stiff, a byproduct of the hospital (they taught him how to walk in a pool, holding onto a rail built into the side, terrified even though he was standing on the bottom). The buzzcut's his parents' idea; Tim keeps waiting for his hair to grow back. The Kyle he knew was working on muttonchops and would never, ever wear a Stop'n'Shop hat. And he's gained weight, always sneaking candy bars (their manager's asked Tim to watch him, meaning Tim pays for them; at this point what does he need money for? "Thank you, Tim," Kyle says blankly). He has glasses now, held on by a black elastic band, and permanent dentures. His face is flat and lopsided. His nose and cheeks aren't real, or his forehead; only his chin is the same, and his hands. He's become someone or some*thing* else, even his clothes a kind of disguise. When Tim goes to pick him up after school, his mother has him dressed in his uniform, the same every day. She packs his dinner in a black lunchbucket with his name magic-markered on a piece of masking tape (sometimes on break Tim will buy him McDonald's, doing the drive-thru in his jeep, jamming his pb-and-j and celery sticks in the trashcan and telling Kyle to keep it a secret, then dabbing at the ketchup on his shirt with a napkin). She treats him like a little kid, but—and it's taken Tim months to admit this—he *is* a little kid. He likes his thermos of chicken noodle soup, he likes his baggie of Double Stuf Oreos. Watching him eat, Tim wishes he could be happy for him instead of thinking it would have been better if he'd just died. (He thinks it every time he sees him, but really he's thinking about himself. Sometimes he thinks it would be easier being Kyle.

Toe thinks he's being selfish. I don't know. Danielle spends more time with him than anyone, but she won't talk about it. She still thinks we can stop him.

Why, Toe says.)

Kyle jangles the last cart over the lot while Tim waits, wondering at the dramatic sky, the clouds dragging across the almost full moon. It'll be cold going home, that's the one drawback to the jeep, even with the hardtop on. Danielle used to complain about the heater when they were making out, and now he can't help but see her face, the two of them kissing wet-faced across the emergency brake, her shirt open, his fingers trying to free her underwire.

(Oh baby! Toe says.

Shut up, we both say.)

The memory makes Tim tired, makes him dip his head to shake it off. He remembers her sitting on his lap that last night, turning his ear to her back and trying to listen to her heart. The music was too loud, and the wind outside.

Behind Kyle, a car turns in at the light—too late, they're of-

ficially closed, the doors turned off. People make this mistake all
the time, with the sign on and the windows lit up; all the other
Stop'n'Shops around here are 24 hours, only Avon still has these
goofy blue laws. Tim's ready to wave the car away, to explain to
the pissed-off driver that they'll have to get their milk at the
Shell, and then the car reaches the first set of lights and he sees
it's a cop.

It's a shock at first. His instinct's to run, as if he's been
caught, and then he relaxes, gives in to disgust—fuck, not again.
He knows who it's going to be. He goes out and takes the cart
from Kyle, trying to ignore the patrol car rolling up on them, its
lights shining through the chrome cages, blasting their shadows
against the wall. There's no escape, but he rams the last cart home
and slips the strap through the handle anyway.

The car pulls into the striped fire lane beside them, facing
the wrong way, close enough to touch. The window's already
down. It's him, his guardian angel, and Tim feels the usual guilty
mix of gratitude and detachment, the bond between them he
wishes didn't exist. The only way to pay him back would be to
save his life (to have died like he should have), and that's not going to happen.

"Say, Kyle. Tim."

"Hello, Officer Brooks," Kyle says in his doughy, dumb-bear
voice. (Duh, Toe says, what about the rabbits, George?

Why do you have to be so mean, Danielle asks.

I'm dead, Toe says. I don't have to be nice.)

"Hey," Tim says, and like always he can feel Brooks reading
his thoughts, looking through the rooms of his brain, slamming
drawers—it's probably just us, but he doesn't know that.

They agree it's a quiet night. No, no trouble here. Brooks

says he'll check around back anyway. Tim thinks he's free when
Brooks leans his elbow out the window again.

"You guys wouldn't know anyone with a white Cabriolet.
Black top?"

That would be Travis; he just bought it off Debbie Par-
malee's older sister who left home to go to Stanford. (Emily,
Danielle says; she was the nice one. Megan I can't stand.
Couldn't, Toe says. *Can't*.) Tim wonders if Kyle remembers the
car, because he and Debbie were friends—are friends—but
Kyle's lost the question, gone off to Kyleland, watching a hardy
moth spiral through the red lights of the sign.

"Nope," Tim says.

"All right." Brooks points to Tim's Wrangler over in the far
row where they're supposed to park, as if he knows it's a lie (as if
he knows every car in Avon). "You know your registration's up
this month."

"I know." He does, actually. It's just one more chore on a
long list he'll never get to. Legally he has thirty days; in reality
he has one (less than one now), and there are real things he needs
to do.

"You guys working tomorrow?" Brooks asks.

"I don't know," Tim says, not wanting to get caught in a trap.
"We might do a half shift."

Brooks doesn't get into the question of parties and whether
their parents will let them out of the house—the same one Tim's
been avoiding. He hasn't told them he's working yet. He doesn't
expect them to like it, but they're not going to tell him what to
do. They trust him, which he thinks is sad. (His mom's called
Danielle up at night three times in the last month, but out of a
sound sleep, as if a deeper part of her knows what's going to hap-

pen. Danielle stands at the foot of the bed, watching her turn her head on the pillow, saying no, no, but Tim's mom thinks it's grief, a memory, not a warning. Danielle waits to visit her during the day, to knock a cup out of her hand at the sink or steal her bookmark—there's only so much we can do—but the call never comes.)

"I'm pulling a double," Brooks says, a threat. "I'm sure I'll see you around. Kyle, say hello to your folks for me. You too, Tim."

"Goodbye, Officer Brooks," Kyle says, waving (Tim wants to pull his hand down), and the two of them watch him wheel around the side of the store.

It takes them longer than usual to get the carts in because Tim's thinking about Brooks and gets the middle of the train hung up on the doorframe and they have to stop and yank the whole thing sideways and then it doesn't go in straight. Kyle stands there while Tim fixes it. Everyone else is punching out, hauling their coats on over their uniforms, calling their good-nights across the registers. Tim and Kyle are left to close up with Darryl, the manager. They turn off the muzak and turn on a boombox to Radio 104 and cover the meat and dairy and produce cases with their canvas drops and sweep the aisles (if it was Friday they'd have to buff the floor with the machine that makes Tim's wrists ache). He thinks he'll miss this—the whole store quiet, his. He doesn't like going home, it's like lying. Here he's closer to the person he's pretending to be, and at times like this—just doing something mindless—he really is himself. Outside—at home, at school—he's like Kyle, an impostor.

It's not so much that he wants to die as not exist like this anymore.

He can't explain it or defend it, even to himself, and so he doesn't try, doesn't risk it. It's just something he has to do, and since he's made his decision he feels relieved, free. Knowing there will be an end to this makes living easier; it's the only thing he's hanging on to—or sometimes songs, the way a chord or chorus makes him feel part of the sound, a larger, ideal world, no longer a body, let alone a person connected to other people and to what happened. (Because we stick to him and he doesn't really want us to go away. Like Kyle, we're his friends no matter what. Danielle's with him all the time; it's only now, when he's concentrating on sweeping an even line of dirt, that he's alone, and even now we're standing by, lined up by the freezer case. A glance at Kyle and all five of us are together again, getting in Toe's mom's car, saying what we said to each other, the fragile weight of Danielle pressed against him, her breasts resting on his locked arms.)

The floor's done, and Darryl takes care of the upstairs. The long lights go off in rows. They grab their coats, and Tim helps Kyle find the right line to punch out on, the purple numbers chunking down. Their parents will get their checks. It's not much, he thinks. (Another reason not to, as if he's keeping score.)

"Tomorrow, gentlemen," Darryl says at his van.

"All right," Tim says, because they're scheduled for a regular shift. After school he'll pick up Kyle like always, and they'll have the whole night to say good-bye.

Just going over it like this is bad luck, makes Tim think it's wrong, bringing Kyle. The key for him is not looking at his decision too closely, to just trust himself. At the last second he can always drop Kyle off—but he would never do that. That would be the worst thing he could do to Kyle. And what about his parents, isn't this the worst thing he can do to them, after everything? Who will understand if even he can't?

No one has to. How could they? And it's too late anyway.

It's like trying to argue with something that's already happened.

The jeep's waiting, the jeep that will be famous, the jeep that Brooks will have to deal with, if Tim can escape him. Kyle gets in his side, his knees scrunched up against the grab bar attached to the dash until Tim reaches under the seat and slides the whole thing back. He helps Kyle with his belt and thinks he won't tomorrow.

(It's wrong, Danielle says, and while she's almost strong enough to get through, her presence makes him miss her more. He doesn't care that it's wrong, or only that it's wrong for Kyle. Sometimes even Danielle understands, like those nights he calls us again and again and we sit through the stupid ride—every single detail, half of them made up—until we *want* to crash, we're actually glad to see the tree. And then it starts all over again.)

Darryl's gone by the time they slant across the lot and past the darkened garden center, the plants breathing dumbly inside the steamed greenhouse. Tim pauses to look both ways at the blinking light. Why? Wouldn't an accident be just as good?

No. He can't imagine anything more irresponsible. There's a logic to his plan, and part of it is not involving anyone else. Nothing's random. (He sounds like Brooks now, getting all cosmic. It was an accident. Why do they keep trying to find meaning in it?

But Kyle's mom does that too, and Danielle's sisters, Toe's mom and stepfather, my folks, Mr. Kulwicki at school. No one can let it go. Look at us, still driving around town with Tim and Kyle. It's limbo, and if Tim pulls this off we'll never get out of here.

I like being a ghost, Toe says.

Jesus, Danielle says, you would.

Seriously.

Oh, Toe.

What?)

Tim has to wait for the light at 44, even though no one's coming. Nothing's open except the Mobil Mart, the cashier trapped in his glass box, surrounded by bright merchandise. Tim uses the extra minute to light a cigarette.

"Tim," Kyle says, then nothing.

"What?"

"Smoking is bad for you," Kyle says, straight as a first-grader.

"It is," Tim says, and unzips his window.

The light turns green and they make the right and accelerate between the Staples and the McDonald's, the Dunkin' Donuts where Danielle worked. The air pours in, freezing, and he tugs the zipper, swerving into the left lane.

"Tim," Kyle asks, "do you think it will snow tomorrow?"

"No, Kyle, I don't think it's going to snow tomorrow."

"Do you like snow?"

Is there an answer to this? "Not really."

Kyle doesn't reply, as if he's lost the conversation, and that's fine. Tim wants to be alone so he can remember Danielle at the drive-thru window, how goofy she looked in her hideous uniform, the stupid purple visor, her hair pulled back. He's seeing her ears and her neck, the gold chain he gave her for Christmas, when Kyle says, "I like snow."

"I wouldn't bet on it tomorrow, bud," Tim says, trying to let him down easy.

Does it mean anything? Kyle can take orders and do simple things like sweeping, but how he thinks is a mystery. All summer he was stuck on lightning, now it's snow. Does he remember it or has he seen it on the weather channel? Have they been talking about it at the rehab, flipping flashcards of Frosty and ski resorts?

"Why do you want it to snow?" Tim asks.

"Because then we could have a snow day."

"Do you know what day tomorrow is?"

"Tomorrow's Wednesday," Kyle says, as if Tim is being stupid. And he is. He wants the day to mean the same thing to Kyle, and that's impossible. He wants to talk to him about that night, and everything that happened after, but this isn't the Kyle that can help him.

"It's Halloween," Tim says.

"I know. We're going to have a party."

"So why do you want a snow day if you're going to have a party?"

Kyle squints at him, unsure, then looks down at his hands as if he's being punished. "I don't know."

And why is it Tim who has to find the right thing to say? Why can't he let Kyle sit there bummed out?

"I think we're supposed to have a lot of snow days this year," he says, a soft lob.

"I would like that," Kyle says.

It's like having a kid, Tim thinks, which makes him think of Danielle and the perfect life they would have had together. (Kids? Danielle says. I don't *think* so.) He used to have Danielle, now he has Kyle.

The night passes outside, the lines and signs and guardrails meant to save their lives. An oncoming car kills its purple brights and the streetlights float up his windshield like bubbles. The radio's playing Garbage—*I think I'm paranoid, and complicated.* The song's wrong; he's neither, just blank, tired. He's driven 44 hundreds of times but feels no connection to the parking lot of La Trattoria or the Acura dealership with its rows of unsold cars. They could be anywhere. He could be anyone.

Ahead, at the corner where the Rotary sells pumpkins and

Christmas trees, a lumbering Chevy from the '80s stops and then pulls slowly onto 44 in front of him—a drunk or an old guy. Tim figures it's going to straighten out and take the slow lane, but it keeps creeping over. He can't believe it—the guy's got to see him—as the Chevy wanders right into his headlights. Tim punches the horn and hits the brakes at the last minute, yanks the jeep right, slipping by on the inside.

"What are you, fucking nuts?" Tim whips his shift hand up and shoots him the finger through the back window. It's over, but his heart is still pumping hard, and the rush of anger gives way to a strange mix of feelings. He's surprised; he didn't expect to be frightened.

"Tim, are you mad?" Kyle asks in that dull, calm voice Tim will never get used to.

"No," Tim says. "Are you okay?"

"Yes."

"Fucking idiot, pulling out like that."

"Don't say that," Kyle says, because he's gotten in trouble at home for swearing. Some of the cashiers were teaching him words, and Tim promised Kyle's mom he'd stop it.

"Sorry," Tim says. "Fuck fuck fuck fuck fuck."

Kyle tries to keep a straight face, serious, pinching his lips—like a little kid, Tim thinks again (because he's got no other way to relate to him)—then breaks into helpless laughter at the hilarious, banned word.

"Fuck," Kyle echoes, testing, and waits to see if it's all right.

"Okay," Tim says. "But don't get me in trouble, okay?"

When Brooks circles back and cruises the Stop 'n' Shop again, they're gone, the sign dark. He's tempted to check up on them, to make sure they're okay. He's followed them home before, has seen Tim drop Kyle off and back down the long driveway, has watched from his car like a stalker as the porch light goes off. Thinking back, it's stuff like that that makes him agree with Melissa, forgive her for leaving him, though he knows how that would sound to her—the start of another argument.

There's too much time on midnights.

He goes up to the Mobil and sits in the glow of the pumps until his legs get jumpy. He can't sit for eight hours straight, so he picks a plaza he hasn't visited in a while, parks across the ranked spaces, gets out his flashlight and does some business checks, the cold air and the distant hum of unseen traffic refreshing. Seeing his breath reminds him that he's alive—the whole mess of bone and tissue and juice working in concert—as if he'd forgotten. (Oh, and don't think he wouldn't trade places with us. But that's too easy, Brooksie, and there's only one of you, and you're old. We've got our whole lives in front of us. We're the future, re-member?)

The doors are locked. He shadows the glass with a hand and peers inside The Artful Framer with its wall of gilded joints, the Bagelz with its empty tables. Something about these places seems makeshift and unreal to Brooks. When he was a boy, none of this was here, the asphalt islands and their shops all farmland. 44 was two lanes with a solid white line down the middle and weedy ditches on both sides. (He sees white butterflies like handker-chiefs—he's time-traveling, another bad habit, trying to escape the present, to go back to an age when everything was possible. It's like Tim remembering Danielle or the Kyle he knew before: Why can't they stay there where nothing hurts? Why do they have to grow up? Why do we have to die?)

He radios in, everything secure. Ravitch copies but has nothing for him.

He checks the time—a mistake, but a break too. In twenty minutes the bars will be letting out. He can waste a good half-hour trolling the parking lots and intimidating the patrons of the First and Last Tavern and the Double Down Grill (a younger crowd, more trouble). If he gets caught up in a good car stop, he could burn an hour or more.

Danielle leans close to him in the front seat, as if to kiss him, to whisper in his ear, and the computer blinks. He sees Tim with his Stop'n'Shop apron, and Kyle, the train of carts.

(No fair, Toe says.)

A familiar feeling of helplessness comes over Brooks, his breath pressed out of his chest, caught in his throat, a charged, ticklish heat as if he's about to sneeze, his sinuses pinched. He rubs his face with both hands, and suddenly, from out of nowhere—and we're always called in to watch, as if this apology is for us—he's in tears. A handful, quickly brushed away, rubbed into his cheeks. He catches his breath again, embarrassed at his capacity for self-pity, blows his nose and tucks the kleenex in the ashtray.

"Christ," he says, the word eaten by silence.

No one blames you, Melissa used to say.

No one has to, Brooks thinks.

(What about us? Toe says. We do.)

His solution is to keep moving, concentrate on the job—the same tactics that frustrated Melissa. He signals and turns onto 44, heads up the strip to do the bar crawl. The heater warms him, the glow of the screen a companion. Here he's connected to Ravitch at the station and Saintangelo cruising District 2 if he needs back-up; at home there's only the dogs and the empty closets. It's amazing how small the world can become, and how suddenly. And it's true, he admits, as sad as that is: he'd rather be here.

What do we call Kyle's mom—Mrs. Sorensen? Nancy? She's Kyle's mom.

So it's Kyle's mom who waits up for him, watching Letterman in her robe, listening for Tim's jeep, then opens the door as he's zombieing up the walk. It's Kyle's mom who waves to Tim (thank God for Tim, what would they do without him). It's Kyle's mom who takes his hat and sets it with his lunchbucket on the marble-topped table and helps him off with his jacket and hangs it up while he waits behind her like a guest.

"Okay," she says, cheery, "upstairs."

"Upstairs," Kyle echoes, pleasant, as if slightly drunk, the whole world amusing to him (because he's thinking of the forbidden word, pulsing inside him like a bomb).

She turns off the outside light and makes sure the door's locked, takes the lunchbucket into the kitchen and checks to see that he's eaten, then follows him up. There's no rush. He goes so slowly, a hand on the bannister, bringing his back foot even with his front, only then going on to the next step. Every weeknight it's like this, with Kyle's dad (Mr. Sorenson, Mark) already asleep so he can get up for the commute. With Kyle working, he only sees him on weekends, as if he's given up custody—as if Kyle's all hers now. The timing's right. She can concentrate on him, with Kelly off at college. He's their baby in so many ways.

"Scrub your face well," she reminds him in the bathroom, because his acne's bad and he'll forget. She leaves the door open in case he needs help. He drops things—the toothpaste in the toilet, a hearing aid in the wastebasket—and then will stand there stricken until she comes to his rescue. Tonight he's good until the handsoap topples into the sink. He watches the faucet run over the plastic squirter; she takes a step in, then stops as he bends to retrieve it, scolds herself for not holding off longer. She needs to believe in him more.

"Do you have to go?" she asks.

"No," Kyle says.

"Why don't you try," she nudges, and for this she closes the door and retreats to his room, turning down the bed and laying out his flannel PJs.

The room is picked up, his desk and dresser clean. She hasn't changed anything since the accident, and the overlapping posters of tattooed and pierced rap and rock stars she doesn't know, so alien at first, seem comforting, almost hers now. She likes to think they might help him recall the world before, charge him with subliminal memories, but so far there's no sign. Like a five-year-old, he loves fast food and cartoons. He sleeps under life-size pictures of people he doesn't know, among CDs and video games he no longer plays.

After the crash, while he was still in the hospital, she helped Kyle's dad search his room. The pipes and skin magazines didn't shock her, or the one shiny knife. She was ready for worse. He liked to think he was a dangerous kid, but he wasn't, just trying to convince himself and scandalize them. Didn't she do the same thing? In a few years he would have outgrown the pose, returned from college an interesting young man, someone they could talk to.

(She's dreaming. He hated everything about this place, especially her, the way she wanted their life to be like Martha

Stewart. He couldn't wait to get out of there, he didn't care where—New York, San Francisco. He'd say he was gone, he was so far gone he wasn't ever coming back, and then laugh, thinking what that would do to her.)

He's taking too long, and she quietly moves to the door and listens.

Nothing.

"Do you need help?" she asks.

"No," he says, and the toilet flushes. At least he remembered. She needs to reinforce it, give him credit for everything. Good job, she'll say. That's the way.

"Don't forget to wash your hands."

Another round with the handsoap, a towel that won't go back on the rack, and finally he's done.

The hard part is letting him do it himself. She wants to rip open the velcro and pull his shoes off, unbutton his shirt, but these are the fine motor skills he needs to work on. The repetition is good for him, but when he struggles she has to force herself not to intervene. Buttons are the hardest. He turns away from her and grunts, frustrated, tugging at his shirt as if he might rip it.

"Fuck."

What?

Not this again.

"Kyle!" she says, and he shies away, hunched as if she might hit him. His fear's real, and hurts her. She wonders where it comes from. He can't be afraid of her. Has someone been abusing him at school, one of the staff members?

(Get a clue, Danielle says. God, she's like my mom.)

"It's all right," she says gently, to quiet him. She can't wait too long or else he won't know what she's scolding him for. "Listen. I don't want to hear that kind of language out of your mouth. If someone says that to you, you tell me who it is, and I will deal with them."

(Fuck you, Toe says.)

"I'm sorry, Mom," Kyle says—his reaction to any discipline. But does he understand why?

It's too late to go into that. She helps him with the tough button, slowly showing him how it's done, then leaves him to finish the last two, pinching each one and slipping it sideways through the hole, her fingers moving in sympathy. He can do his pants himself, his underwear coming with them, then has to sit on the edge of his bed to pull off his socks. She turns from him because he's not modest. He used to be so secretive, locking the bathroom door, covering himself with a towel.

(How's it look there? Toe asks.

Don't be gross, Danielle says. Jesus, you really are heartless, you know that?

It beats being headless.

I am not headless, Danielle says.

Technically you're missing part of your head, right?

Thanks to you. Forget it. You guys can stay here, I'm going to go see what Tim's up to.

Get lucky, Toe says, and then when she's gone he clams up. The joking's transparent. He's had a crush on her since eighth grade, and now she's the only girl he sees. I try to stay out of it, since it's obvious she's with Tim, and not the easiest person in the world, but I'm not blind, I've fantasized sometimes. Who doesn't want someone to love?)

Kyle hauls on his pajama bottoms one leg at a time, falling back and bouncing on the bed in between. The buttons on his top are larger, one reason Kyle's mom bought them.

"All right," she says, and lifts the covers for him. She sits on the edge of the bed and sets the alarm on his nightstand a half-hour behind hers. She's the last person Kyle sees at night and the first one in the morning.

"Sweet dreams," she says, kisses her fingertips and presses them to the rough shell of his forehead.

"Sweet dreams," Kyle says.

At the doorway she looks back a last time before turning out the light. His eyes are wide open. "Go to sleep," she says, and he closes them.

She leaves the green nightlight on in the bathroom—doubled in the mirror and then eclipsed as she leaves. Kyle's dad is asleep on the far side of the bed. (And she hates him then—Mr. Sorensen—pretending to be untouched, his life at the office an island.) Kyle's mom closes the door, hangs her robe on the hook and slides in. She lies there facing the ceiling, waiting for the covers to warm her, for sleep to come—just like Kyle, she thinks.

What does he dream of? What's going to happen to him? She's grateful that he's alive (she thinks she's lucky compared to our parents), but beyond that she can't go, not knowing.

Like every night, she's wide awake.

(Good job, Kyle's mom. Way to go.)

The coachlight's on in the yard—his mom—and Tim thinks of not braking and turning in at the drive, as if it's someone else's house, as if he just happens to be passing through Avon late at night and by chance imagines the family sleeping inside this Cape, identical to so many others on this road—the dark halls and bedrooms, the storm windows lowered against the cold, the furnace in the basement guarding its patient blue flame, the doll-house and the avocado luggage and the boxes of old photo al-bums all waiting along the far wall, their ancient history.

(There are pictures of us here, at least Toe and me, eating cake with sweet cream icing and guzzling Hawaiian Punch from waxy cups with Brandon and Justin and Holden before he moved to Texas and John Bunnell and Ryan until we hit middle school and the parties stopped. The pictures of Danielle are in his room, in the bottom drawer of his desk, in the big manila enve-lope with her letters. His favorite's the one of them when the ski club went to Okemo. She's sitting on his lap in the bus with the TVs in the seats; his face is buried in her neck, and the way she's turned her chin makes her look the way he remembers her, that straight line in profile. He'll take that snapshot out and set it di-rectly under his desk light and sit there trying to read her mind, to recall what they were talking about. And then when he's close, when he can smell her strawberry lip gloss, he's trapped in the backseat again, screaming over the stupid music, and she's gone.)

He could drive right by, keep going until the needle's on E and leave the jeep by the side of the highway, stick his thumb out and hitch. Anything could happen then, instead of what has to. Even now he's not sure, as if the decision has been made by someone else and he has to carry it through. Can't he just forget everything, pretend he's fine? Isn't that what he's been doing?

(Don't be stupid, Danielle says, and for once Toe agrees with her. It's a lie, kind of. He's caught in the classic best-friend's-girl dilemma, torn between what's right—Tim being with us—and what he wants—Danielle being with him. Either way, he's guilty; either way, it's not his fault. Toe thinks he's got it harder than any of us, except maybe Kyle. He wishes he were Tim. And it should have been him, he had the airbag. We were just going too fast. Brooks knows it: over fifty, they don't really help.)

Tim lifts his foot off the gas and the jeep floats, the coach-light slows. He swings in and parks beside the movable basketball hoop he'll never use again and lets himself in the side door, clos-ing it gently, easing up the three crispy linoleum stairs, his jin-gling keys smothered in a fist. The only light in the kitchen's the one above the stove. A click and night fills the house around him. He feels like a burglar, sneaking through the living room. He used to come in late from dropping Danielle off after work, hoping no one would wake up and realize what time it was. (I remember, Danielle says, and takes a step toward him but at the last minute stops—like Kyle's mom—knowing the closeness only makes it worse. Toe stands silent beside me in the dining room, not part of that drama.) Tim navigates the dark, homing in on the red blip of the smoke detector. It's like wading, his shins at risk with every step. The coffee table floats to the surface, and the bulk of the piano. A light from the upstairs hall falls on the rag rug just short of the front door. He squares himself with the stairs and starts up.

"Honey?" his mom calls dreamily. "Is that you?"

Besides the accident, he's never been in trouble, and they trust him.

"It's me," he says, the truth. So why, in his room, does it feel like a lie?

Sometimes you can tell when they're going to swing. Brooks watches their posture, these two Italian dudes he's got leaning on the hood of the little one's Z outside the Double Down Grill.

He's got a mouth on him, this one, talking about how this is unconstitutional. He swings his head on his neck, hunches his shoulders—a comedian. Brooks figures he's harmless, an East Hartford operator crossing the city for some high-class action.

"Actually the law's pretty liberal on probable cause," Brooks says, playing the jailhouse lawyer, making it a civil conversation. He should wait for Saintangelo before he pats them down, but they seem reasonable, well-dressed, and the registration's a match. And there are still patrons filing out, laughing, happy it's someone else getting busted. How's he supposed to know the big one's fresh out on parole, his license an expensive fake?

"Am I going to find any weapons on you?" Brooks asks, stepping close behind the big one.

"Don't answer that," the little one says. "It can be taken as consent."

"Am I going to find anything on you?" Brooks insists.

"I don't give you consent," the big one says.

"I don't need consent to search your person, sir, and what you just said justifiably gives me suspicion, meaning I can go ahead and search the vehicle as well."

"Bullshit it does!" the little one says, and jumps in Brooks's face before he can raise an arm to fend him off. As they grapple, the big one spins and charges, and suddenly they both have hold of him, grabbing at his jacket for a better grip, his arms pinned so he can't get to the microphone on his shoulder. He clamps a hand over his gun (the holster's still buttoned), gropes for his pepper spray. They're bulling him backwards, two linemen mauling a running back; he bangs an ankle and loses his footing, and the three of them go rolling over, knees and feet and elbows.

(Get 'em, Brooksie! Kill 'em!)

He wrestles with everything he has, but the big guy's young

and ends up on top of him, the little guy concentrating on one arm. Already he's blaming himself, thinking he shouldn't have been so lax in his procedure. If he could get to his nightstick or flashlight he'd have a chance, just flail away at them until he hit bone, but they're both throwing punches and it's all he can do to cover up. He can't hear the crowd, meaning they're scared. No one's going to help him, so it's pointless to yell. Fingers grasp at his belt. Someone gets him in the nuts—those fuckers!—and his intestines fill, he wants to vomit. Again, and his vision dims, the world blurs; he can hear himself retching, pathetic. His hands move to comfort the hurt. The fight's over, now it's a question of whether he'll survive the stomping they give him. He's defenseless, his gun unprotected. He thinks of Melissa getting his insurance money and thinks that's fair, and how maybe this is repayment for what happened. It's just dumb; he already ran their tags, he's got the one guy's license on his clipboard. He's about to be killed by the world's stupidest criminals.

And suddenly they're off him, gone—running for the car if he's lucky. The guy probably has a weapon.

"Face down!" someone's ordering him. "Arms straight out at your sides." He tries to comply, to crucify himself, except he can't feel anything but the rupture in his crotch, his limbs rubber. (And here comes Danielle, Brooks's angel, kneeling beside him, laying a hand on his forehead.) He shouldn't look up but he does, and there's Saintangelo in his two-handed stance, drawing down on the bad guys like John Wayne.

He's grateful for a split instant, then thinks: I'm going to catch so much shit for this. He's going to have to file an incident report and he's afraid when the chief sees it he might take his extra shift from him.

"You all right?" Saintangelo is saying.

"Yeah," Brooks says, shaking his head like it might rattle. He pulls and pushes his aching body to its knees, fingers his teeth—nothing loose, no blood. It's just his nuts, red-hot and three times their size. "The fuck took you so long?"

Saintangelo's supposed to laugh at the joke, or make his own (I was busy fucking your mother), but just asks Brooks if he has cuffs, as if he's completely incompetent. Everyone knows Brooks isn't the same cop he used to be. Brooks just thought he was a different person, that he could still do the job, but here's proof.

"I got 'em," Brooks says.

"Then take 'em," Saintangelo says. "They're yours."

We leave Brooks at the station, taking care of paperwork. 44's silent under the buzzing lights. The bars are closed, and the Mobil, only Saintangelo lurking by the exit of Cider Mill Plaza. The sideroads are dark, animals loping across the yellow lines, scuttling under guardrails, rustling leaves. It's the time of night you wake up and don't know what time it is.

In the house on Indian Pipe Drive, Kyle sleeps. Kyle's dad sleeps. Even Kyle's mom sleeps.

On Oxbow, my mom and dad sleep, spooned together on his side of the bed, as if she's pushing him out.

Danielle's mom sleeps in her nightgown. Danielle's dad sleeps on his back. Danielle's sister Lisa sleeps in Danielle's room (a little creepy, even with the new wallpaper). Danielle's sister Tracy sleeps in her own room now and misses Lisa, demands that the closet door be closed.

Toe's mom sleeps alone. In Northbrook, Illinois, on business, Toe's stepdad sleeps in a Best Western, turning on a rock of a pillow, the alarm clock (set for six) bolted to the nightstand.

Tim's mom sleeps, dreaming she's at the beach, a sunny day, the low waves breaking, Tim running around with a bucket (she knows it's a dream because he can't be that young, and it's not a memory either). In his own double bed, Tim's dad sleeps without dreaming.

In his room, with the door closed and the lights out, Tim sits in the dark, his eyes wide open, his mind empty as a highway. Above, a small plane burrows through the clouds. This must be how Dylan Klebold felt, he thinks, knowing he was going to school the next day and never coming home. It's different but the same. He doesn't want to think about it, just do it and get it over with.

(You don't want to do it, Danielle says, next to him, but she knows better. What can she say? He thinks he's doing it for her, for us. How do you convince someone they're wrong about the only thing in the world they're sure of?)

He should sleep. Last year he can't remember when he went to bed, but it wasn't this late. If he wants to do it right he needs to be sharp, start early.

He doesn't need us, so we leave Danielle with him and go outside, me and Toe, walking down Flintlock. The streetlights are far apart, and we don't talk. I don't have to tell you he's thinking about her, that it's eating him like a disease, whether it's real or just something he's made up. (Is it because we're young, because Toe's never really been in love? Doesn't it matter that she's dead? But then this wouldn't be a real romance, would it? Where would we be if love ended at death?)

We reach the corner where the school bus used to drop Tim off and turn up Yorkshire. Already there are pumpkins broken in the road.

Aw man, Toe says. That's fucked up. At least they could wait till it's over.

Weak, recovering (his balls a dull ache, the icepack all water), Brooks can't resist. The night wears him down, and an hour before sunrise he's creeping up Flintlock past Tim's house, checking to see if the jeep is there.

It is, sharing the drive with a basketball hoop. Brooks has his lights on, cruising through slow like he's patrolling. The road's quiet, everyone getting their rest for tomorrow. (What's there to stop him from sneaking up the drive and opening the flimsy door, reaching inside and popping the hood, pulling the right wires? But of course he doesn't know.) He doesn't even know why he's here. He believes it's guilt, but if Melissa's right—and she might be, he concedes—it's obsession, a trait even less acceptable in a cop. And what if Melissa hasn't gone far enough, and it's madness? That's Brooks's deepest fear, even more real because there's no history in his family, no legacy to blame. A gibbering aunt locked up in Norwich State Hospital would give him an excuse, but no, he's done this to himself.

He should go see Gram tomorrow.

He won't have time unless he gets up early—if the chief lets him keep his shift.

Like half of Avon nowadays, Flintlock is a cul-de-sac; at the top Brooks circles the turnaround—two more hoops, a scrapwood hockey goal knocked on its back—and as always, the simple solution of kids presents itself, too late to save their marriage, and impossible anyway. The one time they looked into adoption caused more fights than the two of them could ever remember,

both of them sensitive of their failures (not just their bodies—
their bank account, their house, their half-assed lives), the whole
thing a compromise neither of them could live with, and Melissa
shoved the folder of half-finished forms in the basement file cabinet where they wouldn't have to look at it. But driving these
streets, Brooks is convinced the only reason these people are here
is their kids. Without them the town wouldn't exist, its good
schools its only drawing card. Who would want to live here if
they didn't have children?

He and Gram are the answer to that—old folks and townies,
both of them slowly going extinct. It's not the property taxes exactly, that's just the surface. Avon's changed, gone beyond upscale
and still growing; the roads are packed with Saabs and Lexus
SUVs, and new construction starts at half a million. When he
sees his father's cronies from the old days in Luke's Donuts they
complain like subjects of an occupation, nostalgic and powerless.
Brooks feels he's letting them down, selling the house. Once he's
out, there's no way back in.

He slides by Tim's driveway, makes the jeep again, as if the
kid might have escaped while he was turning around. He checks
the windows upstairs, downstairs, around the side. He wouldn't
be surprised to find Tim watching him from between the curtains, as if everyone is as paranoid as he is.

Why did he argue with Melissa when she was obviously
right? He *is* a mess. He *does* need help. Then why did she quit
trying, wasn't their marriage—wasn't *he*—worth it?

(Here he goes again, Toe says, with his Doc Martens up on
the back of Brooks's headrest. And this guy walks around with a
loaded gun?

Don't start, I say.

What?

It's the worst time of night. We're tired of each other, tired of being here—like there's somewhere else to go. Danielle's still with Tim, Brooks is gnawing on his problems. It should be quiet, a time for us to rest, but there's no break. We won't have Brooks home and in bed before Kyle's mom's alarm goes off. As soon as people start to wake up and remember what day it is, we'll be flying around town, making special guest appearances at breakfast tables, showering with people we barely know. How many parents of our classmates are going to pass the tree on their way to work and make us pose there (say antifreeze!)? We'll be in and out of school all day, swooping into biology and woodshop, smoking in the trees at the edge of the soccer field, hanging out behind Mrs. M.'s gasmart. And then there will be the wreaths and flowers, the cards picked out at the CVS by the misguided and signed, as if we can read them (Toe does, mocking the ready-made sentiments meant for our parents: *May memories keep your loved one near. Walter and Liz Preston*). This is the easy part, just following around the hardcore. In an hour we're everyone's lost children, everyone's best friends.

For now though, Brooks has us in custody. We're his prisoners as much as he's ours. All we can do is sit back and enjoy the ride.

Didn't I tell you this was going to be fun?

So I lied. Go ahead and kill me.)

THE NIGHT TURNS PURPLE TO THE EAST and then a twilight blue slowly fading to white over Avon Mountain (the treetops separating, becoming visible), and the town wakes up. The drunks are long gone, and the singles staying out late, dragging back to their condos. In the hills, along the new, exclusive streets (all of them dead ends), a thousand garage doors magically rattle open. The expensive cars warm untended, billowing enough white smoke for a million suicides.

Surfing 44, Brooks sees his regulars, vans delivering the *Courant*, bread trucks, the managers of places like Bagelz and Dunkin' Donuts going in early to serve the rush hour crowd. They're glad he's there and lift one finger off the top of their steering wheels, a gesture he echoes—a connection, the brotherhood of work.

It's the end of his shift, and he feels it; even the gray light is too much for his eyes. The feeling of being ahead of the rest of the world turns and curdles as traffic picks up; like every night, his brief reign over Avon proves an illusion. In an hour or two he'll be asleep and the future will go on without him. Everyone seems to be passing him, leaving him behind, as if he's stuck in yesterday. It's like dying, or living in another world, a vampire life.

(Do I have to say anything? Like, do you really want to hear "Last Kiss" again?

But wait: that's how it feels to Brooks when he visits Gram, the whole motel-style nursing home a kind of ark caught in a backwater, drifting in time. The cemetery's the same way; that's why Toe's so psyched to be a ghost. What's the alternative?)

Tim's awake way before he needs to be, and *bam*, we're all there—I swear, even Kyle for a second, the real Kyle, cigarette breath, scraggly muttonchops and all, in the Rage T-shirt and black Levis he never took off. Materializes, and then, *pop*, he's gone.

(Yo, where the fuck did *he* come from? Toe says.

He's got to have something to do with it, Danielle says.

Maybe he's supposed to stop it, I say.

Maybe not, Toe argues.

Oh shit, Danielle says.

Oh shit is right. Kyle's way sicker than Toe.)

Tim squints at the clock and lets his head drop again, his breath hot and rotten on the pillow. He feels different, like he might be someone else, but then the plan comes up whole, rigid and inescapable, snaps into place like a website, then drains away.

Why would anything change just because he slept? But it's early, he's still got time. The wall's white—daylight savings messing with him.

He remembers Danielle smiling in the dream but nothing she said. He tries to call back the sound of her voice and can't, as if his memory's going. Every night he goes to sleep hopeful. He hates waking up because it separates them, sentences him to this fake world of trees and streets, houses with people in them, cars going nowhere. The dream was sexy, a question of what they were allowed to do; she gave him the feeling that anything was okay, they'd always be together. Her shoulders were bare but he can't see the top she was wearing—her black bikini? that shiny pink bra? She was happy, reassuring, that's all he can recall, and even that's fading away, overpowered by the light from outside, the sky white as paper, one dead leaf clinging to a twig, too stupid to fall.

He can't get up yet, it's bad luck, like getting out on the wrong side of bed. He pulls the covers over his head, making a cave of breath, and waits for the alarm to start the day again.

Kyle's dad's already in the shower (not thinking of us, never thinking of us), so Kyle's mom throws on her robe, points her toes into her worn slippers and goes downstairs. The coffee's on a timer, hazelnut, filling the cold kitchen with its flavor. It's gray and there's mist softening the woods, a big blue jay hogging the feeder, scattering seeds on the deck, which needs to be stained—and when will they get around to that? Not this fall. It's too much for her morning brain. She gets out the bacon and lays strips in the skillet, stands there with a fork, watching them sizzle and pop.

(It's a perfect time for the real Kyle to show up, the genie of the frying pan. We're all waiting, thinking of things to say to him, like: So where the fuck have you been?)

She flips the strips and the fat crackles like static, a jammed transmission. In a minute she'll rip a paper towel from the holder above the sink and fold it double on top of a plate to soak up the grease (like my mom, like all moms), untwist the tie around the raisin bread to make toast, but for now she stands there blank, not a thought in her head. The bacon spits. Automatic pilot—not again. This is how the days escape her, or vice-versa. She wonders if everyone makes their lives a series of routines they can handle. Only if they have to. The Perlmans (my units) and Stones (Danielle's) certainly do.

(I hate that, Toe says, the way she always leaves me out.

And we don't say: because it was your fault. We say: yeah, that does suck.)

Somewhere, she thinks, people don't live like this. She didn't used to.

One year. Is it possible? It seems she's been tending him her entire life. How many more will she have to give? But she will, willingly. She's grateful he's still with them, she doesn't forget that for one second.

She remembers twenty years ago, when she was pregnant with Kelly, how relieved they were when the amnio came back normal. Not that it would have changed things, they would have loved Kelly no matter what, but that moment, hearing the result, she felt they were luckier than they deserved. Now that the opposite has happened, how can she complain?

Kyle's dad comes down without his tie, his collar undone. He goes out in his shirtsleeves to get the *Courant*, closing the door to keep the heat in (the brass knocker clanking behind him—

a sound she despises), then takes the same seat he does every morning, pulling the sections apart and stacking them in order of importance. Instead of interrupting his routine, she caters to him, rakes grease over his eggs to make the edges lacy, puts his toast in so it will be done at just the right time. She isn't angry with him, or disappointed, because she's not surprised. He's made it clear— in what he hasn't said, hasn't done—that he has no intention of commemorating the day but that she's free to do as she pleases.

"Thanks," he says as she sets the plate in front of him—his first word to her. She knows he'd be content to let it be his last for the morning, that he wishes this wasn't his life. Once they got Kyle off to college they were going to move to the Cape. They used to discuss their future greedily, the stone fireplace in his den, the porch swing with a view of the dunes, how empty the beaches would be this time of year. Now they're staying here indefinitely, their plans tied to Kyle. It's no one's fault, and yet his silences seem to accuse her, she feels she should be able to do something to make things right for them, though she knows by now that she can't. Neither of them can fix the problem, so— and this is his point—what good is discussing it?

She hovers above him a minute, watching him eat, absorbed in the front page, and wonders what she wants. For him to talk, to acknowledge what they've lost? He's done that and gone on, maybe that's what she resents, his pretending to accept this. Because it is not acceptable. It will never be acceptable to her.

"It's very good," he says. "Thank you."

"You know I'm going there today."

Because he's asking for it, sitting there like nothing's wrong, like this is any normal morning—like what they're living is a normal life.

"I figured," he says, looking at her, taking a break from his paper, being patient with her, attentive.

"I don't suppose you want to come."

"When were you thinking of going?" he asks, as if one time would be better than another for him—as if he might change his plans and join her. She can see he's doing it to appease her; he doesn't feel the need to go, he just thinks he should be supportive.

"Forget it," she says.

"No, tell me when," he says, but when she walks away he goes back to his breakfast, back to the important news.

She climbs the stairs, suddenly and helplessly furious with herself for saying anything. Kyle's left the seat up and a wet towel on the floor. He stands naked with the closet door open, stuck, unable to decide. His slick hair hugs his skull like a bathing cap. Every day it's like starting all over again.

"How about some underwear first?" she asks. No realization dawns on his face, he just moves to the dresser and finds a pair of briefs. How long would he have stood there? She wishes she didn't know: until she came and helped him.

Pants, shirt, socks, shoes. In rehab there was a lesson devoted to this exact sequence, and he's retained most of it, but he struggles with every step—tucking in his shirt is a torment—and finally forgets to velcro his shoes closed. She holds back, hoping he'll remember on his own, but when he heads for the door, she stops him. He looks at the floppy straps, his face slack, his lower lip hanging open—catching flies, her mother used to say.

"I'm sorry," he says—again, as if she might punish him, and she worries that he can read her disappointment.

"It's all right, just fix it. And comb your hair. Chop chop. We don't want to be late." She feels false, like she's cheerleading. She can be tired later, when they're gone and she has the house to herself—the hardest part of the day.

Downstairs, Kyle's dad swabs up a last line of yolk with his toast and stands as she guides Kyle to his chair.

"Morning, pal," Kyle's dad says, super chipper. "Ready for another big day?"

"Good morning," Kyle says, delayed. His dad's already at the sink, rinsing his plate. The dishes in the dishwasher are clean, so he leaves it there, another chore for her to do.

"So, what's the plan for today?" Kyle's dad asks, though he knows it (or should).

"Dad," Kyle says. "Do you think it's going to snow today?"

Kyle's dad looks at Kyle's mom like, what?

She shrugs.

"No, Kyle, I don't think it's going to snow today."

"You don't think so," Kyle echoes.

"No."

"Why not?"

"It's not that time of year," Kyle's dad says. "The air's still too warm."

Kyle looks directly ahead of him as if he's thinking, figuring out what he means. Then he looks at the feeder, loses himself in the flurry of birds. Kyle's dad checks with her, as if to prove he's making an effort—as if she can absolve him of his guilt (because he's a different kind of mess, never letting himself remember us, only the problems they'd been having with Kyle right before the crash; he's honest about that in a way she isn't, but it doesn't help).

"I've got to get ready," he says.

"Go ahead." It used to surprise her, how cold he can be (that she can be toward him). Not anymore.

(Come on, Marco, Toe says, these guys are boring. Why can't we hang out with Tim?

Go ahead, Danielle says, a decent imitation of Kyle's mom.

Ouch, Toe says, and clutches his stopped heart.)

It's just the two of them then. Kyle sits with his back to her, silent, as she makes his eggs. She glances over, watches him watching the birds fighting for position. Does any of it register or is it just there, like the TV shows that wash over her at night while Kyle's dad fools with the computer? Sometimes, when Kyle's dad has gone to bed and she sits alone with the TV, she imagines him and Tim having another crash, another policeman knocking on their door in the middle of the night (*not* Brooks this time, doing his duty, making the notifications in person, practicing his sincerity on the way over), another trip to the hospital, except this time there are no survivors. She has to identify him, a doctor in a white lab coat drawing back the sheet. She finds the outmoded tattoo above his left ankle, a tiny cloud shooting a giant thunderbolt (signifying what, she doesn't know). It's a relief, this latenight daydream, a reason to feel even worse, a kind of self-torture she can't avoid, though she knows she doesn't really believe in it. Besides, what are the odds? She's forty-nine. He'll outlive them, and then what? Who'll make him breakfast? Who'll tie his shoes? That's harder to contemplate than this tidy finality.

She flips his eggs the way he likes them (liked them). Her face—her entire body—feels bathed in grease, the pores sealed shut. Her reward for getting them off is a long shower, the quiet light of their bedroom with the drapes pulled. She'll have five hours to fill—two of them donated to the library, one spent making lunch and then watching part of her soap opera. Going back to school she never had time like this, and she's tempted to sign up for a course or two (she's only a dozen credits short of her master's), but she doesn't see how she'd handle the work. She needs her downtime to recharge.

She fixes Kyle's plate, and Kyle's dad comes down with his tie and jacket on, his briefcase fetched from the den.

"What time will you be home?" she asks, because he'll hide out there if she lets him.

"Regular time."

"And when is that?"

"Nance," he says, as if she's being unreasonable.

"I guess I should be grateful you come home at all."

And she can see he wants to agree with her, to hurt her with the weapon she's given him. (This is fucking *ugly*, Toe says, loving it.)

"I'll be home by six," he says.

"It'll be just us," she relents. "Kyle's working."

"Do you want to go out?" he asks, and as the meaning of what he's proposing hits her, he seems to realize what he's done. His face changes, he holds up a hand to cancel the whole idea. "Forget it. I mean—"

"We can." And she's insistent, definite.

"You're sure."

"It's got to be better than sitting around here. You'll have to talk to me, you know. We're not going to just sit there."

"I will. You choose where. And not the Charthouse."

The last time they went out—a disaster. She felt everyone staring at her, the mother of that poor boy. How could she laugh or enjoy a glass of wine? She could either be a freak or a monster, but she wasn't like them anymore. This won't be any different, she thinks, watching him get in his car (it could crash, he could be like Kyle, the two of them needing to be cleaned and dressed every day). Why she's agreed to go out in public with him mystifies her. To get back at him? To prove she's stronger than he thinks?

She waves. He waves and backs down the drive and into the street and is gone, off to another world, and she envies him. Where will they eat dinner? What will they talk about?

In the kitchen, Kyle is finished. He sits with his napkin in his lap, mesmerized by the birds. She has to remind him of the time. The van will be here soon and they don't want to make Peggy wait like the other day.

She leaves him to himself upstairs and takes care of the dishes, makes his sandwich and cleans up, swiping down the stove and the counters, running the disposal and rinsing the sink. She's given him enough time to get everything done, but it's already ten after. She hesitates at the bottom of the stairs, calls up.

"I'm coming," he says, and then it takes another minute.

"Did you brush your teeth well?" she asks from habit, turning away before he answers. He mumbles something, and as she looks back to see if he's lying, he rushes straight at her, raising both arms menacingly over his head, his long hands claws, growling and opening his mouth wide as a tiger to show her his plastic fangs.

It's a joke, though for a second she's honestly startled, shies back from him, unsure exactly what's going on. She's supposed to laugh, because he's laughing, so she does, wondering why some connections still work while others are permanently burned out. How many times in the last year has she heard the brain is a mystery?

"Are you going to scare Peggy with those?"

"Uh-huh." He's pleased, and she can't help but be happy for him—any happiness is welcome in this house. But, a mother, she can't stop herself from seeing him leaving the teeth in too long and choking on them, and as they wait in the front hall for the van she ruins things by telling him to please, please be careful with them.

Outside, the middle school kids are filtering down to the bus stop on the corner, hunched under the weight of their back-packs. She remembers Kyle at that age and envies their parents. She envies everyone, that's part of the problem; by some trick of fate her life is no longer hers, though she's still the same person, mostly. Tomorrow she could wake up on the Cape with another husband, different kids, a different situation, her life restored to her. Not perfect, that's not what she wants, just something liv-able. And then is disgusted with herself for what that idea im-plies. Kyle is alive; she needs to be grateful, especially today. That's why she's going to see the tree.

(And here, as fast as we hit it, she runs through who else was in the car, a little review that comes to her like one of those phrases you use to memorize shit for a test. Every good boy de-serves favor. Tim and Danielle, Marco, Chris.

Toe, Toe says. My name is Toe.)

She wants to leave something, but what, and for who? She thinks of our parents, how they must miss us. Sometimes the best thing is just remembering.

(It fucking sucks being tragic. It's like being famous. People won't leave you alone.)

Peggy's late, gliding to a stop in the drift of leaves at the edge of the lawn. As Kyle pads down the drive, she waves to Kyle's mom through the open door, wearing a witch's hat, and Kyle's mom waves back, her first contact with the outside world.

Does Kyle frighten her? Does Peggy laugh, and the others on the van?

They're too far away to tell. Kyle takes his assigned seat and Peggy folds the door closed. The van pulls out, passing the bus full of middle school kids slowing for the corner. The piercing squeal of its brakes is an alarm, the old reflex still part of her—Kyle will have to run if he's going to get on.

She closes the front door and locks it—against what?

The world. The day. The *Courant's* on the kitchen table, but the news means nothing to her. Wars and ads for dinette sets. She climbs the stairs again, heavy, carrying all of us. In the bathroom she turns on the water and hangs up her robe.

(And we can't look—dude, it's Kyle's mom—and we can't look away fast enough. Danielle sits on the pot. Toe tries to find himself in the mirror. Shampoo, rinse, conditioner. She likes it hot, and steam rolls across the cottage cheese ceiling, fogs the cold window and drips, leaving clear streaks of the pines outside.

Get ready, I say, because we've been with her long enough to know what comes next. This is her reward for waking up another day, having the faith to go through the motions. She's clean, and twists the nozzle to massage, turns her back to it and hangs her head, her eyes shut, and lets the pulse warm the knob of her spine. The shower washes the morning from her, and the past, makes the present a dark calm, only the drumming of the water on the tub, summer rain clunking through a downspout.

And we're ready, you know we've been ready this whole time. The second Kyle's mom lets us go, we leave her and sneak through the bedroom and into the carpeted hall, down the stairs and outside, and then we're running across the lawn like when we were little and late for the bus, free, for a moment, in that

world in-between home and school, of the sadness and hassle
of adults.)

Traffic's thick now, the cars anonymous, and Brooks is counting
the minutes, sticking close to the station, hoping to time it just
right. He can't refuse to answer a call, and there's always a
gap between the official end of shift and checking in the Vic
when he's defenseless. They don't get paid for running over,
not even comp time, so he circles the town center, trying not
to be obvious, waiting for the churchbells to tell him to punch
out.

     Brooks rolls through the shopping village with the Mail-
boxes, Etc. and the Japanese takeout he sometimes has for breakfast at night (and then regrets, tasting soy sauce with every burp).
Both are closed now, that part of the day not quite started yet.
He's hungry but doesn't know what he's got at home—one of
those frozen rice bowls, he hopes.

     There are the bells—his watch is dead on. He speeds to the
far end of the village as if he's on a call, then has to wait at the
light to join 44 again. The radio's quiet, and he imagines Ravitch
straightening up the console and handing the chair off to days
(the way he wishes he could hand us off to someone else).

     There's almost no traffic going away from the city, and
Brooks makes the light by the town green easily, signals and
swings into the department lot, too fast. He's got his own spot, or
the cruiser does. The scanner blinks its red dotted line a last time
before he kills it. He closes up his screen and fits his clipboard in
his briefcase, secures the shotgun in the trunk, locks the doors
and then doublechecks it, the Marine in him seeing that everything's squared away.

Inside, days is already gone, the locker room all his, a gaunt-
let of closed doors. He leans over the bench and lifts the metal
handle of his locker gingerly, ready to roll clear. He imagines a
flock of bats packed in there all night, mad and trying for his
eyes. Brooks lifts it so it clicks, pulls the door open and braces for
the onslaught.

His shirt hangs on the hanger, his jeans on the hook, his
boots facing the back wall.

He dresses in a hurry, hoping to clear out before Saintangelo
shows, knowing he won't make it.

And he doesn't. The door opens, letting in the chatter of
keyboards, a beeper peeping, and there he is. He nods at Brooks,
and Brooks dips his head. For a while the two of them concentrate on their lockers, a mutual truce. Brooks wonders if
their paperwork has reached the chief, and what his says. He
can imagine; he's written up his share of probies. Officer's disre-
gard for procedure precipitated dangerous situation—meaning
he fucked up bigtime. Meaning they should cut him, trim that
dead weight.

"Thanks," Brooks says, because he does owe him that much.

"Hey," he shrugs, non-committal.

"No, I appreciate it."

"I was just backing you up like anyone."

I'm fucked, Brooks thinks. It's not Saintangelo's fault, and
he's not sorry it was him; it would be harder if they were friends.
(What friends is he thinking of ? The guy who runs the Dunkin'
Donuts?

Mr. Arnold, Danielle says.

Whoever.)

"Look," Saintangelo says. "Maybe you ought to take some
time off."

"If I could afford to, I would." But, like any pathetic confession, it's only half true. What would he do all day?

"Don't get me wrong, but from where I'm standing, you can't afford not to. Seriously."

"I understand."

"*I* can't afford it."

"I know," Brooks says. He wants to promise he'll get his shit together, that when it comes time to back him up, he'll be there, but he has too much pride to do that right now. He's finished dressing and they're finished talking. "I'll see you tonight."

"You will," Saintangelo says.

Fucking prick, Brooks thinks, hitting the crashbar, won't cut him any slack. But it's not true, they've been carrying him the whole year. Every night he tries to forget that fact, tries, shift by shift, to redeem himself. It's not Saintangelo's fault it hasn't worked.

(And it's silly. What kind of candyass lets a carful of choppedup teenagers mess with his head? It's part of the job—for Christ's sake, Brooks is a reconstructionist, he's paid *extra* to take pictures and measure how far the dead are tossed from the wreckage. Before we showed up, he loved to race to the scene and duck under the yellow tape, the flares throwing his quivering red silhouette into the trees, the adrenalin filling him. Everything's easy when it's not your fault.)

Brooks stops at the roster board in the hall to move his magnetic disk across his name to the OUT column. The chief's in, and he detours around his office, sneaking out the back way by the recycling, then walking around the fenced-in dumpster to his truck. One of the new supercharged Tahoes slides by—Phil Eisenmann, young guy. Brooks worked eight years to make day shift; now he can only wave as the kid rolls out.

Warming up the truck, he wonders if everyone knows about last night, the gossip ricocheting through the station. The chief might be calling a meeting right now, talking with the town manager to see what kind of retirement package they can get away with, the old golden parachute. Brooks decides not to hang around and find out.

44 is engulfed in the full flood of rush hour, the eastbound lanes backed up past Stub Pond. Brooks gets off and winds his way through the calm backwaters of the sidestreets, waiting behind a flashing school bus, a kid in the emergency exit dressed like Nomar, tagging the window with his mitt. When he was a kid, the buses were round as Airstream trailers, he wanted to be Yaz and this was all woods.

(Dreamy Brooks, retreating—like us?—into the idyllic world of childhood. We're tempted every minute to stop and appreciate the homes and roads we know, the picnic table outside the library with our initials carved into the top, the path through the pine trees behind the tennis courts, the Zax convenience mart where we'd stop after school and buy a Big Grab of Doritos.

This love isn't justified; it's just time passing. When we were here we never said, isn't this great? We had too much to do, or not enough, or something; it was just scenery, and—ask any of our friends—boring as shit. It's still boring as shit, but what else do we have? We miss everything. You would too.)

The bus peels off at my street, Oxbow, and the only cars Brooks sees after that are fathers coming the other way, speeding to make up time, hoping 44 won't be jammed. (Not Kyle's dad, he's ahead of schedule, already over the mountain and nosing through West Hartford.) Mothers power-walk in pairs, wearing pastel tracksuits and talking with their hands. A younger one jogs, listening to headphones (Mrs. Lindsay, who we'd peek at at the swimming pool, pretending we were sleeping). The houses stand there dumb and inscrutable, set back from the road like mansions. It's here, alone and out of uniform, passing the neatly kept Capes and saltboxes, that Brooks feels like an outsider, maybe even a criminal, the holstered gun under his arm illegal, a potential murder weapon. Because his life is so far from theirs, and going in the wrong direction. Because they have everything and he has—what? A house he can't sell. Why should he protect them, just because he's sworn to? Melissa swore she'd be with him forever, and where is she? He can see why guys walk into offices and kill everyone they've worked with for years; it's because they think they've been screwed out of what they deserve.

And what does he deserve?

(Us. Sorry, Brooksie, fair's fair.)

He can't answer because he doesn't know (because Melissa's right, that's why), and as he lets the question sink deeper into him, a crow flies up in front of the truck, skimming the hood, buzzing the windshield. He brakes, locks 'em up, afraid he might hit it—fat, black omen—then when it's gone, winging through the woods, he wonders if it's really a sign or if he's just jumpy, his nerves fried from being up all night.

He zips down his window and spits in the crow's direction, a superstitition he picked up from Gram. He's not taking any chances today.

(And, swear to God, it wasn't us.)

Brooks just wants to get home now, to let Ginger and Skip out and feed them. He's not freaked, he's too tired for that. He wants to eat something decent and go to sleep, put yesterday behind him, forget, for a minute, that we're waiting for him today. He turns right onto Crestview and right onto Woodhaven, left onto Musket Trail, the houses smaller now, rundown bungalows and early ranches—one reason why he can't get rid of his (that and the cracked driveway and weeping shingles). The right onto Steeplechase and he searches for his mailbox, ready to lock onto the three red reflectors like a fighter pilot, except he can't find them. He's past the Bonners', he should be able to see it by now.

And then he sees why—it's lying smashed in the grass, the post headless, decapitated.

He slows, expecting the trees to be festooned with TP, the windows sticky with egg yolk, but that's it. He stops at the bottom of the drive and hops out. The box is bent in the middle, curled around whatever they used, the metal stretched. Whoever did it wasn't kidding.

(Travis and Greg, Toe says.

And you let them, Danielle says.

What was I supposed to do?)

At first Brooks is more surprised than angry (angry that he's surprised), but can't shrug it off, not like the crow. It doesn't matter that it's Cabbage Night; this is a message for him, and he knows what it says. He can hear Ginger and Skip warning him—probably been barking all night.

He picks up the crumpled box and tosses it in the bed of the truck, hops back in and guns up the drive. When he brakes, the box bangs the liner right behind him, and now he's pissed, now he is *pissed*. He slams the door and grabs the box, jams the key in the front door and shoulders it open. "Back off!" he orders Ginger and Skip, the two clamoring at first, then turning tail, scrabbling to get out of his way. He splits them, headed for the kitchen (spotless as always for Charity), where he tears the lid off the garbage and shoves the box in on top of an almost full can. He kicks it and it spills, and he kicks it again, sends it skidding off the cabinets. He tracks it into the corner and works it over, stomping on it, breaking its ribs, then stands above it, huffing, still angry.

"Fuck you," he says to nobody. "Just fuck you," he says to everyone and everything.

And like that we're beamed halfway across town to the high school, through the bulletproof windows and into the principal's office, where we stand behind Mr. Fischer (The Hook!) as he goes over the morning's announcements on his blotter. He sips his coffee and decides against asking for a building-wide moment of silence. There's no sense inflicting this on the kids again.

Yet it seems wrong not to remember us somehow. A picture in the trophy case, maybe. A stone bench with our names etched in it. Something tasteful and unobtrusive.

(Interesting, since he doesn't know our names or faces. They've slipped away, lost among thousands of other kids that graduated the normal way, kids not in his office every week, not field hockey stars or leads in the stupid musicals or members of the National Honor Society. Kids that sat in the back and skipped gym. Kids that blended in. The Hook only knows us like you do—we're the kids in that car wreck—but since he's the head of the school he feels responsible, a distant, surrogate father.)

Next week there's a Driver Safety Day sponsored by the police department, but mentioning it would be too obvious. He skips down the page with the tip of his pen—tickets for the fall formal are on sale, the chess club is meeting in the library after school, at four there's a JV volleyball game against Simsbury. We don't fit with anything; there's no easy segue. At the end he'll just

remind everyone to please be careful tonight and hope they all
have a safe and happy Halloween.

It's not the last time Tim is leaving the house—he'll stop in after
school and have the same handful of cookies, the same OJ in the
same Patriots gas station glass—but it's the last time he'll see his
mom and dad, and he doesn't want to give it away. He'd like to
tell them it's not their fault (the way Danielle tries to tell him it's
not his, the way we don't blame Toe), and all through breakfast
he feels jittery and sick. The little TV is on, Scot Haney guessing
at the weekend weather, laughing for no reason. Tim plows
through his cereal, the milk reacting like acid when it hits his
stomach lining. He can't hang on to the plan tightly enough, and
checks the clock. Time will drive him, all he has to do is stay on
schedule.

He was late that day—he was late every day because Toe's
alarm clock had a snooze bar. Toe slapped at it and rolled over,
five more minutes. (No one knows this better than Brooks, who
interviewed everyone we came in contact with 24 hours prior to
the accident for his big report.) So Tim thinks he's early. He can
afford some extra minutes with his folks, minutes they might
need later. But they're not doing anything special, and for him to
do something—to touch them, hug them—would seem suspicious. Jim Carrey is on now, goofing on the set's phony living
room, promoting his new movie; his is the only voice in the
kitchen, as if they've agreed to let him take over their lives.

He seemed fine at breakfast, they'll say in private, away from
the neighbors.

How can he stop them, in the future, from reading everything as a clue? Because they will, even though he knows from Danielle that it's useless. He won't leave a note (what could he say that wouldn't crush them?), so whatever he says now is even more important, something to remember him by.

"We're having leftover pasta for dinner," his mom announces after searching the fridge. "If that's all right with everyone."

"Oh joy," his dad jokes, mugging for him, and from habit Tim plays along, sticking his tongue out, uck. Why, all of a sudden, is he sorry? It's all a lie—summer was, and the two months of school he's sat through, taking notes, doing homework, building his cover. He's been waiting for today for too long. Now that it's really here it feels stale, not the pure relief he imagined. But it will be.

"I'm working tonight," he says, certain his look down into the half-empty bowl has given him away.

"That's convenient," his dad says.

"You driving Kyle?" his mom asks.

"Yep."

"You be careful, they say it's going to rain."

She's busy with a cantaloupe so he doesn't have to answer. She'll see it as a prediction, he thinks. "Fucking slow down," he told Toe, but it's different.

(I wasn't going that fast, Toe argues, but Brooks's equations have us leaving the road at fifty-five, a good twenty above the limit.)

And who'll believe it's an accident, just a coincidence? He wants to protect them from the rumors, from the truth, but how can he protect them from himself? He'd have to split in two, one of him alive, the other dead.

It's too late, that's already happened, only they don't know it. He's almost glad it's going to rain, as if he's gotten a break, but not really.

Wet flakes stick to the side of the bowl, a slick of specks in the middle. He'll be sick if he finishes, and then he thinks he'll be sick anyway. He gets up, holding the bowl high enough so his dad can't see how much is left (like when he was little and didn't want to eat his peas), takes it to the sink and rinses it, washing the evidence down the disposal.

"This guy's a nut," his dad says, amused by Jim Carrey lying sideways across a chair—the same shtick Tim has seen him use for a hundred interviews—and Tim wonders what it would be like to be famous and have everyone love you.

(Everyone does love you, Danielle says.)

It wouldn't change anything important. His mom and dad love him. Danielle loved him.

"Better get your rear in gear," his mom says, pointing a knife at the clock on the stove.

His dad's done too, and follows him upstairs, a second set of footsteps. When Tim was little, his dad would make a race of it, thundering up behind him, crowding him out roller derby style, but now they climb at the same pace, and at the top they go their separate ways.

In the bathroom, everything shrieks with meaning—the striped wallpaper he picked out when he was a kid, the brand new toothbrush his mom just bought him (and there, in the wastebasket, its plastic package). The worst is his face in the mirror, the zit that's been growing on his chin, a hard nodule. This person. This flat double of him. He can't see what's in his mind, what he thinks he's doing. It was that way even before the accident; he never felt the way his reflection looked, as if one of them was false. The mirror fooled him—it's been him all along.

His room is stocked with artifacts. What does he need? Not much. The top of his desk is empty. He's got his cigarettes and

lighter in the outside pocket of his backpack. Sunglasses, gum,
pens. Books, notebooks. He's even done his trig homework.

"Five after!" his mom calls.

This time his dad beats him to the stairs. Going down, Tim
has a view of his bald spot, the fluffy crown around it. What will
his dad do? He can't see anything past the funeral, the procession
of just-waxed Cadillacs. They'll go on living somehow. He could
if he wanted to. It isn't that hard. You wake up and do what
you're supposed to do and go to sleep, over and over. All you
have to do is make sure you don't do anything stupid.

Their keys are on a pegboard in the back hall. His dad kisses
his mom, and he's glad he sees it, that he can be their witness.

"Have a big day," his dad says, and flashes him a wave, his
keys in hand, briefcase weighting the other.

"You too," Tim says, and that's it, he's gone, the door to the
garage closing with a hollow clap.

"I don't know what you're going to have for dinner," his
mom says.

"I'll get something there."

It's time to go—past time—but he's stuck. What can he say
to apologize, to make them understand? Just a hint so it makes
sense to them. He stops in the middle of the kitchen as if he's
forgotten something, but really he's stalling. If he's late, maybe he
won't have to go through with it. The thought lingers, a curios-
ity; he holds it, turns it over. He's all caught up in school; he
could just go on living. Could it really be that simple?

(It's Danielle touching a hand to his forehead, a mother
checking for a fever, fogging his mind. The effect is temporary—
(we'll do it to Brooks too), a split second of intense questioning
followed by emptiness—what was I just thinking of?)

"Are you all right?" Tim's mom asks, coming over to him, cocking her head to look into his eyes.

"Yeah," Tim says, but now she has his arm, holding his wrist gently, as if it might be broken.

"I know today isn't going to be easy," she says, "but I know you, you'll get through it."

She's so wrong he almost wants to laugh, it's that sad. Who is this person she's thinking of? The Tim who takes care of Kyle, the Tim whose grades are better than last year's, that's who she means. Not the Tim who wakes up at three and is disappointed it was just a dream. Not the Tim who's been counting down the calendar since school let out in June. She doesn't want to know that Tim.

So he says, "I will." Because he doesn't want her to know him either.

He has his backpack. His coat's in the front hall closet, a replica of the one his mom tossed with all of his other clothes from that night, even his Timbs soaked through. He's got his new ones on, and upstairs in his closet a new blue flannel waits beside his uniform. Brooks isn't the only reconstructionist in this.

It's cold out, the sky white above the trees. The air smells of mushrooms and rotting leaves. Tomorrow's November. Then December, the days growing shorter, night coming early.

"Drive safe," his mom says, then waves behind the storm door. He waves, a no-look over his shoulder. He wishes he had a basketball to shoot at the hoop. A swish—would that be a happy memory for her? Could anything be?

Sometimes she blows his dad a kiss. That would be good, but when he turns, the front door's shut.

He shoves his backpack across the emergency brake and climbs in, leans forward to turn the key and the jeep fires up.

While it warms he untwists his safety belt and clicks it home, smooths it over his shoulder. He can't believe it—he's free.

It's Kyle who calls up the real Kyle this time. A kid getting off the van in front of him trips and can't free a hand in time to stop his fall. It's a major faceplant, the kid kisses the curb and there's blood, and there we are on one side of the crowd gathered around to help and the real Kyle on the other.

It's him, in black jeans and his leather jacket, but he doesn't recognize us, doesn't seem to see us, like Peggy and the teachers yelling for everyone to make room.

Hey, you loser, Toe calls, but already he's fading, we're fading, the whole scene is dissolving. We're being called away.

To the tree—big surprise. Someone in a car, it's impossible to tell which one, traffic's so bad. We stand there for the family photo, three teen angels.

Maybe his memory's coming back, Danielle guesses.

I don't think so. I think he needs to be here the same as we do.

He's in-between, Toe says. It's like part of him's here. His body. The rest of him's dead.

So what does that mean? Danielle says, and Toe looks at me like I should tell it.

Hello? she says.

Obviously she doesn't watch the right movies. It means he's come to get it back.

It's so busy Mr. Arnold is doing the drive-thru. Most everyone is a regular, but the dark-haired girl in the Toyota he doesn't know.

She's small, maybe college age, young enough to remind him of Danielle. She's not, of course, but once she's gone he can't get rid of her.

He worked with her that night, and remembers her friends coming in while they were mopping up and bugging her for some freebies. Maybe they were stoned, he doesn't know. None of them seemed drunk. (Thank you for suspecting it anyway.

Leave him alone, Danielle says.)

He remembers her boyfriend because he used to visit her when she was doing the drive-thru. He'd have his mother's wagon and he'd pull up to the order board and just talk to her. He survived, she didn't. It's a bitch of a world, it is.

"Yoo-hoo, anybody there?" the headset fuzzes.

"Welcome to Dunkin' Donuts, may I take your order?"

He punches it up and prints it out, preoccupied the whole time, an instant's trance of a daydream. He sent flowers to the funeral home, hoping that was proper. He'd never lost an employee before. They were shorthanded for a few weeks; he doesn't remember who he found to take her place, the turnover's so high. It seems longer than a year. How does that happen? It's Monday and then it's Sunday and the whole thing starts all over again.

The woman pulls up and he makes change, hands her the bag with her croissant and a tall decaf with cream and sugar. They're polite, warmly impersonal with each other, the perfect retail relationship, keep things moving. He folds the window closed and glances at the black-and-white monitor—someone's coming. The rush is almost over, though; pretty soon he'll have to start putting together the soups.

Danielle stays with him, and Toe with her, like he's interested. No one gives a shit about ol' Marco so I walk around back where there's a scraggly guy my dad's age in an apron and a paper hat making doughnuts. They're raw and white and knock against each other in a big vat of grease, like bobbing for apples. A machine makes the dough and shapes it into O's; the guy just puts them on a stick and dumps them in. What a sucky job.

But he's alive. He'll go home and eat dinner and watch TV.

Those doughnuts were the last thing we ate; they were in the accident just like us, DOA, thrown smack against the walls of our stomachs. Halloween ones, with orange and black icing—bad luck. I wonder . . . and yeah, there are some out front. They must be popular, half the tray's gone, rows of ghostly circles on the sheet.

Hey, check these out, I say. It's the same ones we ate.

Oh man, Toe says, 'cause it's his kind of joke.

I didn't eat any, Danielle says. No way. I've seen what goes on around here.

It's like a secret mission. In the basement, one at a time, Kyle's mom shoots hot glue on our faces. Caught for all time on the creaking stage of the auditorium (our classmates mocking from the front rows, moving up like Stratego pieces, one cheek-numbing seat at a time), we're airbrushed and dull, as blank as the plain gray background. Only seniors get color. Kyle's mom thumbs us into place on the doily, a trinity, Danielle in the middle. I look stupid with my hair short, and Toe is completely retarded in a tie and sweater combo.

Who dressed you? Danielle says, leaning close to see better.

Shut up.

She laughs: this is sweet. And you know everyone who stops at the tree is going to see this. Christopher Murphy, dorkus malorkus.

Shush, he says, but he's right behind her, leaning in, her clean hair inches from his lips. These dreams we keep. How do you tell someone they're doing something stupid?

Kyle's mom's craft table is as neat as their living room. The doily's on a black piece of construction paper on a square of plywood left over from some project. Kyle's mom pries the metal top off the clear shellac and swirls it with a stirrer, brushes it on thick. She wants us to last.

Waiting for us to dry, Kyle's mom stops on the page with Kyle (my own vacated spot neatly filled from underneath by Moriah Reeves). He's unshaven, sticking his chin up, looking tough. We all look around, expecting him, but there's nothing, just his dad's workbench, a box of extension cords, an old rocking horse in the corner.

Now she's the one that's stuck in the past, an indulgence she only allows herself in private, a secret drinker proud of how long she's gone without. In the picture he's wearing a black T-shirt, but it's impossible to tell what band, the tops of the gothic letters are chopped off. She has it upstairs somewhere, she has all of his old clothes, though they no longer fit him. Every couple months she goes to Bob's and buys him new blue jeans one size up, folds the old ones and piles them on the shelf in his closet. (Forget that Kyle wore black jeans, that Kyle hated sneakers, that Kyle liked the idea of frying the power grid for the whole East Coast.)

Looking at the face she remembers, she pictures him in the hospital, the first time she saw him after the accident. The doctors had explained that his injuries were severe, but even the sight of him cocooned in bandages, a fountain of tubes jutting from him, didn't convince her. It was only when they cut away the shell to irrigate the grafts that she understood he was different now.

They've done what they've had to. She was a fool then, thinking there was a choice, just as she was wrong in thinking she was alone. When they went out to Denver, every family there was going through the same thing, working through the stages. Physically Kyle was in better shape than most of the kids, and he didn't have the problem a lot of them had adjusting mentally—a fact she's still not sure she's grateful for. The hospital provided a suite for them, and every afternoon while Kyle was walking in the pool there were separate classes for them, facilitators and parents who'd been through it giving them tips, always ending with a little peptalk, the importance of keeping a positive attitude. She remembers coming out of one of those meetings and seeing a boy in a wheelchair in the concrete courtyard practicing flyfishing, whipping the hookless line swishing back and forth above his head with his one arm. It seemed such a hopeful gesture, and so necessary that she transferred it to Kyle, saw him and Mark down on the Farmington River where the old railroad trestle goes over, back behind the Dairymart and the carwash (where we'd park and get high during school), the two of them sailing their lines into the glassy flats just above the riffle.

What other promises did she want to believe? That this would bring them together as a family, make them stronger. That Kelly would take the rest of the semester off and stay home to help her. That there was a larger, unfathomable purpose behind it. Because she would have believed anything then.

What's changed?

She's alone here, the neighbors unsure how to approach her. There's not a whole floor full of parents who know what she's going through, with new families showing up every week, devastated, ready to listen. In some ways, the hospital spoiled the rest of the world for her. And the vast improvement they all but promised—that she expected, keeping that positive attitude—hasn't happened. It's been a year.

Looking at the old Kyle, she tries to remember what her life was like then, right then—what she was doing the moment this picture was taken. In class. At the library. Driving somewhere, mindless. It's impossible, as if she could call back the feel of those lost days, breathe that stale museum air.

She knows some of the other faces on the page, recognizes names, but they seem to belong to the past as well, like the high school itself, there but no longer a part of their lives (the swim club, the rails-to-trails bike path they used to cruise). Only Tim comes to the house now, and Noel the Mailman, steady as a metronome. She sees her old friends at the library and they talk across the counter, trading harmless gossip, recommending best-sellers, but it's rare that one of them invites her anywhere. For a long time she didn't feel right accepting even lunch offers—it was just too soon, she had too much to do—and she thinks her nearly hermetic self-involvement has probably driven them off for good.

Kyle. Shouldn't she make something for him? Or would that say something about her she'd rather not reveal?

She flips to Tim, the lucky one. Spared. But there's been a change in him too. He's still the nice, quiet kid he was before, but now he seems singled out, apart, more mature, the teenager drained out of him. He'll never be the same either. All of them.

(But notice how she barely thinks of us, the ones she's putting up, too far gone to deserve her pity. The glue dries on the backs of our skulls like blood.)

She takes a plain wreath of vines and tries it on for size, the hole showcasing the three of us. Not perfect but good enough—the other one's too light. A thread of glue stretches like a web from the foil pie plate to the tip of the gun until she breaks it with a finger. As a last touch, she adds a black velvet bow, and is happy with the colors. (Mourning by Martha Stewart. Kyle would stop the car and punt it into the woods, jump up and down on it.) She's torn between leaving it up and reusing it, having it up just for the day, making it a yearly thing. There's already a wire loop to hang it; all she needs is a hook to screw into the tree. She finds a silver one in her cubby.

(And voilà, we're immortal.)

Brooks makes eggs for dinner and canned corned beef hash that looks like dog food. It's all he's got. Ginger and Skip watch him as he watches the weather channel in his bare feet, chewing as the maps pass, cold Bud from a can easing him toward sleep. It's a ritual, soothing; it's as much excitement as he can handle after being on all night. The other shows babble at him; this he can understand without sound. There's already snow in the Rockies, a truck jackknifed in Loveland Pass. (And—cue the shivery music, cue the dead kids, sitting right beside him on the couch.

But we're always with fricking Brooksie. He's like part of our clique, another fuck-up, just older, held back indefinitely.

This shit's making me hungry, Toe says.

It's so nasty, Danielle says. I hate coming here, this place creeps me out.

It's not dirty, Brooks is good at battling the dog hair. She means how bare it is, unlived in, like the houses built out in the desert for the atomic bomb. Because it's on the market, Brooks tries to confine himself to the back bedroom, and even there his things are stashed out of sight, the surfaces polished. Maybe it's working, because Charity left a note by the sink saying she thinks this new couple is serious, transfers from Virginia with kids. Brooks has already heard this song a dozen times, has learned to ignore her chirpy sales pitches.)

No, here's what he's really been waiting for, the blue screen of the local forecast with the phases of the moon—"Local on the 8's," dependable as breath, giving his day some desperately needed continuity. He'll watch it again when he wakes up, the channel waiting faithfully on the cable box while the TV sleeps.

Cloudy and cool, a chance of light rain late in the day, showers lingering well into the morning hours. Different. What he remembers from last year is the wind, the way the yellow caution tape bellied out, leaves cartwheeling into the darkness beyond the portable lights. The road was dry, the friction coefficient hefty enough at a reasonable speed.

(Here he goes, Toe says.)

We know the routine. Because Brooks is drawn to what went wrong, thinking if he can understand it he'll be able to fix his own smashed life—the accident and Tim and the commendation and then the allegations in the paper and the quiet demotion and night shift again and Melissa leaving and the dreams that haven't stopped since midsummer. A zombie, he's drawn to the door in the hallway and down the rickety basement stairs, drawn to the makeshift desk under the stuttering fluorescent light, drawn to the black file cabinet he bought at the department auction, drawn to the rubberbanded folder fatter than all the others. He still has his plate but the dogs are afraid of the stairs so he's alone. It feels like night down here, windowless. (They could tunnel to each other, him and Kyle's mom, burrowing under the hills and roads and fiber optic lines.)

He knows it's late. He knows if he takes the rubberbands off and starts leafing through the report that he'll be here for hours (he needs to wake up early and visit Gram), but knowing isn't enough. It's an addiction—we are—and today of all days he can't help himself. And anyway, it's not like he'd sleep.

He opens the folder, and there are the contents broken down into an efficient alphabet of sections and subsections. Involved Persons. Interviews/Statements. Scene Diagrams. Mechanical Inspect. He knows his own words, but there's a satisfaction in reading them again. Here are the formulae he got right, speed and energy and distance, the conservation of momentum, the free body diagrams, the evidence location chart cleaned up from his scribbled field notes. He'd forgotten the CD case, launched like a cannonball at impact. And the ice scraper, the empty Dunkin' Donuts cup. Contents of ashtray. A whole page of Vehicle Lamp Examination Notes—*Photo Y/N.*

He's done with his Bud. Outside, the white sun is up and Avon's bustling, everyone rushing, but there's no time underground, and Brooks is sinking, heading for the center of the earth. Beside him, his eggs go cold. As the pages rattle past, the fat congeals in white blobs, and he elbows the plate away. Appendix I details the roadway profile (cracked, local DOT maintained, posted 35 MPH, two way, solid center line, curve, hillcrest, bituminous concrete). Appendix II lists the weather conditions (overcast, dry, moderate to heavy wind, dark, artificial illumination absent). Crush deformation, vehicle search, release of medical records. You'd think we'd be bored, knowing it so well (having so many places to go), but there we are at the very end, gathered around Brooks, looking over his shoulder at pictures of ourselves, laughing and making snotty comments, as if this is a family album. Not because it's fascinating (it's really not that interesting, told so dryly). No—because it's about us.

That day Toe picked him up first, so now Tim has to swing by my house, rolling up Oxbow. It feels illegal, like Brooks with his gun. Everyone else is going to work, doing something constructive; Tim's just out there, on the loose, no future to worry about. The world is simple and thin, numbers on a clock. He stops at the bottom of our drive, counting out time, how long it took me to get in, Toe being an asshole, pretending to take off as I reached for the door handle.

(I was waiting in my jean jacket, telling my mom—yelling back at the house—that I didn't need a coat.

And where are my parents? Why aren't we following them? Why don't we get to chew on every delectable morsel of their grief?

Because *I'm* telling the story, all right? You don't think it's hard enough just being here? We're all Scrooge in this one, we're all Mr. Magoo.)

Tim gives me a minute and then we're off to Kyle's, our last stop.

What did we talk about? Brooks doesn't have that. There was a rumor at school that Amy Rubin was sleeping with Mr. Bailey, our gym teacher (it was true too, it was one of the first things we learned when we came back). We were cracking jokes about that, making crude guesses at how they arranged it, the love notes they passed, their hiding places. Mr. Bailey was short and used too much mousse. We were outraged and jealous and letting our imaginations get nasty with it. Mats and gym equipment, the desk in his office, the way the shellacked basketball court gave you brushburns.

(Marco, Danielle scolds, but she knows Amy Rubin too—stuck-up, too good for us. In the cafeteria, the day after, she laughed. "Oh phew," she said, "I thought it was someone important.")

It was just a regular day. We didn't care that it was Halloween, we didn't need an excuse to party. Toe had Rancid cranked, headbanging over the wheel as we drove down Oxbow. Tim was shotgun because he was the first one in; later I'd be sitting there, and he remembers this like it was his fault. None of us were wearing seatbelts, but he has his on now, being careful. Outside, nothing's changed—the lawns and houses are the same, the driveways and rock gardens. Nothing moves. The only signs of life are birds, and he has to search for them. Everyone could be dead, the earth deserted. That would be fucked up, he thinks—if he were the last person in the world. But it's like that already.

A Cadillac with an old guy in a hat passes the corner of Surrey, ruining the illusion. Tim crosses Country Club and worms back through the maze, taking Stagecoach to Indian Pipe. Mounds of leaves from the weekend are piled in the gutter, waiting for the town truck to vacuum them up. He stops at Kyle's mailbox. Their grass is unnaturally green, chemically healthy. The bare trees look like hands reaching through the ground, and he feels stoned, insulated from outside by the zippered windows and the machinery beneath him, the interlocking gears and steering. He waits for an imaginary Kyle to come hunching down the drive, his fists shoved in his pockets, the belt of his leather jacket hanging loose (and here he comes, on cue, the real Kyle, like Tim, duplicating that day. He pats the hood and the engine hiccups. He tips the seat forward like he doesn't see Danielle there, climbs in and sits smack on Toe's lap.

Get the fuck off me, Toe says, but Kyle's poking his head between the seats, talking to Tim, his lips moving but nothing coming out. (What did he say that day? Nothing important. Is this the same?)

Kyle, man, Toe says, like he can wake him up. Kyle!

He keeps talking. We're not here for him any more than we exist for Tim, like we're on different planes.)

Tim looks over his shoulder into the backseat like he's forgotten something, like he can hear Kyle, and there's the fear that he's stronger than us, that all we can do is watch. Danielle gives Tim the Vulcan neck pinch—it was a thing between them—and he looks back to the house. The garage door is lifting.

He searches for first, jams it in and hits it, the jeep slipping on the leaves, peeling out—not *too* suspicious. He bolts for the hill, and then, on the far side, thinks it was dumb of him to run. What's going to happen if they catch him? He hasn't done anything yet.

Kyle's mom has just pushed the button for the door and is walking toward her Pathfinder with the wreath when she hears the screech of tires out front, heart-stopping. She expects a thunderous crash, glass tinkling, a silent aftermath, but there's nothing, an engine revving and then gone before the door's halfway up. They're lucky no one's been killed on that hill, with the Fiedlers' drive right there; the place is a speedway in the morning.

She clips the thought off, aware that she's being paranoid. All cars do not crash.

(Only Toe's.

Eat me completely.)

She sets the wreath on the seat and carefully buckles up, checks her mirrors like a pilot and inches back, tentative. Mark's commented on it. She's been a different driver since the accident, quick to yield. One of her persistent daydreams is that she will kill someone with her car—another driver, a child on a bike. She wishes she could avoid driving altogether, do everything over the internet, but that's just not possible, despite all the promises on TV. Her days are a series of errands dictated by the layout of Avon, the loop she uses to connect the library on Country Club to the Mailboxes and post office in town center to the liquor store and bank and Blockbuster and Stop'n'Shop on 44 and then home again. She knows the backroads in case there's a problem, how Old Albany Turnpike will take you by Secret Lake and hook up with Parkview when the dip by the golf course floods, but lately she tries to consolidate her trips, ventures out in mid-day when traffic's thinnest. Some days she leaves the house only to walk to the mailbox.

It will all change in time, she thinks. She has to believe that. A glance at us assures her: she's lucky.

The door rumbles down in sections as she backs into the turnaround. Closed, the house admits nothing, stands there blank and well-cared for, like any other on the road. Is that what they're hoping for, to be normal, the same as their neighbors, to pretend everything's fine? How can a house—a road, a whole town—be a lie?

She makes it to Stagecoach unchallenged, gives way at the stop sign to a new green Beetle—cute but impractical; she'd never take one on the highway, that would be asking for it. She pays attention to what she's doing, sitting up straight, both hands on the wheel, her mobile phone off. There's always a line on

Country Club, and after waiting she joins the tail, hanging back, riding high above the other cars. She's prepared to miss the light at the bottom of the hill but it waits for her. She could be going to the library—Alice is in early, her Volvo parked at the far end— but she passes the entrance, fends off the old cemetery on her left with its lichened tablets and granite obelisks from before the Civil War. She could make the right onto Burnham Road and get there quicker taking the back way, but she doesn't. She's like Brooks. She's like Tim. She wants to do it right.

She slows for the white stripes of the golf cart crossing. Later the retirees will be out, hunting for their Titleists among the brush, but it's too early now, too cold, the grass frosted a spruce blue. While she's climbing the long rise to the 18th green and the remodeled clubhouse, she passes a spot on the right where Brooks sometimes hides, the grass worn away there, bare mud rutted with tiretracks. Mark used to warn her in the mornings, since he came the same way; it was a joke, a game, evading the police like teenagers.

(Like us, except we didn't evade shit. We couldn't evade a fucking tree.

Stop, Marco, Danielle says. Just stop. It wasn't Toe's fault.

I didn't say it was, I say. And Toe's all mopey, you can see he's playing it up for her.)

The long flat crossing the top of the hill is easy, her mind finding nothing charged to feed on—jack-o'-lantern trash bags stuffed with leaves, orange and black streamers wound around a coachlight, a vestigial wishing well, a covered above-ground pool—but coming down the other side, she slows for the curve before the rails-to-trails and there's the telephone pole those two girls from Simsbury hit. (They shimmer into existence by the roadside, our closest neighbors, standing shoulder to shoulder

like the twins in *The Shining*—weakly, as if their signal's fading.)
It's cruel, she thinks; it hasn't been five years and she can't remember their names. There are more every day; every little town
in Connecticut loses a few kids each year, every graduating class
has its missing. As hard as it is for her to admit it, the truth is she's
not unique. Neither is Kyle. This should be a comfort.

Over the rails-to-trails and down the steep hill, braking, to
the stop sign at the T of Old Farms Road. A bleached poster on
the pole beside her advertises a fire department carnival from
August. A left would take her into town center with its busyness,
the Mailboxes just opening its doors, the back of the post office
smelling of coffee. Across the intersection they're building a new
gated community around a pond, the plywood shells of houses
up, bundles of tiles grouped on the roofs. There's no decision for
her. She signals (for who?) and follows us through the ruined pillars and into the woods.

It *is* a dangerous road, all switchbacked curves and no shoulder, trees encroaching on both sides, no visibility. A couple
of the worst trunks have reflectors nailed to them at waist level.
Someone has given the leaping buck on the deer crossing sign
wings—a Pegasus—while someone else has supplied it with a
stiff penis. Because that's what kids do, they fool around, thinking
everything's a joke. They don't expect a deer to come slamming
through their windshield, that only happens to losers.

(And don't think we're not tempted to flush one into her
path for this little lecture.

Or how about a dog, Toe says, and then has to deal with
Danielle, who misses her two.)

Like everyone, Kyle's mom wonders what we were thinking
in those last minutes, sure we were oblivious, a bunch of stupid
kids taken by surprise. Who wouldn't be? At least she knows Toe

wasn't drunk. It's small consolation, knowing we were just going too fast. For a long time she couldn't believe it was that simple, but, turning through the curves, she can see how easy it would be to lose control, how narrow the road, how little room for error there is. Every tree's a potential killer.

Why doesn't the town cut them back? Why aren't there guardrails? Why aren't there lights?

She knows the answers but doesn't accept them. In the end it all comes down to money.

The people she feels sorriest for are Chris's parents. She sent them a note with her condolences; she hopes they know that no one blames them. (For what?

For me, Toe says.

It's a circle, a spiral, a whirlpool. She's sorry for my parents because I'm their only child, and sorry for Danielle's because she has two sisters. She's so sorry for herself that it spreads to everyone else. But she doesn't want other people to feel sorry for her. It's enough that she does.

Okay, it's unfair of us. Our parents are just as crushed and messy, and she's the only one who made something for us. And really, Kyle's so fucked up that we still feel sorry for her.)

There's nothing to look at in the woods, so she's dreaming, memory overtaking her. She used to drive Kyle to mites this way, and she remembers the hollow boom of the puck hitting the boards, the slashing sound their skates made. The Whalers practiced there. Banners hung from the rafters with the names of the private schools she and Mark later debated sending him to: Andover, Choate, Loomis Chaffee. (They should have—another what-if.) What happened to those early Saturday mornings, freezing rain and bad coffee at the snack bar, the other mothers stopping their conversations to cheer as their kids wobbled past?

She's going too slow because there's someone riding her bumper, a maroon Jaguar, and she speeds up. It's not fast enough; the car behind her slips over the yellow line to peek around her. "Don't be an idiot," she says. She's tempted to just touch her brakes to make him back off but knows it could get her killed. She thinks she'll lose him at the school; he's probably on his way to work, taking the back way to Route 10. She can see the out-buildings of Avon Old Farms fleeting through the woods, the half-timbered mock-Tudor garages and dormitories, and then around a final curve the giant red-brick silo rising into the pines. The turn comes but he stays with her, locked on, as if this is a chase.

This isn't how she wanted to approach the tree, being driven from behind. It's not far—a jog right, a dip and then a rise—but she's going too fast, there's nowhere to pull off, and suddenly she's going past it, it's here and gone, the cards and ribbons and flowers whirling by like a bright carousel.

"Get *off* of me," she says, and brakes, waving the idiot around her. "Come on, you jerk."

The Jag whips past, its horn swearing, and just as she thought, it's an older man, treating her to the finger.

"Yeah," she says, "fuck you too, buddy."

(Go Kyle's mom! Toe says.)

Stopped, her hands still on the wheel, she lets out a breath, shakes her head, pissed off. This is how she's remembering Kyle.

And no one else is going to do it. No one would care if she opened the window and threw the wreath into the bushes and drove off. Life would go on. That's the worst thing. All around her are things existing dumbly—squirrels and trees and bushes—and she resents them. She can't help it.

She has to do a three-pointer, nervously checking both ways, has to pass the tree going the other way and then turn into Avon Old Farms, easing over the speed bumps as if she's heading for the rink. Breakfast is over; boys in their blazers and backpacks are walking on the quad. White shirts and identical ties. (I know, it's creepy, someone's weird fantasy of high school, but Kyle's mom thinks it might have been safer, sending him away. It's what Kyle's dad wanted, tired of dealing with his shit. But who would have kept an eye on him then?)

She'd like to stay—how long has it been?—but turns around in a handicapped spot and makes her way back to the road. This is better, more deliberate. She takes her time, the car quiet, tires climbing the bumps. She waits at the entrance until she sees it's clear, then takes the dip and the rise at her own pace. She pulls off as far as she can, one set of wheels in the leaves.

It's an effort getting out, to stand there breathing the chilly air. People driving by will see her with the wreath. She can hear the rumors creeping through the hair salons and pizza parlors, passed from row to row at the next band concert. Did you hear about Nancy Sorensen? She shouldn't care how people see her, but she does. Even at the library she feels separated from the rest of Avon. If she could just make a connection that didn't involve her being a victim—because she's not. It's impossible; they've talked about moving, but she's afraid of ending up with nothing.

She's been here before but is surprised to see how ugly the place is, how insignificant, not the great stage of a tragedy. The grass is a wrack of dust and muddied cigarette butts. Beneath the faded notebook paper and the stapled pictures, the tree seems smaller than she remembered, harmless, not a murderer. It's a sycamore, patches of scabby bark holding poems, pennies, an old ticket stub from *Les Miz*. Some of the flowers are new, and she wonders who left them (the yellow rose is from Mr. Kul-

wicki who had Danielle in chorus and band). She wonders if
there's anything for Kyle, but doesn't bend down to check the
cards stuck on with rusty thumbtacks.

She wonders where our parents are, why they're not here.
She thinks they might understand. (She's right and she's wrong.
Like her, our parents have their own problems no one can share.)

A minivan passes, trailing its own shift of wind. Around her,
the tall trees creak, their bare branches fanned like nerves against
the white sky. She picks an empty spot about eye-level, facing
traffic. She takes the hook from her pocket and digs the point
into the tree, screws it through the tough skin until it's solid. She
holds us up with both hands, evenly, hangs us like a picture in the
living room (and here we are again, the photos you know us by,
those kids from the high school, eternally seventeen).

The ribbon twists in the wind, and she fixes it, steps back to
see how it looks. The pictures are too small, and she's glad she
thought of the wreath. People on the road will know, and that's
the whole idea.

She looks up the trunk to the peeling limbs, the fingerlike
twigs and dangling seedballs, calculating the tree's age. It could
have stood here fifty years before we ran into it and made it famous. Why this tree? Why not the next one, or the next? But
that's the definition of an accident, isn't it. She doesn't blame the
tree, just as she doesn't blame Kyle.

Is that true?

She needs it to be.

She should be more like the tree, untouched, untouchable,
stand there and let the weather blow over her year after year,
hopeless, waiting for nothing.

She's going to leave, she says, addressing the tree one last
time, straightening the wreath, already cocked in the wind.

There, that's better. Touching us, she has the sense that someone is listening, that someone *must* understand. (And right beside her, dropping a hand on her arm, Danielle says yes.) She steps back, sure that she's lost it. And then, as if she's from another planet, this world a mystery, she lays her hand on the trunk of her enemy, on the rough bark, as if she might feel, beneath its wooden skin, a beating heart.

TURNING IN WITH ALL OF US CRAMMED INTO THE JEEP, the first thing he sees are the goalposts and the dead scoreboard beyond the end-zone, the painted lanes of the track and the deserted erector set of the bleachers with its control tower of a pressbox where we used to smoke. No signs of life, just the shag of yellow grass trampled to mud between the hashmarks. On the far side, an acre of parked cars. Sitting square and slit-windowed in its maze of chainlink fences, the school looks like a factory, a brick prison. Two flags fly from high poles in the middle of the circle by the front doors. The buses are gone, the lot taken up, even the raised dividers at the ends claimed by four-wheel-drives. He has to troll around back for a spot, just like Toe did, though the one he finds is closer to the woods than to the baseball diamond. Nothing is going to be exact, he thinks, but silently blames himself anyway.

He's late enough, and reaches through Danielle for his back-pack, then hesitates, the gray trees framed in the windshield, sending him a message. Certain pieces of the world—or are they visions?—still have a touching density. He thought leaving his parents would be the hardest part of the day, but now he sees it will get harder with every step. He doesn't want to have to deal with people. The plan seems foolish, unnecessary. He could drive to the tree right now. It's Halloween, that's all that matters.

At the same time, he wants to honor those promises he's made to us (to Danielle—to himself, really). What's the rush? He's done five months like this, pretending he's interested; now that the day is finally here, he should relax and enjoy it, that private knowledge lifting him above everything else. And he will; it'll be like going to class stoned. Plus he's like us. He wants to see it all one last time.

That day, Kyle stayed behind. He said he had to meet someone (meaning he had to sell some bud) and went off into the woods along the outfield fence, following the trail there. That's what he does now, probably headed for Mrs. M's gasmart to make a delivery. (His dad found the rest of his stash and ditched it in the garbage before his mom could see how much product he was sitting on.) So we know he's running the same game that Tim is, replaying the day. It's almost a relief; it buys us some time (like time matters).

It would be nice if someone could keep an eye on Kyle, but we're all walking with Tim around the side of the building, his entourage. Cruising through in his Blazer is Jamie Weeks, and immediately we fly across the parked cars and slip into him, switch like a jumpcut, watching Tim as we glide by—and then jump back, Tim's again.

It's like that inside; everyone who sees him summons us. Only the freshmen don't know, and even some of them pull us away, we're that famous. The hallways haven't changed, the lobby with its backlit glass cases full of lame student art, but it's Tim that's on display, a marked inmate. People watch him from their lockers. He's not paranoid, they really do stare, taking x-rays of him, inspecting the scars on his heart. It's been like this since the accident. Usually Tim resents and resists it, whatever it is—pity? fear? a misplaced envy?—but today he feels a vicious satisfaction, knowing this moment will stay with them, that years from now they'll see his face and they'll wonder, they'll guess, but they'll never know. It's his revenge, unexpected and sweet, leveling everyone, burning the school to the ground.

(Because he still doesn't understand how the world goes on, how the building will still be here tomorrow and then through winter and spring and graduation and the next class and the next. He expects it to disappear with him.)

The warning bell has already rung, because the period bell— a single held *bing* like when an airplane reaches the gate—clears the halls. Everyone bangs their lockers shut and runs for it. His timing's right; he needs a late pass, and has to brave the office.

It's quiet after the hall, and warm, the wall of teachers' cubbies filled with leaning mail. The varnished wood of the counter is dented with the impressions of words. Beyond the desks and their glowing computers, on a shelf along the back wall, the chrome microphone the Hook uses to address the school stands on top of an amplifier, and he imagines vaulting the counter and turning it on.

What would he say?

"You have a note?" Mrs. Camilleri asks.

"No," Tim says, Toe says. "My alarm didn't go off."

He says it with a shrug to provoke her, but he's a senior, and she doesn't give him the lecture ("I'm going to have to mark it as unexcused," she told Toe). He leaves with the slip, disappointed, and leans through the heavy door into the windowless box of the hall, empty as a dream, an echo of footsteps fleeing him. On the wall some girl's taped a poster with a drawing of a volleyball: *Go JV, Beat Simsbury!* He passes windows full of rows, faces opening and closing, laughter that puzzles him. Everyone's in class and he's the last person on earth.

This is why he's here, this floating feeling of being a ghost (dude, you don't even know). It feels illegal, free. He expects a teacher on hall duty to turn the corner or come down the stairs and bust him, his late pass a see-through excuse. On the landing, in between floors, a slant of sunlight tries to stop him, chopping off his legs, bright bent stripes falling up the steps in front of him, specks of dust drifting like fish in an aquarium.

He has to pass by Mr. Kunkel, who's on duty, sitting like a plump sentinel between the doors to the main hall, grading papers. He can't remember who it was that day (it was Mrs. Pistorio with her tinted hair), but knows it's not the same.

"Let's pick it up, Mr. Morgan," Kunkel says, ignoring us. (Toe pokes him in the gut, the big old doughboy. Don't, Danielle says, but it's funny.)

What else has changed? His locker's new this year, and his combination, and when he opens the door there's not the picture of Danielle and him at Six Flags at eye level, the two of them flashing by the camera on the Superman, their hair pulled back from their faces by the sheer speed. That's at home in the envelope with the other ones, and nothing's taken its place, no mirror or calendar, no stickers or posters. There are no extra clothes or jackets hanging from the hooks, no Snickers bars or bottled water stockpiled way in the dark back of the shelves, no trash or matted papers cluttering the bottom. On the top shelf are his books and notebooks for the morning; on the bottom shelf are his books and notebooks for the afternoon.

The notebooks he'll throw away. The books the school will give to someone else. He hasn't written his name in them, so there's nothing to white out.

What will they do with his homework? They won't hand it back to his parents. (Some of them will keep it for a while, then they'll chuck it and feel shitty for a minute.)

He fits his books into his backpack and heads for class, passing Mr. Kunkel again, except this time Kunkel says nothing. His footfalls bounce down the stairwell. The sun's gone, the sky overcast, the color of dirty snow. The Hook is beginning his announcements; his voice comes from everywhere, as if the building's speaking. In the hall Tim catches fast frames of other rooms, bright behind glass.

And then the moment he dreads, facing the door to Mrs. Alpert's room, knowing what's waiting for him on the other side. He hesitates, thinking he can still turn around, that so many things are different now that this doesn't count. And then what, just go do it without Kyle? He thinks of the police notifying his mom at her work, and his dad, the questions they'd have. What was he doing driving around? Why wasn't he in school? They'd know immediately. They'll know anyway, but there's a difference. He can make it one more day.

He leans forward and grabs the handle and pulls, turns and lets the heavy door slip past him. There's a second before he steps in when no one can see who it is, just the door, and then he crosses the threshold and the whole room zeroes in on him, holds him there as we flash into them, completing the circuit.

Because they know what day it is. And it's true, what Tim thinks, pinned by twenty sets of eyes—it's not his imagination. They've been waiting for him.

The pictures of Danielle's hair stuck to the window pillar convince Brooks he needs a second Bud to get to sleep, and there's no one to say no. He cracks the cold can, foam tickling his nose, then lets the dogs out and stands at the storm door, watching them hunt for a spot among the trees. He just raked the yard this weekend, and it already needs it again. Next to the shed, a stack of Melissa's plastic flowerpots lies on its side, another thing to take care of. How much does a mailbox cost? He drinks, and the beer fizzes on his tongue, cools his throat, but it doesn't get rid of us, the glovebox broken open, maps scattered like napkins. He took the pictures himself, so why do they surprise him?

The one that comes back isn't a nasty close-up of us, a ruler inserted to show the scale of our livid injuries, but a long shot, the Camry and the tree, and off to one side in the leaves, his own yellow slicker spread over Danielle. And even that isn't so bad; it's the lighting, the absolute darkness of the background, the flash bleaching what it can reach with the flatness of fact, the night world burned down to a car, a tree and a body, simple cause and effect, except he's not in the shot, he's the one taking it.

Ginger's quick, squatting and looking back over her shoulder; Skip has to do his own and save enough to cover hers. They come bounding across the yard, expecting a treat, and he's touched, as always, by their faith in him.

"Okay," he says, "hold your horses." The box is almost empty. He makes them sit, makes them wait and then take it gently. He finishes his beer, watching them eat, the clock above the sink rushing him. Rinses the can and pitches it in the recycling bin. Have to be neat for the buyers.

The machine's on, the sound turned down. He goes to the front door and chops the deadbolt across. The dogs know what that means, and lead him to the bedroom. He pulls the blinds against the light, and still it's only dusk. Pulling his undershirt off, he feels the beating those two assholes gave him. In the bathroom he can see the damage in the mirror, his skin just beginning to blossom, but what hurts worse is the memory of Saintangelo, and knowing he's right.

It seems every night he goes to bed with a question: What are you going to do? And there's no answer he can see, no plan of action that will change what's happened to his life. He's fifty-three, in debt, alone, a mess, and he needs to start all over again. The impossibility of it sets his mind spinning. The only thing he can hold on to is his next shift, the routine of punching in, the womb of the cruiser, and one look at Saintangelo's write-up and the chief will take that away. They can't suspend him, but they can make him take time off, like Manos after his shooting. That was mandatory, department policy; this would be voluntary sick leave, a more serious admission.

He knows they want him gone. He's an embarrassment, and though none of our families have filed suit, a huge legal liability. Seventeen years, day-in day-out, and now it's like he has two strikes against him. He needs to be careful, and yet he's tempted to just say fuck it, blow them all off with a single insane gesture like driving the Vic through the front doors of the station— I quit.

(See why we love this guy?)

At the same time he thinks if he can stick it out, keep his shit together on a minute-by-minute basis, the days will pile up, and the months. He'll sell the house. Everything will work out.

He knows both of these are fantasies, but can't come up with something in-between. Quit and find a new job, but the idea makes him twitch and shake his head. He's a cop. What else can he do?

Outside, the birds are talking to each other. Ginger and Skip are sacked and sighing. When Brooks shifts, the bed's cold. He has too much room, too many pillows. He tries one side and then the other, his back, his front. The clock jumps ahead a minute, ten; it makes him tired just contemplating waking up.

Finally Danielle bends to him, touches his forehead like a mother, and he sleeps. We stand around him like doctors, like angels, waiting for the dreams to begin, the sirens and screaming tires, the night country flying in his headlights as we chase him, racing to the tree. It might seem like revenge, except it's not ours. Brooks is easy to haunt. We don't have to bring him nightmares. He has his own.

"Here you go, man," Greg says, and tips the can of Bud over Toe's grave, foam puddling in the grass at his feet. He takes a sip and passes it to Travis. Travis balances a pack of Marlboros on the stone; it has just the lucky one left, the one you flip upside down at the beginning. He adds a pack of matches with just one left, but the combination's too light, and the wind knocks them off. They go right through Toe's hands and land behind him; from reflex he bends down like he might pick them up.

Travis searches around for a rock, puts it in the pack with the matches and sets the pack on Toe's stone again. The two of them stand back, trading the beer can, Toe looking on with them, peeking over their shoulders. There are no old bouquets or candles like at Danielle's, just the cold grass, mismatched along the seams. Toe's mom will bring something later and tell his real dad over the phone.

"I still can't believe it," Greg says, and it's not clear who he's saying it to—the stone or Toe or Travis.

Travis isn't saying anything.

"We miss you, man," Greg says.

(Don't fucking cry now, Toe says.) Because for a second it's close, Greg ducking and shaking his head. Then Travis takes over, stepping up and setting the half-finished beer next to the butts.

He steps back into place like it's a ceremony, and they're quiet again, an honor guard. The rear of the cemetery edges the Farmington Woods golf course; from a distance comes the soft roar of some greenskeeping machine. The few trees left as a fence tilt in the wind, and leaves wheel past. One catches on the stone, then slips off, gone.

They take it as a sign, turn and weave their way back to Travis's Golf. A chewed Louisville Slugger lies across the backseat, nudging a cooler with the remainder of the twelve-pack. (Toe can go with them but doesn't, just watches them curve along the narrow road and through the wrought-iron arch. We wait for him beside an eyeless angel, and when he comes back he gives us a look to let us know he'd rather be with them but understands we have work to do.)

She reshelves yesterday's returns from a rumbling steel cart, going row to row with an armful of books, tracing the typed numbers on the spines with a finger, making space for them. There's been a run on nonfiction about the circulatory system, a middle school health project. She doesn't have to recall the times she drove Kyle here to do research; she accepts that he can ambush her anywhere. Better here where she can distract herself than at home.

Her problem is filling up the time—the exact opposite of her other life. Before (isn't that a nice way of saying it?), she was torn between school and taking care of her family, the commute a nuisance. They had takeout three nights a week, and she couldn't watch TV or she'd never get her reading done. Now she pieces together her schedule, glad to have these hours at the library, a true volunteer.

Morning is when the older men from The Mews and Sunrise Village read the newspapers. Some days the van shows up early and they're waiting outside, huddled like numbers runners in their polyester slacks and hats; she's stood with them under the overhang, an honorary senior. "You should have your own key," they say, and she agrees. Sometimes it seems she's here more than the regular staff.

There's a quiet mindfulness about the library, a clarity, the arched windows letting in the sun, the functional carpet and ceiling tiles softening the smallest sound. Every surface is the bland tan of nougat, the books the only color. The stacks are close, honeycombed. She feels insulated by so many pages, safe in the thoughts of others. The precision and repetition of the work soothes her, a kind of therapy. Everything she does brings about more order, helps someone else find what they desire. On the calmest days she fools herself into thinking her love for the place is uncomplicated and gentle instead of necessary and desperate, a fugitive running for cover. Either way, she'll take it.

She stands on a metal stepstool like an overturned bucket to slide a study of breast cancer onto the top shelf. She's been spared that, thank God, and the wall of illnesses beneath it. There are no books on Kyle, only a looseleaf binder at home from the rehab in Denver, and it just deals with the physical, how to change a dressing, how to give a shower. She steps down and picks up the next book, checks the number. The cellophane jackets on the new arrivals up front are smooth and clear; back here they're smudged and cracked, dust magnets. Spines are cocked and buckled, pages fitted back in. Everything medical is badly out-dated, careworn. Ultimately the unloved ones will be culled for the book sale; she's helped Alice go through the stacks with a cart, looking for anything that hasn't been checked out in five years. It seems a waste, and occasionally she'll take one home just to save it, guiltily returning it unread.

Through the Dewey decimal system and into 92, biogra-phies, too easy, separated from the rest and arranged alphabeti-cally. Billie Holiday, Vivien Leigh, Golda Meir. Their thick, heroic lives take her away from her own, transport her like the posters in the stairwell promise, a pirate ship full of little kids—READING IS AN ADVENTURE. She feels boundless here, surrounded by the world in concentrated form. Just holding the books does it for her.

(And while she's relieved she isn't thinking of us, we're still here, on reserve. We stalk her from a distance by the Fiction, peeking through holes in the shelves, playing hide-and-seek like we used to, Toe flirting with Danielle, and then Danielle turns a corner and suddenly pulls up, and there standing right in front of her, a good foot taller, is Kyle.

Toe's like a hero; he grabs Danielle and runs the other way, plowing through an older woman who looks up from her book, then keeps reading.

It's the same Kyle, with his T-shirt, his wallet on a chain. He doesn't see us, he just follows his mom up and down the rows, looking through the books at her the same way we were. We don't know what to think of him showing up. We thought he was at Mrs. M's, but maybe he's like us, flying all over Avon, a wild card. Maybe he's watching Brooks snore, or like that night, wandering the woods.

He follows her around the curved circulation desk and through the knee-high gate into the back. Toe looks to me, and Danielle; I see they're done holding hands. I shrug—how would I know what's going on? There's nothing we can do but tag after him.)

Kyle's mom has her routine. Her third cup of coffee's waiting in the break room, in the NPR mug from home. The bright box is the silent heart of the library, hidden from the patrons. The old 30-cup urn percolates under the bulletin board. The table's a bake sale. Because of the holiday there are extra treats—cupcakes with pumpkin faces, orange sugar cookies, a dozen crullers from Luke's. FOOD AND DRINK ARE NOT PERMITTED IN THE LIBRARY, a sign on the door warns. She avoids the candy corn and the basket of miniature Hershey bars as if she's on a diet. It's a shame; it used to be her favorite holiday.

(Me too, Danielle says, and runs her fingers through the candy corn.

It's still my favorite, Toe says, defiant. How 'bout you, Kyle?)

But Kyle's sticking with his mom, hunching over her and whispering as she freshens her cup, making her turn around as if she can hear him, touching her hand to her throat. She peers into her coffee before taking a final sip, as if there's something in it. She leaves it on the table and fixes her hair, hooking it behind her ears, and she's ready to face the public again.

She works the circ desk, waving to the mothers arriving

early for storytime, ushering their costumed children upstairs (a
hobo, a dragon, Obi Wan Kenobi). Four- to five-year-olds today.
She hasn't decided what to read yet. Yesterday was two- to threes,
and she did *Go Away, Big Green Monster!*—a hit with the flannelboard. The four- to fives are more sophisticated, into irony and
wordplay, great fans of the pun and the running joke.

She's weighing *The Hallo-weiner* (too goofy) and *The Scary
Party* (too cute) when a younger mother she's seen before slides
a pile of travel guides across the counter. The woman's heavily
made up and dressed in a fitting black suit, as if she's stopped on
her way to a fundraising lunch. Her nose is so pointy it has to be
fake, and she has a pair of driving gloves in one hand.

"Paris," Kyle's mom says. "Very nice."

"Thanks," the woman says, not interested. She hefts her
purse onto the counter to dig for her wallet. By the time she
finds her card, Kyle's mom has the back covers open for the
scanner. She turns the card over and holds the barcode under
the red light. Usually the computer responds with a peep like at
the supermarket, but this time it plinks like a xylophone.

The tone is supposed to alert her. It means the patron has a
book on hold, or an interloan, something on reserve. A look at
the screen and Kyle's mom sees there's a block on the card.

"Is there a problem?" the woman asks.

"It says you have an unpaid fine, is that possible?"

"I don't think so."

"*Hot Air Henry?* It says here it's been reported as lost."

"My daughter," the woman explains, as if that solves things.

"I'm afraid there's a block on your card because of the fine."

"She probably returned it to the school library. That happens
sometimes."

"If she did, they'd send it to us directly."

The woman looks to the ceiling and sighs, and Kyle's mom sees she's trying to keep from exploding. Is it wrong that she's enjoying her power? (What worries us is that Kyle has climbed over the counter and is standing beside the woman, leaning in, giving her the crazy eye.)

"This is stupid. I'm not paying the fine. We'll find the book."

"I'm sorry," Kyle's mom says, and does the cruelest thing she can think of—hand the woman her card.

"Look," the woman says, pushing the card back at her. "I need to check these out now. How much is the fine?"

Kyle's mom takes her time with the screen, makes her wait even though it's up already. "Eighteen ninety-five."

"Eighteen ninety-five," the woman repeats to herself, and swears under her breath as she digs in her wallet, shaking her head. There's a line behind her now. She finds a twenty and slaps it on the counter. (Kyle swipes at it and it slides off, lifted by an invisible current, and falls to the carpet. Oh shit, Danielle says.) The woman has to bend over to get it and comes up red-faced. Kyle's mom leaves her to go make change from the lockbox under the center station. She counts it out in front of the woman, clears her account and scans her books through, the computer peeping. She stamps the return date as the woman tugs on her gloves. Neither of them says a word.

"They're due back November twentieth," Kyle's mom reminds her, but the woman stalks off with her arms full, hustling out the door as if she's late (Kyle right behind her, giving her the finger sideways). The next patron who steps up raises her eyebrows and makes a face, and for a second she and Kyle's mom— the whole library—are allies.

(Toe still can't believe it: moving an inanimate object. What else can he do that we don't know about?)

In the break room, Kyle's mom laughs with Alice.

"Don't mind her," Alice says, peeling a cupcake. "You get that from time to time."

"She got so irate over nothing," she says, as if she's amazed, amused. She can't tell Alice the truth. She's been treated so gently by everyone that to feel that kind of hatred is a relief. The woman didn't see her as pathetic and special, just another person. It's what she's fought for; now that she's succeeded, there's no one to share it with. She thinks of calling Mark at work, but even he might not understand. And, thinking of the wreath and how thoroughly she enjoyed torturing the woman, maybe it is a little crazy.

It's five minutes to storytime, and she still needs to choose. *Five Little Pumpkins? The Haunted Dollhouse?* She needs to pick something they can use the flannelboard with, the children coming up to affix the felt cut-outs, something fun. (She needs to pick where they're going to eat tonight, but that can wait.)

Alice is in reference and knows everything.

"What do you think?" Kyle's mom asks, holding up her two finalists, letting Alice make the decision—*By the Light of the Halloween Moon.* (And should we be worried? Kyle chose the same one.)

Upstairs the walls of the craft room are papered with Q-tip skeletons and witches with yarn for hair. It's an overflow crowd, the kids sitting on their purple mats—angels and cowboys, hockey players and black cats. They quiet down for her, and some of the mothers filter out to browse downstairs. She sets up the flannelboard, spreads the chained legs of the easel, opens the baggie and sorts the cut-outs before taking a seat, the book flat on her lap. She waits until they're done fussing, sitting stone-still with her hands folded. They watch her as if it's part of the act—and it is, a trick she picked up from one of her own teachers.

(Kyle sits in the front row of little kids at her feet. We stand in the doorway like guards, as if we can stop him from leaving.)

She's deliberate, in control, a different person, the way an actress is changed by the stage. "*By the Light of the Halloween Moon,*" she enunciates, and holds up the cover so the whole room can see. She reads, calling up demons and fairies with a witchy curl of her finger to stick the cut-outs on the board. Waiting to go on with the story, she looks out at the masks and painted faces, their eyes intent on her, and for the first time she can remember, she doesn't wish they were hers, these perfect, unmarked children. For these few precious, simple minutes, she's theirs.

He's dreaming he's playing wiffle ball in the halls of a fancy hotel with the winning quarterback of the last Super Bowl when the phone rings next to his head. What the fuck? It's a reflex; even though the machine's on, he reaches out of his sleep to pick it up.

It could be about Gram; they're supposed to call whenever they take her to the emergency room for her dizzy spells. It could be the chief telling him not to come in, Melissa wondering where this month's check is, Charity trying to set up a time to show the house. He's been sleeping on his side with his hand tucked under his cheek, and his fingers are rubber. He has to roll the other way to free his arm from the sheets.

"Hello?"

The line is silent, dead air, then clicks, breaking the connection. They've fooled him again. (It's not Kyle like Toe thinks, just Travis and Greg from Greg's cell phone, thinking we'd dig this.)

"You suck," Brooks says to no one, and drops back into the pillows, exhausted. He doesn't bother with star-69, doesn't look at the clock, afraid of what time it might be. The insides of his eyelids are sliding red screens. He buries his head and stretches himself flat; it feels like he's been run over by a steamroller, and last night comes back, a shoe aimed at his face—the fuckers— but, punchy, going under, he can't be angry, can only touch on it softly, almost pleased that he remembers, a last, lucky guess at a baffling question.

He grunts, rolling over, rubs his nose and scratches his ass with his eyes closed, twists his head from side to side, then lies still, willing himself to sleep. He was dreaming something, doors and long hallways, a carpeted staircase and curved brass bannister. He empties himself to enter it again, his mind working back- wards and then not at all. (We watch as his mouth goes slack, his eyes shuttle beneath the lids. Finally his breathing subsides.)

And then the phone rings.

Tim's learning that nothing is the same. It can't be, a year later; his schedule's different and his friends are dead. Just being here in the halls is like time-traveling, visiting a museum. Between classes, watching the stampede between the lockers, he has the feeling it's being staged for his benefit, a re-creation like shooting a movie. Everything's off just that much, fake. If he opened the wrong door he'd find a room full of extras having their make-up retouched. And then he thinks the opposite's true—he's the one that's unreal, a ghost walking among them, a monster in disguise, *I was a Teenage Frankenstein.*

He felt that way the day after the crash, and the suspicion's

never left him. It's like *Final Destination.* There was a mistake; he
was supposed to die that night, one of us.

He knows most people secretly think that. It doesn't seem
fair that he walked away unscathed. (I'll admit it, we think it too;
we belong together, a team.) He's heard the worst rumors—that
he was drunk and propped Toe in the driver's seat after it happened, that he used Danielle as a shield. (I know who started that
one, Danielle says, like she's already taken care of them.) At first
they hurt him, but now he understands; people need a scapegoat
and he's the only one handy. That's what makes the plan so perfect; it completes things for them *and* gives him his revenge.
Everyone's happy except his parents.

There's nothing he can do for them, no apology that will
convince them it's not their fault, and that bothers him. He
wants things to be neat. He wants the impossible: for this to only
be about him.

He lets himself be drawn along with the flow, keeping the
same pace as the backpack in front of him. It's sick how easy it is
to pretend everything's normal, it's like they're all sleepwalking.
At the same time, he envies them, the freshmen especially; he
wishes he could be that innocent again, that anonymous, passing
through school unmarked, moving toward some unseen future
far from here, becoming someone else.

He's on time for bio and takes a seat at his lab table in back,
trading a wobbly stool for a good one. Outside, the day is dark-
ening, clouds right down on the woods, making the room seem
artificially bright. The drawers are locked, the gas nozzles turned
off. Up front, Mrs. Blaustein is wearing rubber gloves, making
even stacks of aluminum baking pans. He recognizes the vine-
gary stink of formaldehyde and panics. He totally forgot: today's

their lab practical, and he hasn't studied. All that time doing his homework, wasted. What else has he spaced?

His partner's Sean Campbell, a lacrosse jock who uses mousse so his hair spikes up in front and wears a lame Dave Matthews T-shirt. He's a starter and barely talks to Tim outside of class, which Tim actually prefers. He doesn't want new friends; he'll just lose them.

Mrs. Blaustein sets the pan between them, the pink, ringed worm already pinned at the ends. They'll share a scalpel and a pair of tweezers, a dozen numbered flags for the organs. As Mrs. Blaustein is passing out the sheets ("facedown on the table, please"), she warns the class that she's created three different tests, so looking at your neighbor's won't help. "All right," she says, back where she started, "you can turn your papers over."

He wants Sean to lead, but neither of them reaches for the sheet. Finally Tim flips it, revealing a list of things they need to find, an ugly scavenger hunt.

"You want to cut?" Sean asks.

"Whatever," Tim says.

"Why don't you cut, you're a better cutter." Meaning he hasn't studied either.

Tim takes the stubby blade and slides the pan closer, trying to ignore the smell. The waxy block is gouged and pitted, a thousand old holes from how many dead things. (He can't help it, he pictures us laid out on stainless steel tables, the autopsy room in *Silence of the Lambs*.) He has Sean hold the pan as he slices into the worm lightly, drawing his arm straight down, the wet skin splitting around the incision like lips, parting like a zipper to show a dark vein underneath, the mushroom-colored bulge of some organ. Formaldehyde bubbles out like cider, filling the holes in the brick.

"Pin it open," Tim says, and Sean spreads the skin tent-tight on both sides so they can see the worm's plumbing, a straight line from its mouth to its anus, the organs knotted around the five arches that make up the heart. He knows that at least (five hearts, as if he could have four more chances).

"Is that the liver?" Sean points.

"Hang on." Tim marks the heart (number 1, a gift) and checks the sheet to see what they're looking for. Brain, crop, setae, nephridia. A couple of them are common sense, the rest is guesswork. He shouldn't care, but there's a part of him that doesn't want to fail this last test—proof that he knows what he's doing.

He spears the clitellum, crosses it off the list.

"Which one's the ovaries?" Sean asks, leaning in close.

The pink nodules glisten, and he thinks of us cut up and stitched together again (it was only Toe). He imagines Danielle lying on a table, her front split down the middle and opened wide like two doors, her regular face watching him from above. The dead smell rises like heat from the pan, and he hears someone choking, someone gagging. A metal stool goes over, and he turns, scalpel raised, to see Tracy Paley running for the door, a hand clamped to her mouth, her other arm straight out in front of her like a halfback. Sean's already started to laugh, like the rest of the class, her dash a necessary comic release (a convenient chance to glance at your neighbor's paper). Tracy shuts them up by not making it, suddenly stopping short of the door and doubling over, the first burst gushing through her fingers, splashing at her feet, making Mrs. Blaustein rear back before pushing her into the hall. The door closes slowly, letting in another grunt. Then nothing.

"That was fucking *nasty!*" Sean says, triumphant.

"Wait'll we do fetal pigs."

The vomit sits there, a present for the janitor. Everyone's laughing, re-enacting the scene, nakedly trading answers. Tracy's saved them, and Tim wishes he could save her back, that what he's going to do will make everyone forget what just happened. He knows it won't. They'll both be remembered, but with a difference: Tracy will have to learn to forget hers, and how do you do that? He's tried. People—things—don't let you.

He and Sean mark the organs, going over them one by one, learning. Here's the nerve cord, here's the subneural vessel. It makes sense. Once they've finished, the parade of flags in place, Tim realizes they'll cut him up like this, and Kyle, but in his relief he doesn't care. All he wanted was to pass, and that's done. Now he can go back to sleepwalking, biding his time, keeping his secret beating inside him until it's too late for them to pluck it out.

It's the kid who pulled the faceplant off the van who sits next to Kyle at lunchtime. Zack. He's about twelve, skinny with a big forehead, mouth open as if doped, and maybe he is, drifting on Ritalin. They've cleaned him up, slapping a square patch of a band-aid above his eye, but Kyle recognizes the brown crust stuck to the inside of his lower lip, a chocolate high tide line separating wet from dry, can almost reach with his tongue and taste that speedbump of blood again.

(That night, we were there in the room with his parents after the nurses left. He was alive, asleep under the octopus of tubes, and they were both hopeful, both doubtful, trying to read each other and come to some answer they could believe. In the morning, where could they go? Not home, that would be a trap.

Kyle had turned into their world, every operation a death sentence they were required to sign. They stayed there, shaky and afraid, forgiving him everything, while our parents were calling Vincent's, talking coffins and visiting hours, the number of floral sprays. It wasn't until we were underground that Tim visited, touching his still fingers, careful of the IVs wired into the back of his hand. Kyle's mind was like a pond in a blizzard, Tim's like a microwave cooking nothing, the empty carousel circling in the buzzing light. A blast of Danielle came every minute, draining him like a taser, while Kyle's brain waves penned miles of straight lines. Everyone wanted him to get better, everyone wanted him to die.)

"Does your head hurt?" Kyle asks.

"No," Zack says, and goes back to his cookie, holding it with both hands like a sandwich.

Kyle picks his up, and the two of them are completely occupied. (Are they happy? Why does anyone have to be? It's lunchtime, they're eating cookies and slurping chocolate milk through bendy straws, that ought to be enough. You know how much we'd give to be doing that?)

"Finish up," their student teacher Libby says, and already we're fading, disintegrating, our outlines flickering with bad *Star Trek* special effects. There's no one to remember us here, so we're gone.

We meet in the woods behind the scoreboard, but the Hook is on the prowl. He's loud, his suit and bright tie flapping as he stalks the parking lot, calling people by name so they know he's seen them. It's third lunch so no one's officially cutting until the bell rings. Kids flick their cigarettes under cars, jam their one-hitters into glove compartments. In the jeep, Tim sees pieces of him shifting through windows of other cars, a kaleidoscope. He tracks him past the smokestack before losing him and decides to wait a minute. He's got time. On the windshield, clear dots appear, each holding the world, then join and run between the others.

The warning bell rings, his signal. The sidewalk's gone brown, and there's no sign of the Hook. Tim twists to see through the plastic window in back, checking his wavy escape route.

The wind is like a cold breath. It didn't rain that day, but there's nothing he can do about it.

He takes the same matted path along the outfield fence, cuts across the creek at the same place and slips into the woods, safe now, protected from the rain. He was with Danielle, the two of them walking single file through the bushes, but he can't remember what they talked about, as if the crash has knocked it out of him.

(I don't remember, Danielle says, but she says that all the time so she won't have to talk about it. She doesn't believe in what we're doing; she's only here for Tim, something Toe shouldn't forget.)

We were already at the clearing, the rest of us. Greg and Travis had just left, going over to Greg's house to play pool. Kyle was stoned and wanted to get some frozen burritos and go hang out by the river, it was so nice. Toe said he was up for it, and there was no way to say no.

What if it had been raining? Tim replays the decision to go with them as if it means something, a necessary link in a chain, stands there facing the same trees he did a year ago, the cuffs of his jeans wet from the grass. He and Danielle were holding hands. She had on her suede jacket with the ripped pocket and her hair smelled like pears. He waits, sure someone will catch him standing in the rain like a psycho, then when the bell for class rings, heads back to the parking lot.

As he's leaving he passes a 4Runner stopped in the circle by the front doors—someone being picked up—and thinks of his mom at her office and the school picture of him in the knitted frame next to her computer. He's smiling and has a tie on, his zits airbrushed away. He's always thought the person in the picture wasn't him; now he knows. He's tempted to drive by her office to see her one last time, say good-bye right.

There's only one way out, watched by a hired security guard, an old guy in a windbreaker with gold patches on the shoulders and a walkie-talkie—another half-assed Columbine precaution. The guard stands in the road by his little Buick wagon from a hundred years ago, checking everyone coming in or going out, like anyone couldn't just run him over. He leans in to see Tim's parking permit and the card on the dash that lets him leave school property, then waves him by.

The rain's light, his wipers impatient, scraping at the glass. At the stop sign he has to wait for a string of cars, and drops into his mother's office again, wonders what she's doing. (She's in line at Bruegger's Bagels, choosing what she wants on her Santa Fe chicken sandwich, vetoing a bag of chips. There's orange and black crepe paper wound around the soup kettles; the day's inescapable—*we* are.) For the millionth time he thinks of a note, and then is pissed at himself. He needs to follow the plan. He breaks out of his trance by focusing on cross traffic, letting it clear his head, just in time to see a familiar gold Pathfinder flash by. The woman driving waves to him—Kyle's mom.

He waves back without thinking, an uncertain flip of his

hand, then lets it drop. Luckily there's another car so he doesn't
have to pull in right behind her.

Kyle will have a chance to say good-bye.

Not really.

There's a gap, and he pulls out, his blinker clicking off. Kyle's
mom's three cars in front of him. (We can fly between the two.
Kyle's mom's happy she ran into Tim; like the library, it's one
more thing grounding her, making her feel she belongs here, that
her life in Avon will go on somehow.) The car ahead of him signals for Hollister, and he thinks of turning just so he won't have
to see her. But the plan is stronger than he is, all his will given up
to it, and he stays straight.

She's two cars away as they close in on Thompson Road. The
mouth of it opens to their left, and they both note it. They both
know every dip and bend that will lead them through the dis-
used fields and past the M. H. Rhodes plant and across the rails-
to-trails and over the creek to the altar that holds us all hostage.
The road's an invitation to revisit it, another opportunity to pay
tribute and admit what rules their lives, and for that reason they
have to pass, let it slide by as if it means nothing. Tim thinks that
after tonight he'll feel nothing, a relief. Secretly, Kyle's mom
thinks this too, that time will let her forget. (They're both wrong,
but how can they know? Nothing changes, no matter how much
you want it to. You're still you.)

It's ridiculous to think she's following him when she's ahead
of him. Tim's afraid she'll stay with him all the way down Brick-
yard, but as they brake for the three-way stop, he can see her signal. There's no wave this time; the Pathfinder rockets off. He
edges up and waits, edges up. She was glad to see him, and again
he doubts himself. How could he ever explain it to her? He

thinks if he could leave here and start all over—but it would be the same, he'd be pretending.

We were listening to one of Toe's CDs (Alice in Chains's *Best of the Box*, Toe informs me), but Tim lets the silence accumulate. He needs his mind clear. He's sure of what he's doing only when he remembers us.

Then, it felt free, like running away, leaving everyone back in class. Now he follows automatically, making a right at The Keg, cutting under the old railroad bridge with its spray-painted banners made from old sheets (HAPPY 16TH CLAIRE BEAR, AVON JAYCEES HAUNTED HAYRIDE). He curls into the DairyMart and parks nose-in the way we did, goes in and nukes two beef-and-bean burritos, picks up a twenty-ounce Mountain Dew.

It's in the script. Instead of getting back on 4, he goes left, by the run-down houses and the DEAD END sign. He rolls past the empty stalls of the car wash and the leaf-dotted ballfields to the curbless turnaround, aims straight across it and bumps over the asphalt lip onto the dirt road the fishermen use. He rocks all the way to the end, thinking the rain will keep everyone away, but there's a white Cherokee there, nearly pulled into the bushes.

The river's dark as motor oil, the sound constant, rain on concrete. He scopes the banks like a narc, but can't see anyone, just the upturned cage of a shopping cart in the rocky shallows.

He takes the path back into the woods and climbs up the steep grade, the bag with the burritos clutched in one hand. The hill's slippery; he grabs at roots and gets his other hand muddy. On top, the stones of the old right-of-way clash with every step, but there's no one there. The town was going to use the bridge for the rails-to-trails until they ran out of money. A few years ago they put up a fence to keep people from walking on the trestle (there were no post-prom tragedies, no paralyzed divers, it was just obvious); already it's history, split down the middle, the limp chainlink two accordioned doors daring him to walk out onto the ties. From here he can see across the river, the way it narrows to a sluice under the bridge, the smooth dark swells before it spills foaming over the ledges. The rain makes pooling circles; leaves surf the current, accelerate into the narrows and disappear, re-emerge and twirl, caught in lazy backwaters.

He hooks his fingers in the fence and steps out. The ties are slick, the creosote a shoe polish blue with an oily hint of rainbow. The river sounds louder out here. Beneath him, swallows chase each other through the girders. He's still over land when the obvious hits him: if he fell, would it kill him? Peeking down between the open ties to the black iron latticework streaked with birdshit, the spike-like treetops, he thinks it's a possibility but not a sure thing. It would fuck everything up, so he inches across, crouching for balance, bringing his feet even before moving on, holding the bag out to the side like a timebomb.

(There was a game we used to play when we were walking the ties. You'd be concentrating, trying not to look down, and suddenly from behind someone would grab your shoulders, scaring the shit out of you. "Saved your life," they'd say.)

In the very middle, facing upstream, there's a tie with a hole just the right size to hold a beer bottle—Kyle's favorite place. Tim doesn't think he could get Kyle out here now, but saves the seat for him anyway, sticks the Dew in the coolie. He still doesn't see the fisherman anywhere beneath him. He lowers himself slowly, sits and lets his legs dangle over the edge. The wind yanks the napkins out of the bag; there's nothing he can do but watch them flutter and swoop, spastic as birds. So what—nothing's perfect. He unwraps the first burrito and tucks in.

The river makes a gap in the trees, opens up the sky so he can see the far hills of Burlington. It's sprinkling, and he's not sure if he wants it to pour, for lightning to reach down and shake him. The first hit of the Dew gives him the hiccups—and not just one, he's really got them.

"Just fucking great," Tim says.

Kyle's mom is late and doesn't take off her jacket, just wipes her feet on the mat so she won't track up the kitchen floor. Tosses her keys and her purse on the counter and shoulders around the corner into the living room, giving the coffee table a little hip-shake, scoots down the hall past her twin in the mirror and swings into the TV room. The clickers are on the ottoman. She palms them and spins, drops her bottom onto the couch as she's firing—doing a two-fisted John Woo fadeaway. ON, CHANNEL, VOLUME. The box responds, and she's not late, she hasn't missed it, she's there as Blair peels off her top to put the moves on Max. The scene cuts strategically in the middle and the theme music comes up, comforting as a lullaby, the stars' windswept credits reassuring as a family album. She's back in Llanview, and we're nowhere —like the song says—because we only have *One Life to Live*.

Ginger is the freaky one. Even sleeping she can hear us coming through the woods and pricks up one ear, her eye slowly opening, the dark membrane drawing back like a shade on the bloody white, and like that she's barking—hard, waking up Skip, who joins in before he knows what's going on, and then Brooks, lurching straight up from the sheets like a jack-in-the-box Dracula, that Parris Island training kicking in (sir yes sir!).

"Hush!" he commands so he can hear, and we freeze. He looks around the shadowed room, his head hollow with sleep. "You're all right," he says. "There's nothing there." The clock says he has three minutes until his alarm goes off—really two hours, but he needs to see Gram. Three minutes. He collapses back into the pillows with his eyes closed, then forces himself to roll out, his feet searching for the floor. He has to sit on the edge a second, rubbing his face, thinking: It's Halloween.

He doesn't notice it's raining until he's shaved and dressed, opening the blinds on the backyard (and there we are, staggered across the grass like a bad album cover). When he lets the dogs out, they circle, barking, their ears flattened back. "Why are you guys being so weird?" he asks, just as the phone rings.

He lets it ring three, four times before picking up, then says nothing.

"Hello?" a woman asks—Charity.

"Hey," he says, covering.

"I didn't wake you."

"No."

"Are you ready? They've made an offer."

"Wow," he says, "that's fast," genuinely stunned. She's the first human he's talked to today, and the size of the decision intimidates him.

"I told you they were serious. So here it is."

He braces for the number, prepared to say no to the lowball.

It's way low, lower than he expected, lower than he could ever accept, even if they did bump it up.

"I know, I know," Charity says. "It's not exactly what we were hoping for, but it's something. Did you want to come back with a counter-offer? You don't have to right now if you want to think about it. Why don't we think about it?"

What Brooks is thinking is that after her commission and the lawyers' fees it won't cover the mortgage; it's not even close. Just the land's worth that much, according to the town's latest appraisal, and only going up, thanks to his neighbors. If he tries to stick it out, the taxes will bleed him dry. What's the difference? Already he's down to the truck and his clothes and his computer. Sooner or later he'll have to give the house up.

"Let me think about it," he says.

"Not too long," Charity coaches. "You've got my cell on my card. Call me whenever you're ready."

Strapping on his holster, he can't get past the simple arithmetic. He doesn't see how it's come to this. He's worked hard, it's not his fault, yet at the same time he understands this is failure, the closing off of options, the helplessness. All in a year, he realizes, the car and the night returning like a forgotten thought.

He locks the back door before leaving. "You be good," he orders the dogs, standing there as if he might take them with him.

In the truck he notices something balanced on the stump of his mailbox—white and black, the size of a dead cat. Fucking punks. (Roadkill, we hope (like us!). We wouldn't put it past Greg and Travis. They'll do what they have to do.) Brooks rolls up slow, expecting the worst. It's become a habit with him. It's only when he's right on top of it that he recognizes the wet, rubber-banded bundle. It's his mail.

How fast the day passes, not like when we lived here. Part of it's daylight savings—fall back; it feels later because it is, the clock tricking the sky. Part of it's the weather, the low clouds imitating the gray before dusk, and the change that happens every day about now, the manic anticipation of Avon's first rush hour. And okay, we'll admit it, part of it's us; we wish we could stay here forever—the exact opposite of Tim.

At the high school it's last period. The office is busy signing kids out for the orthodontist and piano lessons. In the cavernous Dattco barns behind Rotondo Concrete, bus drivers lean across the green seats and pinch the windows closed before rolling out, their lights on, their wipers going. Strong as an armored column, the convoy skirts the self-storage and the Towpath condos and (where we went straight) takes the turn up Country Club, snakes over the hill and through the soggy golf course, the lights of the clubhouse on, getting ready for tonight's big party. Once the buses load up and fan out to do their routes, the roads will be stop-and-go, the whole town at the mercy of their flashing lights and folding stop signs. The routine takes two hours, the same buses hitting the middle school and then the separate elementaries, crisscrossing and backtracking, stopping at the exact same stops.

The rain screws up everything, adds an urgency to the usual holiday confusion. Already there's a line of minivans outside the middle school. On 44, traffic thickens, moms finishing their errands (or behind schedule, leaving the drycleaning one more day), racing to beat the kids home. The library braces for an onslaught of students wanting to use the computers; there's a pen tied to the sign-up sheet. At Roaring Brook and Pine Grove, the kids are having a parade in the hallways, all of them in costume, trick-or-treating room to room as the P.A. plays spooky sound effects records.

But before anyone's let out, before the buses circle and idle outside the high school, the widebody handi-van with Kyle inside breaks the town line by the cemetery, making Peggy cross

herself. The rain keeps her leaning forward, nervous. Kyle has his
teeth in his hand, menacing the girl behind him, who just laughs.
Her name is Cheryl, and she wears a pink jacket over her cat
costume and has the bulging eyes and pug nose and thick limbs
of Down syndrome. Kyle likes her. He snaps the teeth at her and
she shies back, her hands up to fend him off.

(She's like *twelve*, Danielle says.

And don't hold it against her, but the handi-van creeps
Danielle out. Toe's not saying much either. They can't get used to
Kyle being here—unlike Kyle.)

"Everybody, look," Peggy instructs from the front, pointing
to the split-rail fence running along the road. The corny wooden
cutout of a cow its owner dresses for every holiday is wearing
a stiff cone of a witch's hat, and they've hung plastic jack-o'-
lanterns from the tree.

The van laughs and claps, goes wild for a minute. A cow!
With a witch's hat!

(Jesus, Toe says, and scans around for the real Kyle—
nowhere, but we can feel him.)

"All right," Peggy says, "calm down," because one of the kids
is slapping at his window. "Don't make me stop."

A warning's enough. They obey until the next kid's dropped
off (his mom waiting at the bottom of the drive with a golf umbrella), then a Yankees cap comes flying from the back and lands
in the aisle next to Kyle. It's a favorite game, keepaway, and he
snatches it up and tosses it over the rows. Peggy checks the mirror above her head and taps the brakes, making everyone nod.

"That's two," she says. "Give it back *now*."

Kyle's so occupied by her scolding that he's forgotten his
teeth. He had them in his lap, but when he reached for the hat
they fell on the floor, and Peggy's braking sent them scuttling

under the seats. Right now they're three rows in front of him, right by this little kid named Jared's shoes. They're neat, so Jared picks them up and puts them in his pocket.

There's no more trouble; Peggy's tough. The van drops off and pulls out again, winds through the hilly streets, past the corn shocks teepeed by the mailboxes, the Indian corn hung from door knockers. (My people call it maize, Toe says.) Cheryl bumps up the aisle and down the steps, her mom waiting in the open door of the garage, arms folded. Kyle leans back in his seat; there's no one left to talk to.

The day has changed. The buses are rolling, brakes sighing like violas as they swing through corners, then the gruff diesels powering up. It's snack time, TV time, even if there's homework to do. It's raining, and the den's dark. Drop the backpack, grab the clicker and snuggle under the blanket, lie down and sink deep into the couch, flip around. *Batman Beyond* is on, and *Digimon*, *TRL* on MTV.

Kyle's mom's show is over. She's watching *GH* just to fill up space, listening for the van to pull up out front. One of her fears—or, popping up so often, is it a sick hope?—is that he'll miss the van, wander off somewhere and get lost, like the Alzheimer's patients she sees on TV, helicopters circling the woods as night falls, the temperature dropping. But they'd call.

She notices a shred of leaf on the carpet and thinks she hasn't gotten anything done today. The house is a mess, and there's always laundry. She has to pack Kyle's dinner and make reservations, and the two nagging tasks combine, a guilty mix.

This is when the real Kyle appears, taking the far arm, not really watching the TV. He looks at his mom as if he can read her mind, then looks back to the set, but doesn't see us, as if we're on a different plane. And he does seem more solid than us, more present. What does it mean, and should we worry?

(Yes, Danielle says. We should definitely worry.)

He moves to the window. A second later his mom follows, the two of them standing in the same place, a double exposure. Far down Indian Pipe, the van has just turned the corner, slowly growing, crushing leaves as it comes. She turns the TV off, and the two of them glide through the dark house and outside, wait on the stoop as Peggy swings into the driveway, her last stop. The van slows, the door opens.

Kyle's home.

Brooks stayed up too late reading, plus he's up too early, and now his head hurts, as if his brain's a muscle. He hits Luke's for a maple cruller and a tall coffee, nods to the trio of oldtimers who anchor the stools. Even they seem cool to him, as if they've heard what happened last night. He can't go emptyhanded, so he stops in next door at the Zax and selects a tin of butterscotch drops. Handing three dollars to the clerk, he doesn't understand how this money is related to the offer the buyers have made, and then to Gram (he's in charge of her checkbook), but it's all one in the end—his ability to keep everything together.

In the truck, munching the cruller as he pulls into traffic, he remembers the one murder he's had the bad luck to clean up after, a husband who shot his wife so she couldn't divorce him for his money, then shot himself so he wouldn't have to live with it. One of the big new places on Thornwood, a stray slug in the bottom of the fancy dishwasher. Now he can almost see the logic. But none of this is Melissa's fault; it's all his. The oldtimers have to know about that. Do they feel sorry for him or think he's a schmuck?

"A schmuck," Brooks says, testing it as he drives past the high school. No, he thinks, both. He searches for Tim's red jeep, a sweeping glance at the line coming out. Probably gone already. Check in on him at the Stop'n'Shop.

The home's not far, just past the Baptist church with its new wing. If he patrolled Zone 2 he'd pass it ten times a night—overkill, since he already feels guilty for visiting her only once every couple of weeks. It's all he can handle. The last time he saw her she didn't know him. Now he wishes he'd brought flowers for her room, something to cheer her up, even if she can't see them.

GOLDEN HORIZONS OF AVON. There's the carved sign and the flag out front, like it's a country club. The sign advertises that it's a health care center, not a nursing home. The building's low, red-brick with white pillars, a colonial motel. The lawn's neat as an infield, sculpted shrubs and a skinny wraparound parking lot, convenient fire hydrants. The cars at the far edge of the lot by the dumpsters are sporty, obviously the staff's: a Firebird, an Eclipse, a jacked-up Ford pick-up. Brooks parks close so he doesn't get soaked, takes a gulp of coffee for energy, then trots across the lot. Before he opens the front doors, out of habit he gathers a last breath of fresh air.

Inside, the lobby's made-up for the holiday, as if anyone here cares. It's not the spoiled smell that gets to him, or the sudden smothering heat, but the quiet and the washed-out fluorescent light. The halls are long and narrow, and the carpeting softens every footstep. Against one wall, a wheeled walker with brakes like a mountain bike waits for its owner. Most of the doors are closed, a soap opera muttering in weird stereo as he passes. And

zero security—he's penetrated to the nurses' station before anyone makes him, and that person only smiles, as if she's seen him
before. Brooks smiles back, his weapon heavy against his ribs. He
thinks they should at least have a metal detector; this is not a
good place for people to have access to guns.

(Look who's talking, Toe says.)

Her name is on her door, spelled out on a piece of cardboard
in black magic-marker like in kindergarten. If that's not enough,
there's a Beanie Baby lobster hung head down under the room
number to jog her memory—a trick you'd use on a child.
Brooks knocks and then pushes the door open because she can't
hear if she's listening to her tapes.

He didn't call to say he was coming, so they haven't had time
to clean her up, and when he finds her asleep in her chair with
her headphones on, the tape player nattering away, he glances
around the room for the smallest hint of neglect. The bed's made,
her radio on the night table, her pill reminder on the walnut
hutch from the old house—out of place, like her dresser and the
1950s pictures of his mother and his young uncles (all dead) that
he's known since he was little. Everything's clean and neat, the
lights on, the drapes open to a view of the birdfeeder and the
groomed back lawn, yet it still seems wrong that this is all that
remains of a world he remembers as rich and mysterious. In his
mind he can revisit those rooms, see the hand-painted plates they
ate off, the screenhouse and the stone cover of the cistern in the
backyard, her kitchen garden she defended against rabbits and
groundhogs, the musty basement where Grandad tacked up covers of the *Saturday Evening Post*. His history. He's the only one left
to remember it.

Her lips are pursed, her face a net of wrinkles except for a
dark scab on her forehead where she fell a couple of months ago,

still not healed. She's snoring, a faint scraping in her sinuses. He draws a chair up as if he's interrogating her.

"Gram," he says, then takes her headphones off and tries again.

Only her eyes open, watery, a light blue, and then her mouth, her lips working, moving to shape words but saying nothing. "Is it time for dinner?" she asks.

"No," he says loudly. "It's Johnny."

She doesn't seem to understand, even when he repeats it, but accepts a kiss. She smells of talcum powder and Ben-Gay, and he can see her pink scalp through her crown of hair. Around her neck is an alarm she can squeeze if she falls down again.

"I brought some of that candy you like." He wants to give her the tin but doesn't trust her hands. He unwraps the cellophane to make it easier. "I'll set it right here for you."

"Where's that sister of yours?" Gram asks, and he's glad she can't see his face.

"My sister."

"You know the one, I forget her name. What's she up to now?"

Does she mean his mother, thinking he's one of her sons? "You mean Millie?"

"Who? No, the other one, I can't remember her name."

"I'm Johnny, your grandson." He goes to the wall and retrieves the picture of himself in his red Roy Rogers outfit, twin six-shooters in his hands. He turns it to her and she leans forward, lays a spotted hand on the glass. "This is me—Johnny."

"Johnny," she repeats, but it's still a question.

"How are you doing?"

"I'm okay."

"What did you have for lunch today?"

"I had a sandwich," she says.

"How's your arm?" he asks, because she bruised it when she fell.

"My arm."

He peels back the sleeve of her sweater. The bruise is still there, brown now, dull under the thin skin. "It looks better. How does it feel?"

"Do I have to see the doctor?"

"Not unless it hurts. Does it hurt?"

"It's not too bad," she says.

He sits back down, and the conversation stalls. He wants to tell her he might have to sell the house, but there's no reason.

"That sister of yours," she says, amused. "She was a character."

Brooks plays along, hoping she'll drop clues. When she mentions how she loved to go to the dump with Leonard, he realizes she's remembering someone from fifty years ago, her mind retrieving what's been lost. Maybe she needs to, he thinks. He wishes he could go back in time and change things.

(Too late, Brooksie. It's one way the whole way, and knowing things and changing them are completely different.)

Gram subsides again, and the two of them sit. Half the visit is silence, weighing what to say, what can be understood. He doesn't ask if she's happy or what year it is. Time is tricky in here.

"What are you listening to?"

Her tapes are a mess, and he helps put them in order, fitting them into their cases so the home can mail them back to the Library of Congress. He uses the bathroom, an excuse to check its cleanliness and secretly consult his watch. He looks over the familiar knick-knacks on the hutch—the creamer shaped like a cow, the brass elephant toothpick holder; they soothe him the way they're supposed to comfort her, a connection to a better past, but one so far gone that he feels guilty. When was the last time anyone called him Johnny?

His sister, oh, she remembers the time they went to the shore that summer. He supposes she's making sense on some level and feels it's his fault for not inventing his side of the conversation. It's not as if she's speaking gibberish.

"Do you need anything?" he asks before he leaves.

She doesn't, and this is perfectly in character. She doesn't want to be a bother. Brooks leans down and holds her hollow body, kisses her goodbye.

"Bless you" are her last words, ones he's sure he doesn't deserve.

The hall is another world, a limbo, in-between. (It's creepy for us too, all these rooms filled with people who have nowhere left to go, the real living dead.) Brooks feels the same way, just wants to be gone. It's wrong, walking away, and outside, in the drizzle, the sky and trees even darker now, he wonders why he expected things would be different. And he thinks it's simple: because he wanted them to.

No one's home, so so far the plan's working, Tim just has to focus on it, not let himself get distracted. He comes in through the garage but doesn't hang his keys on the board. Usually he gets something to drink—OJ, and some cookies—but not today; a glass in the sink would be too cruel. He doesn't want to leave a trace, still wants to be blameless, as if that's possible. Crossing the living room, he steers clear of the furniture, and when he climbs the stairs he doesn't touch the bannister, as if his fingerprints aren't all over the whole house.

Upstairs it's gloomy, the bathroom haunted, the shower curtain dark. He closes his door, leaves the lights off as he changes into the blue flannel—new, but good enough. In the mirror it could be last year.

He sits at his desk and opens the bottom drawer. He still has the little manila envelope the hospital gave him, the string wound around the cardboard circle. He clears out one front pocket, trades his new bills for the unlucky ones, the change too. He's bought a black lighter to replace the one he lost, and he's burned a CD for the occasion, a mix of our favorites (Natalie and Smashing Pumpkins for him and Danielle; Black Crowes with Jimmy Page for Toe; Zero Tolerance for Kyle; Everclear for me).

He knows he shouldn't look at the pictures, that they'll paralyze him. It's not in the plan, and he can't afford to get caught here, even if he has time. He knows what they look like, can flip through them in his mind, but it's not the same—the difference between thinking about food and eating. He's broken into them so many times the tape he used to seal the envelope doesn't work anymore.

He turns his desk lamp on and bends over the glow, leaning on his crossed arms, gazing straight down, his nose inches from the fat stack of pictures, muddy instamatics in with regular prints.

This isn't part of the plan, and he wonders if it's bad luck, but there she is, undeniable, leaning against the jeep in her shorts and halter top, twisting to wave from the ski lift. Those days come back with their weather, her suede coat, the way her hair blew across her face, a single thread caught in her lips.

(Danielle walks away, stations herself at the window, watching the needles of the pine trees drip. He'd say she's the reason he's doing this—for her, because of her—and she thinks it's unfair. She hasn't asked him to do anything. And she's not that strong. If she could stop him, we wouldn't be here.)

The lamp heats up and smells of dust, an electrical burning. He should be downstairs, on his way out instead of hiding in his room, going over these for the millionth time. This is what he wants to stop doing, but here he is again, an addict.

And nothing will move him. Not Danielle and not us, not the day. For the few minutes it takes him to get to the bottom of the stack, he's outside of time and with her again, and when he's done, he's ready, convinced. He stuffs the pictures into the envelope, bundles it into his pocket like a wad of cash and closes the door to his room.

Downstairs he doesn't let anything register. He stalks through the rooms like a murderer, intent, heads straight outside, gets in the jeep and drives off for the last time without saying good-bye.

Saintangelo's in; Brooks spots his Acura across the lot and decides to try the back of the building. The Vic's where he left it, a safe haven if he can make it through roll call. Have to gas up—he'll drive a couple hundred miles tonight. He checks his mirrors and over his shoulder, waits until he's sure no one's around before getting out. Aware of his paranoia, he locks the truck, then lifts the wet packet of mail from the bed and chucks it in the dumpster, in the dark far corner where no one can see it.

He can't hide inside, has to say "Hey" to Eisenmann at the roster board.

"Love that doubletime," Eisenmann says, and Brooks thinks he can read something false in his voice, as if Brooks hasn't earned this extra shift. When he was Eisenmann's age, no way he'd be pulling a double; it was straight seniority. Now this kid's busting his balls.

The chief's in—the chief's always in—and Brooks takes the long way around (like us, running from the Hook). He slips into the locker room, goes to his row, and there's Saintangelo buttoning his cuffs—busted.

He sees Brooks but doesn't respond, a snub.

"What's up?" Brooks asks.

Sandy concentrates on his wrists, and Brooks thinks he's fucked. "I couldn't lie," he finally says.

"I didn't ask you to lie."

"I wrote it up just the way it happened."

"Good," Brooks says—fuck you too. Or is Sandy telling him this because he feels guilty? Brooks knows it's his own fault but part of him wants to blame Sandy, even if he did save him. "I screwed up. It happens."

"No. *Maybe* you get your ass kicked, but you don't lose your weapon."

"I misread the situation."

"Two drunk-and-disorderlies in a parking lot. With back-up en route."

"Yeah?" Brooks says, and hears how lame it sounds.

"You're not that stupid. You need help." He holds Brooks's eyes so he knows he's serious (and seriously embarrassed for both of them), drops the bomb and he's gone.

Alone again, Brooks wants to argue with him, to say he knows he's been sloppy, that he hasn't been sleeping much, but even he doesn't buy these excuses. And Sandy's cutting him a break; he could take it straight to the chief or file a complaint with the union. Brooks should be grateful this is just a warning.

He pulls on his uniform, already tired. The report can't be that bad; otherwise he wouldn't be here. The chief will call him in, tell him to sit. Carelessness, at most a reprimand, and as always, at the heart of the argument, unspoken between them, the reason everything's gone wrong—us.

Filling his pockets, he finds Charity's card stuck in a wad of bills and wonders if she's still in her office. He can't stretch his head around the idea of selling the house and getting nothing out of it. Short term, it makes more sense to keep it. Long term, he doesn't like his odds anyway.

Roll call takes longer than it ought to. Brooks wonders if swing shift knows. They take up the front row, the smart kids in class. He sits in the back of the squad room, a visitor, jotting notes on his clipboard, sneaking peeks at Saintangelo, who won't look at him. The chief says they should expect weather. It's good news, bad news. The rain will cut down on the funny stuff, but the commute's going to be a bitch. Swing will stick with its regular assignments, Saintangelo's the floater, meaning Brooks pulls traffic detail. SNET's doing some line work over on Lovely Street; the chief needs him there until they're done. It's an insult, a babysitting gig, standing in the rain with a plastic shower cap over his hat, waving people through with a flashlight.

"That's it," the chief says. "Let's roll. Brooks, in my office."

There's no low oooh like at school, but the feeling's the same, the whole room knows he's screwed. The chief doesn't wait for him, straightarms the door, all business. Saintangelo and swing shift flee as if he's diseased, and though he expected this, he's still surprised that it's happening, a bad dream.

The chief's door is closed, and he has to knock.

"Come," the chief says.

He has his half-glasses on and is reading a folder opened on his desk, an incident report. Brooks takes a step in, his hat in his hand, eases the door closed behind him.

"Have a seat," the chief says.

Kyle's mom wipes the flat of the knife against the edge of the jar, then dips it into the jelly, spreading it thin, painting the square of bread, the holes soaking it up. She matches the two slices, cuts the crusts off, then saws it diagonally in half and bags it, seals the seal. He likes it, he'd flip out if she gave him anything else (he refuses to eat cold cuts, which he used to love), but she hates to think of herself doing this twenty years from now, making the same sandwich for a boy who never grows up.

Kitchen thoughts, not real. She busies herself peeling carrots, splitting them into sticks. He's in the den, watching some Japanese cartoon she can't follow. She knew he'd lose his Dracula fangs at school—anything that's not attached. Rain spatters off the birdfeeder, the rail around the deck. The day's dark, making the light over the sink seem warm.

The doorbell rings as she's rinsing the sticks.

"Can you get that?" she calls. "It's probably Tim."

She listens for his footsteps to cross the living room. The bell rings again, something Tim wouldn't do, and then she hears Kyle open the door, and the tentative, overlapping cry of "trick or treat"—the first little kids, way too early.

She dumps the knife in the sink, grabs at the towel on the handle of the fridge and hurries to the front of the house, waggling her hands to dry them. Even the neighborhood kids will point at his remade face and run from him, and she curses herself for not thinking. She's been trying so hard to remember the day, not like Mark.

The bowl of miniature Snickers bars should be on the hall table, but it's gone. Kyle stands in the doorway with his back to her (and, what she doesn't see, for a flash before he disappears, the real Kyle inside him). She expects to find the children terrified, racing for their parents, a mother with an umbrella headed for the door, ready to confront her.

Kyle's got the bowl. The children are navigating the slick stepping stones with their bags—a chubby Spiderman lifting his mask to see where he's going and a tiny angel with a halo of crushed aluminum foil. A van is waiting for them in the driveway, and she recognizes Andrea, who works the reference desk at the library. Kyle's mom waves.

"Thank you," she tells Kyle, replacing the bowl, amazed. As a reward, she gives him a Snickers. Just one can't hurt.

"You're welcome," he says, unaware that he's done anything special. (And he's not. He couldn't tell you why he picked up the bowl before he opened the door. The real Kyle's gone.

We are in deep shit, Danielle says.)

Fluorescent red would be the best but black's not bad, and Travis's dad has an extra can. In the basement, Travis shakes up the Rustoleum—the ball inside clatters—and tests it on a cardboard box. The line's fat and drippy, the smell like licorice, deliciously toxic, melting braincells.

"Is one going to be enough?" Greg asks.

IT'S TIME. Time to light the pumpkins, time to put on your costumes and paint your faces, time to rip open the plastic bags and dump the Blow Pops and Tootsie Rolls and Nestlé's Crunches in the big bowl. This is all supposed to trick us into leaving your mortal soul alone, make us stay away, but no one remembers that old stuff, druids and bonfires, sacrifices to the harvest gods. No one takes it that seriously here. How can you be afraid of Charlie Brown and "The Monster Mash"? It's just fun, an excuse to dress up and forget about real life for one night, a game of let's pretend. So let's.

Let's pretend no one ever dies.

Let's pretend no one ever wants to.

Dusk comes fast, dramatic. The gray deepens, evening filling in the trees. Coachlights pop on, windows glow. It's not even five o'clock, and the anticipation is killing. Traffic's bad; fathers who work in the city are just getting home, changing into their jeans.

Dinner's simple—hot dogs and mac'n'cheese, maybe takeout; no one feels like eating, they're so revved up. Leave the dishes. Come on, the little kids are already out there. Dad loads batteries into his flashlight. Let's go, we're ready, but no, mom wants everyone to stand still for a picture.

In school kids used to draw maps like battle plans, claiming their territory, shooting to break their record for pieces of candy. (How can we hate this day, this place? It's everything we love.)

At the last minute there's a flurry by the door. The umbrellas are in the bottom of the closet. Does anyone need gloves?

And the warnings: Be careful on the stairs. Be careful crossing the street. Be careful not to trip over your robe. Can you even see your feet? Be polite. Don't forget to say thank you. Don't run across people's lawns. Don't run ahead. Don't eat anything that isn't wrapped.

The air is cool enough to turn breath into mist, and the boards of the porch are slippery, the wind blowing rain between the pillars. Already the top of the pumpkin is charred, the stubby candle guttering, a black match shriveled in a clear puddle of wax. Nightfall softens the driveway, the coachlight throwing shadows through the rhododendrons. On Indian Pipe, packs of kids rove from house to house, trying to decide who's home. Their bags are light, rattling as they jostle along. At the far end of the street, two minivans lurk with their parking lights on, parents guarding their charges as if they can make everything safe, and for now it's true, they do. The night is young and there's candy for everyone.

No wonder we love Halloween so much; for one night it lets us pretend we'll get everything we want.

So let's pretend we can stop here.

Let's pretend nothing bad can happen.

———

Tim slows and turns onto Indian Pipe, sticking to the middle of the road, aiming away from the umbrellas and ghost-green glow-sticks and jack-o'-lantern-capped flashlights. In his headlights, in their jackets and baggy costumes, hunched from the rain, the kids waddle like dwarfs. He thinks of Kyle—the new Kyle, the Kyle that's alive—and how people see him as a freak. He wonders if he does, if that's why he thinks Kyle should go with him tonight. What if he was fine?

He doesn't have to decide now. There'll be time after their shift ends. It's not like he's actually been sticking to the plan.

Kyle's porchlight is on, water rilling down the drive, a spill-way. Tim has to wait for a gang of older kids, then pulls up and sets the emergency brake, takes his keys with him. There's no pumpkin on the porch, no decorations—just like at his house (at all our houses; Danielle's sisters aren't allowed out). He's uncomfortable in the light, as if someone might see him. He rings the bell and looks back at the street to check if anyone's coming.

The door opens, and there's Kyle's mom with a bowl of candy. "Tim, come on in. Have a Snickers. KY-ull!"

"No thanks." Already he wants to apologize to her, stands there wiping his feet, sure she can tell something's wrong.

"How bad is it?" she asks, and for a moment he doesn't understand.

"It's a little cold, that's all."

"These kids come to the door shivering. It's crazy."

He doesn't know how to answer this. He's gotten too used to being alone today.

Kyle saves him, diverting her attention. She tucks his uniform shirt in, circles him like a tailor, then helps with his jacket.

Tim thinks he should say something important to her, like this morning with his parents, but she's busy giving him the number of the restaurant where they'll be, in case there's an emergency.

"And straight home after," she says, "okay? You call if it's going to be past midnight. I don't want to worry." She's holding the door, and a bunch of trick-or-treaters are hiking up the drive. It's his last chance (not really).

"No problem," he says.

Brooks stands in the rain like an idiot, the Vic's lightbar spinning so drivers slow and stare and wonder why they're paying him their hard-earned tax dollars. The telephone truck's half off the road, its yellow light going, the lineman's canvas-covered bucket a cocoon on the wires, leaving just enough room for two lanes. Brooks is stuck here till they're done. There's nothing for him to do except stay inside the cones and think of facing the review board, of what he could possibly say to them.

He motions with both palms down for people to take it easy, but everyone's in a rush to get home. His old yellow slicker's heavy and cold, and the rain has found its way in through a crack in the back of the hood. He has to twist his neck to stop the drops from running under his collar and down between his shoulder blades to his waist.

He's never been in front of the board before. Just being called is proof he's screwed. It's flip-flopped; now the *best* he can get is a formal reprimand. They wouldn't dismiss him, he hasn't done anything that bad (he thinks, searching his memory, suddenly unsure). They can suspend him without pay and make him take a psych evaluation, that's probably worst case. It's what Melissa always wanted, for him to talk to someone professional.

He doesn't believe it would change a thing, and it's too late anyway. Nothing can bring those kids back.

(No one but you, Brooksie, our own doofy Scrooge. Your little pictures and diagrams keep us alive, chained down in the basement like some experiment gone wrong.)

Cars file past, tires swishing. It's freezing, and he wants to sit in the Vic—would if he didn't think he'd be seen. He's not superstitious, he's just had that kind of luck lately. He wonders what Sandy said in his report. The truth would be enough. He doesn't blame him.

He paces, caged, imagining a clean break—selling the house, quitting, leaving town (leaving us). He'd have to come back to visit Gram, even if she doesn't know who he is anymore. He's running through his arguments for and against when he recognizes the car passing right beside him, not ten feet away, a white flash topped with a dark roof—the Cabriolet from last night.

He turns and watches it snake up Lovely Street, its license plate blocked by the rest of the line. A drop of water skims his back, and he shivers. It's only a car, he thinks, maybe not even the right one, but can't shake the bad feeling he has—as if he's seen a ghost.

(While inside the Golf, Travis and Greg look at each other like, Holy shit!

"Aw, *man!*" Greg says. "You should have fucking hit him.")

"Tim," Kyle asks in his dim monotone, "do you think it's going to snow tomorrow?"

"I don't know," Tim says, "maybe so," because it's freezing in the jeep, even with the heat cranked. "I bet we still have school."

This quiets him, and Tim looks over. Kyle holds on to the

crashbar attached to the dash with both hands like he's driving with it. They're coming up on 44, the red light smeared across the windshield. He stops and the jeep idles beneath them, only his own hands sticking out of the shadows, chopped off at the wrists, disembodied killers. The Staples is open, and the McDonald's across from it where they'll get dinner. He's got the money in his pocket.

"It's Halloween," Kyle says from the darkness, and Tim turns down the radio.

"What?" Tim asks, but can't see his face, just the glint from one lens of his glasses. (Which Kyle is it? We don't see the real one.)

"It's Halloween," Kyle says, innocent.

The light's green, and Tim goes. "What about it?"

"I like Halloween."

"What do you like about it?"

"I like getting candy."

"Do you remember Halloween last year?"

"Yes. I got lots of candy. I was a werewoof."

"Wolf," Tim says, relieved.

"Wolf," Kyle says.

Kyle's dad is late and tired from the drive. He comes in from the garage, mumbling something about traffic, construction in West Hartford. The details aren't important, it's just a warning shot to signal his mood, proof it has nothing to do with her. They kiss, a clinch in the middle of the kitchen, formal as a minuet. Kyle's mom relieves him of his briefcase and takes his coat, as if she can lift the weight of the workday off of him. She's afraid he may have changed his mind, that he'll use this as an excuse—or maybe she's hoping he'll call it off. She's still wearing what she had on this morning.

"When are our reservations?" he asks, flipping through the bills.

"Seven-thirty. You've got time."

"Good." He cups his eyes, rubs his face with both hands and totters down the hall like an old man. She takes his briefcase into his dark office and sets it flat on the spotless desk so he can open it when they get home—exactly what she doesn't want. Tonight she needs him to forget everything else and concentrate on her.

"I didn't know we were giving out candy," he calls from the front of the house.

"Why not?" she hollers, but he's already climbing the stairs.

She stands by his computer with its screensaver cruising through space and listens. It seems they're always talking to each other from different rooms, that one or the other of them is always walking away. What will they say to each other at dinner, where there's no escape?

The doorbell startles her—she's forgotten the rest of the world again (the great danger of living here, holed up in our cozy little burrows).

"I got it," she calls, and scoops the bowl off the table, tries on a Betty Crocker smile.

There's a policeman at the door—she sees the blue uniform and understands in a flash that something's happened to Kyle, another accident—except the policeman's only a boy, backed up by a witch and a mummy. "Trick or treat!" they yell.

She recovers, hiding her confusion behind a smile. "Take two," she says, as they all grope in the bowl, the mummy lifting his mask so he can see. She doesn't recognize any of them, but she wouldn't, they're so much younger.

"Thank you," they say, "Happy Halloween!" and they're gone over the stepping stones, shadows on the road.

She closes the door and sets the bowl on the table, catches her face in the mirror and composes herself before going upstairs. Tonight, of all nights, she doesn't want to look thoughtful.

Everything else in the mall is closed for the night, the lights off, the alarm systems armed and blinking. At the far end, set back from the road, the Stop'n'Shop looks isolated, an island surrounded on all sides by darkness, a likely stronghold against an army of zombies. And here they come, one by one, careening across the lot for the front doors, ignoring the stop signs and lined spaces, leaving the Explorer idling cockeyed in a handicapped spot. No, no cart, they're only here for one thing, hungry as junkies, ravenous as the undead.

Like any decent monsters, they're insatiable. They need candy, but the right kind—no Heath Bars or Mallo Cups. The shelves have been ransacked, picked clean down to the bare metal. The floor is slick with their footprints, a hazard, and Tim is called in to mop it down and set out the yellow cones.

Here, under the dull, tireless fluorescents, anonymous in his ugly pine-green uniform, he feels safe. The place is empty and Kyle is doing the bottle room cardboard, breaking down boxes for the recycling guys. Tim swings the mop from side to side, navy-style, leaving neat swirls, flipping the heavy head at the end of each stroke, rinsing it and squeezing it clean in the press. His mom's always saying he's so good at it he should do it at home, a joke he's kept as a compliment. (She's making dinner now, talking to herself as she nukes the clumped pasta, rifling through the deli drawer for the block of parmesan.)

There's always someone who comes and has to step on the wet floor right when he's finishing—someone's dad ("Sorry"), tiptoeing as if that makes a difference. Tim goes over the spot and then dry mops the whole thing again, the tiles drying in swooping streaks by the time he's done. He leaves the cones, knowing he'll be back, rolls the bucket away, using the mop to steer.

The shelves are tall enough to block out the clock, but time is running, seconds ticking off like at the end of a game, a self-destruct sequence. Everything he does brings him closer to us— to Danielle, her face from the ski trip riding in his jeans pocket beneath his apron. (It's not me, Danielle says; it's just a picture.) Is it possible that no one will stop him? He can't believe it, feels out of control and then totally calm, as if this is a regular shift.

He checks with Darryl to see what's next. Usually they'd be bagging, but the place is dead, a couple of guys hitting the beer aisle, people needing cigarettes; the express line's steady, its reader's spastic peeping the only relief from the happy muzak.

"I got yogurt you can stock," Darryl says. After that it's a dolly of Pop-Tarts, heavy jars of pickles still cold from the truck. Tim almost drops one, traps it against the lip of the bacon and hot dog cooler with his hip. "Big save," he says.

Kyle's done in the bottle room and they work on straightening, a job Kyle is surprisingly good at, matching the cans and boxes by the pictures on the front. The only thing he can't do is soups. (The real Kyle doesn't help, just stands there at the end of the aisle like a gunslinger, wearing what he wore. An older woman walks through him and stops as if she's forgotten something, then goes on.

Danielle sticks close to Tim, leans in as if listening, touches him in the middle of his back as he's working. Toe's ready to go, tired of waiting around all day. I'm not. I want to walk through the store and handle everything, follow everyone home. I want to be one of the undead.)

Straightening—it's the most boring job in the world, and totally absorbs Kyle. His broken, sewn-together face is all concentration as he lines up a train of gross canned macaroni and cheese. Tim works on the SpaghettiOs and Beefaroni, wondering what goes on in his mind. What does he know, what does he remember? Maybe it's easier. If Tim didn't remember us, would he be fine? Life would just go on. He'd wake up and feel nothing; it would just happen over and over again, like *Groundhog Day*. He could live like that. He used to play games when he was straightening—what if he was trapped in the store during an earthquake, or after a nuclear war? How long could everyone left survive? Unpacking peanut butter or baked beans, he'd decide the best way to organize their resources, where they'd make camp and how to defend the doors against foragers, playing it all out like a movie. That was before. Now as he neatens the shelves he wonders how long he'll have been gone when whatever mom finally pulls this can out of the cupboard and feeds it to her kids.

"Why don't you guys take five," Darryl says when he comes by. Kyle has to finish the row he was doing, and then the two of them go up front so Kyle can pick out a candy bar. It's ridiculous paying for one on Halloween, but Tim dips into the right pocket (the money that lived through the crash—sacred, untouchable), forks over the quarters and hands Kyle his Nutrageous.

"Thank you, Tim."

"You're welcome, Kyle," Tim says, a routine that Luisa the cashier smiles at.

They go all the way to the back of the store, duck through the plastic curtains into the guts of the meat department and then down a hall of boxes stacked on pallets three high, the fork-truck parked for the night. There's a regular door between the two roll-up garage doors of the loading dock, propped open by a milk crate.

Outside it's chilly and the rain is spitting. They slip into the shadowed bay of one of the big doors to stay dry. A stench of curdled milk and rotting vegetables comes from the ribbed, industrial dumpster, long as a boxcar (rumored to have crushed a drunk prospecting for cans). Tim pulls out his black lighter and stokes up a Marlboro, sends the smoke out into the thin drops. Kyle munches his Nutrageous. The lot's empty, presided over by a high light like the ones in front, a weak sun at the top of a pole. Employees are supposed to park back here, but no one does; the truck drivers are nuts, and people use this as a shortcut from the other side of the mall, whipping through going fifty. (Roll call. We're all here: the real Kyle, me, Danielle and Toe all huddled under the overhang. We're like the crew shooting a movie, following the stars wherever they go.)

"Smoking is bad for you," Kyle says for the millionth time.

"I know," Tim says. "I'm going to quit soon."

"You promise?"

"I promise."

But what is he promising him?

He's promised himself tonight for so long; now that it's here it feels hollow, as if he's still waiting, leaning forward, the reason behind all of this forgotten. But it's not. It's there with him all the time, part of him like his skin. To get rid of one you have to get rid of the other. The problem isn't the decision—he's gone over the reasons for months, mostly how he feels, and the answer's always the same, and solid—it's holding on to it, believing enough in himself. He needs to have faith.

(Don't, Danielle says, a hand on his shoulder. It's a mistake. It was an accident.

And we don't stop her, don't tell her it's useless, that she looks like a fool, the clingy girlfriend. She knows. It's been a year; all of us have fallen back on the obvious with him at some point, the sappy platitudes—life is better than death. Sometimes it's hard to stand by, even when there's nothing you can do. Ask Kyle's mom about that.

And then there's the real Kyle over in the corner in his black jeans and T-shirt and Doc Martens, his Harley wallet on a chain, looking tough, saying nothing, just like in real life. People who didn't know him thought he was creepy, and maybe that's why we're afraid of him now—we don't know what he's up to.)

A car Tim doesn't recognize cruises by, jolting over the puddles, its lights flying through the fence at the far end, catching in the bare branches of the trees. He and Kyle stand there like us as it splashes past, invisible and enjoying the feeling (and sometimes he does wish he could be like us—here but not here, hovering above his own funeral, visiting his parents afterward to tell them it's okay). The car brakes for the corner, taillights flaring. Once it's gone, the quiet of the night returns. The rain's almost stopped, a thin mist drifting down through the high light, fine and slow as snow.

Kyle's too busy finishing his chocolate bar to notice. Tim leans over and hangs a hand on his shoulder, points with his cigarette.

"Hey," he says. "What's that look like?"

Brooks is just warming up. He's two lights from the Stop'n'Shop when he gets the call: MVA with multiple victims, Route 44 and

Deer Cliff Road, Code 3. He's still got his cop reflexes; the adrenalin kicks in and he has the rack wailing and the Vic floored before he processes the details. It's a spot on the mountain notorious for head-ons, a poorly banked curve where the road bulges around an outcrop of rock. Always the same place, and always in iffy weather. No one around here knows how to drive. He's emptied a good box of flares there over the years, the stumpy guardposts along that stretch bristling with rusty nails and metal baseplates from past accidents.

People are slow to pull over. Rush hour's done but he still has some traffic against him. He swings wide at the light and guns it up the vacant turning lane, half-looking for a way back in. It's like racing, a kind of tunnel vision, picking up anything that moves directly ahead of him, anyone that might pull into his path. And then at the light by the Mobil all five lanes are full and he practically has to stop and blast the klaxon so he can sneak through.

A head-on means extrication, facial lacs, blunt trunk injuries. He has one C-collar in back if he's first on-scene (probably not, whoever's on Zone 1 will beat him, maybe Sandy, floating close). He expects an ejection—worst case, an unbelted child. Two. Babies in cheap carseats, bodies on the road. Whatever it is, he'll be ready and professional. As he blows by the Wal-Mart he's reviewing his med-tech procedures, breaking them down step-by-step in case he needs them. Check for dilated pupils, stabilize patient's neck, clear airway. (I told you, he's our hero; it's what he does for a living.) He's concentrating so hard on what's in front of him and what he might find that for an instant he's completely filled and he remembers why, for a long time, he was addicted to this, the rush of helping people. It's only when he passes Stub Pond that he realizes he's going our way.

He remembers pulling up and seeing the Camry on the wrong side of the tree with the door torn off and Danielle lying in the road. There was someone screaming, trapped in the backseat.

The memory falls on him like a weight, makes him let up on the gas, and the Vic slows, floats a second, threatening to break loose before he gets it under control. "Easy," he says, and like that the adrenalin cools and dissipates, leaving him confused and too careful, afraid he might cause another accident trying to get to this one. He balks at the next intersection, looking both ways before crossing Old Farms Road, last Halloween and then the Cabriolet rising before he leaves us behind.

The straightaway of 44 is clear to the base of the mountain, the westbound lanes empty. They must be diverting traffic, meaning it's a bad one. It must have just happened; otherwise there'd be someone at the light by the inn stopping people going eastbound—there's no shoulder up there to squeeze by. Brooks takes the light at a reasonable sixty-five, then opens it up as he climbs the hill, refocusing.

SLOWER TRAFFIC KEEP RIGHT, a sign halfway up says. The Vic automatically shifts into overdrive, fighting the slope. For the first two curves, there's no one, just the streetlights and the dark trees, runoff trickling down the gutters, and then, as he turns for the long approach of the rock outcrop, he sees the scene far ahead, a double line of eastbound traffic backed up a hundred yards, the stuttering blue and red lights sweeping the pines and then, as he slides into the oncoming lane and past the gawkers and slows, he sees the circle of cruisers and Tahoes, and at the center, where they came to rest, the cars involved—neither of them a red jeep, as he half feared.

Head-on. Bad, the front of one smashed flat.

He yanks it into park, leaves the rack spinning and the keys in the ignition. The air is frantic with the chirping of a dozen open radios. Even before he can see if anyone's hurt, he notes the final positions of the two cars—an Acura and something else that took the brunt of it. The crash is textbook; he's probably got it on his computer. Vehicle coming down went wide, vehicle coming up cut the corner; one of them braked, probably the downhill, pulling to the left, and bam.

The smell is what gets him, that hot mix of steaming anti-freeze and gasoline. Glass scratches underfoot, plastic bits of grille and molded bumper. There's no one in the cars. They've got the drivers laid out on the pavement, already being worked on, a woman's face in a forest of legs, and Brooks turns away before he sees more, searches for the person in charge.

An ambulance pulls up from the other side, its siren winding down, EMTs in rubber gloves doubletiming it with a backboard. West Hartford's here, doing mutual aid right over the town line. Brooks looks for Saintangelo, since his Tahoe's sitting in the middle of the road, but finds Eisenmann instead, who passes him off to the supervisor from swing shift—Mason, who they gave Brooks's sergeant's stripes to when the shit hit the fan. Mason's all right, Brooks has no beef with him, it's just bad luck, old history. He's kneeling, shining a light into the ruined Acura.

"What do we got?"

"Looks like the guy was impaired."

"They gonna be okay?"

"Yeah, just a lot of blood." Mason aims the light at the driver's seat and the floormat to show him, and Brooks can take it. He's recreated accidents that would give coroners nightmares—rollovers, decapitations, impalements. Multiple multiples. It doesn't explain why he's suddenly angry at Mason, as if this is his fault, or why he feels the urge to run.

"Where do you want me?" Brooks asks, all business, as a flatbed from MacDonald's Garage rumbles up.

Mason points to the stopped traffic. "Get these people out of here, then shut this side of the mountain down."

At first Brooks is secretly relieved, but by the time he's cleared the scene of civilians and has parked the Vic across both lanes at the foot of the mountain and set out a line of flares, he's deeply insulted and Mason is an asshole. He's crashing from his adrenalin high, his nerves spent. He's helped no one, and feels hollow, but that's the job. It seems strange to him that he used to get a thrill out of this intensity, as if he were sick then, twisted. Or is he sick now?

An ambulance comes flying down the mountain, lights wheeling, and he has to go out and block the intersection to let it through. It's his good deed for the day (too late). He watches it take the straightaway into town, splitting the Exxon and the Sunoco before he leaves his post. In a minute it's gone, traffic filling the lanes again.

Not all the drivers seem to understand the road is closed. They roll down their windows and want to know why—one guy in a lion suit. Brooks clings to the last of his patience, tries to be polite (tries not to get himself fired by midnight). "Accident," he says, and marvels at how one word can have so much power. He knows better than to let himself think too deeply, afraid he'll get stuck on us (Gram, the house, the review board). He stands in the rain in his slicker, waving people away, signaling them not to stop, come on, let's go, keep moving.

"You look nice," Kyle's dad says in the car, in the dark, his eyes fixed on the road. It's his all-purpose compliment, rolled out whenever she dresses up, and even if it's delivered sideways, she doesn't call him on it. She's gone all out tonight, down to her best underwear (Go, Kyle's mom!), and she deserves anything she gets.

"You do too."

"So where is this place?" he asks.

"It's right in Farmington, just over the river. The *Advocate* gave it three stars."

And it's new, a good enough excuse. Still, she's worried that her strategy's transparent—somewhere out of town, a place they've never been, as if they can escape their history. Even here, right outside her window, the neon of the Chinese across from the driving range makes her think of how the kids loved dim sum, the two of them vying for the last fried dumpling, sword-fighting with forks, Kelly finally giving in to Kyle because he was younger. It seems so far in the past it might have never happened, a false memory she needs to believe in—her happy family enjoying a normal meal. That's not what she wants back, nothing miraculous, just a night out, a few hours away from the house, some adult conversation for a change, having someone else cook for her.

It's a pleasure just not driving, seeing things she misses when she comes through by herself. On her side the strip is a carnival, the new liquor store next to Pizza King doing big business; on the other, the darkness over the golf course stretches like a lake. She glances at his face, his profile moonlike in the oncoming headlights, his receding hair, and thinks he's still the man she married. He's only doing this for her. He'd rather be at home in his jeans and a flannel shirt, dealing with his e-mail or crashed in front of the TV.

"Thanks for coming out," she says.

"I invited you."

"Technically."

"Not true," he says, joking, and looks over so she has to admit this was his idea, at least partly. It's both of theirs, reached separately, and she's pleased. She lays her hand on his leg and he covers it.

They cross the river—running high and black underneath them—and swerve to miss the sunken storm drain in the right lane.

"Nice," she says. "That one always gets me."

She lets a blue hospital arrow slide by without comment, hoping he doesn't notice. "It's up here on the right," she says, pointing past the bay-windowed colonial storefronts of the muffin place and the real estate office—and there's the waist-high sign for the restaurant and the driveway. She takes her hand away so he can downshift.

The spotlit lot in back is full, a surprise that gives them something to talk about on the way in. The rain's almost stopped, the downspouts trickling. He holds the door for her, mock-formal, and she thanks him the same way, a vaudeville team.

Inside it's warm, and loud with conversation, all hardwood floors and black tables and delicate track lighting on wires. "Fancy-dancy," he whispers, his breath tickling her ear. From the open kitchen in back comes the flash and bustle of creation. It's too upscale for holiday decorations, and as the maitre d' leads them to their table, she's glad to see the crowd is their age, maybe a little older, mostly couples. (This is boring, Toe says. Can we go?

No. Not till she lets us. You know the rules.)

Their plates are already there, massive handpainted platters just for show. There's a votive candle burning in a sapphire glass holder, and a single violet in a skinny vase the same color. "I like the napkin rings," she says. "Very modern." The menu is a list of things the kids would never eat and that she loves—morels and capers and truffle oil, wilted escarole and grilled portabellos. The maitre d' brings Kyle's dad the wine list, a server right behind him with a dish of marinated olives. (Boring, boring, boring, boring.

I think it's sweet, Danielle says. They're on a date.)

"It all looks so good," Kyle's mom says, leaning across the candle as if it's a secret. "Can we order some wine?"

"What kind?"

"Red, please."

"A bottle?"

"I'm up for it if you are," she says.

He is, and chooses one they've never had before, shrugging like it's a wild guess. While they're waiting, the server brings them a roasted head of garlic to spread on strips of salty foccacia still warm from the oven.

"I won't have to order dinner," she protests.

What a luxury it is to be here. She'd almost forgotten. It feels like an occasion, and she wishes she had some big news to announce. The waiter comes and cuts the bottle, presents the cork for inspection. Kyle's dad lets her test the first sip.

"Excellent," she says, and it is—big and rich and plummy, making the room seem even warmer, the voices that much more buoyant, as if this is a party. Halfway through her first glass, she finds his foot with hers, grazes his calf with her ankle.

"Check, please," he jokes.

(And we're gone.)

———

There's no one on the rails-to-trails at this hour, nothing but blackness and the cascade of raindrops from the trees, leaves plastered to the asphalt in the weak bull's-eye of the flashlight as it hovers in front of their Timberlands. (*Much* better, Toe says.) Greg and Travis march along under their backpacks, wearing camouflage ponchos so they don't get soaked. They've humped all the way in from Stony Corners Road in the dark and they're sweating; the turnoff can't be much farther.

"I smell a skunk," Greg says, and stops. "Hold up."

It's impossible to hear with the rain. Travis shines the flashlight to the side and keeps going, silent as a ninja. Greg hustles to catch up.

"Know what would be cool?" Greg says. "If we caught a skunk and fucking chucked it through his window."

Travis has to laugh at how stupid it sounds. They've been wasted since this morning, and he can picture the surprised dogs watching the skunk and the broken glass come flying right at them. It's like a cartoon, exclamation points over their heads.

"You're fucking whacked," he says, "you know that?"

"It would be cool, admit it."

And he must be fucked up, because instead of thinking of Toe and remembering the big times they had (monstro, broham), he's wondering if the dogs would jump on the skunk and kill it or whether it could spray them and hole up under some furniture. Either way it would make a huge fucking mess. It *would* be cool.

"I can't believe you've got me thinking of that," Travis says.

"I'm telling you," Greg says. "I wish we had one of those traps."

They're discussing the possibility that the skunk might not be heavy enough to break the window—that they might have to use a rock and then toss the skunk in like a grenade—when the flashlight dies.

Total darkness. Outer space.

"Shit," Greg says, his voice coming from nowhere.

They stop, faceless (the three of us right behind them), and Travis whacks the flashlight.

It comes back on, but dimmer, the color of iced tea.

Greg asks if he has more batteries.

"No," Travis challenges back, "do you? Come on, it's right up here."

They jog past the oil-black beaver pond and over the creek, the beam of the flashlight bouncing, the straps of their packs digging in. The can of charcoal starter is like a brick. Travis is afraid they've gone by the turnoff, but there's the old railroad signal box with the door hanging open and its guts torn out, and then, off to the right, the sandy cut of the mountain bike trail leading up into the woods. The ground is soft, and by the time they clear the rise they're breathing hard.

"This is like boot camp," Greg says.

They take the bike trail back to a wire fence with NO TRESPASSING signs posted by Avon Old Farms, and then when the trail curves off to rejoin the asphalt path, follow the fence to the end. At the corner they go straight, ferns reaching out and wetting their hands. After a while the narrow trail disappears. Single file, they pick their way through the woods, turning their ankles on stones and fallen branches ("Fuck," Greg grunts behind him), slipping on moss, highstepping over rocks and rotted logs. Going downhill, it's slick and hard to balance with the pack, and he has to take baby steps.

They're supposed to go a hundred yards and then turn right for another hundred, then left until they reach the backyard. The first hundred he's pretty sure of, the second hundred they get wrong, because they end up in ankle-deep muck, a swamp of skunk cabbage he doesn't remember. "Keep going," he says, and then, when he starts sinking deeper, "Go back, go back."

The flashlight hangs tough—the one thing that goes right. The beam picks out an old stone wall like a pile of skulls, a white trash bag torn in half, a shelf of gray mushrooms on a birch tree. He's counting his steps in case they have to backtrack.

Greg falls—"Ow, shit"—and gets up wiping his hands on his poncho.

"You okay?"

"Yeah."

"We're going to go straight another twenty yards, then turn left. We should be seeing some lights."

But they don't. Travis thinks it's impossible, that if they keep going straight eventually they'll hit something. This is Avon, not Vietnam.

Neither of them says they're lost, even when they come to the stream. It's wide and high, gurgling at their feet. It should empty into the river, but that's on the other side of Old Farms. They couldn't have overshot that far.

They turn back. Travis tries to retrace their steps exactly, but everything looks the same—wet leaves and deadfall. His pack is heavy, his face and hands are freezing. The flashlight's not going to make it. They turn right and go a hundred paces. No birch tree, no trash bag, no stone wall. They turn left.

(What a pair of losers, Danielle says.

Whoa, Toe says. I don't see any of your friends helping.

Like they're helping.

They're going to, I say.

Well, I'm not going to help them, she says.

You don't have to.

You don't have to do anything, Toe says. You can blame it all on Tim the same way you blame me for everything.

Did I ever once say I blamed you? No, so just shut up.

Stop arguing, I say. God.

And in the end, as usual, I do it. The floodlight on the corner of the backporch is blinding, silvering the grass all the way past the clothesline to the metal shed. I cross the yard and climb the steps, and Skip and Ginger come charging from the front of the house, their teeth bared.)

Travis stops, so Greg stops.

"What?" Greg asks.

Travis holds the dying flashlight straight up. "Listen."

"232, this is dispatch."

Traffic's done, the cars hauled off, the road open again; Avon's home for the night. The wind is setting off alarms, kids are egging windows—little bullshit calls, and Brooks is handling all of them. See owner for code. It's as low as you go, on the chief's shit list and mopping up someone else's shift, and driving to the new address gives him time to wonder what it means. He's still mulling over the accident on the mountain, how that burst of adrenalin dried up in him. It's dangerous to think this way, because it all comes back to us.

Because Brooks isn't dumb. He knows what's up, or feels it, darkly, some cop part of him tuned to the justice of his own ruin. Maybe he deserves it. Maybe he's been prosecuting himself all along, as Melissa insists.

(Maybe he's being haunted for a reason. Tell me, Spirit!)

The alarm he's been called to isn't a business but a construction site, one of the massive homes going up in a hilltop development called Orchard View Estates. When Brooks was a kid, it was just a rundown dairy farm set back on a ridge. Even then the orchard wasn't worked, the windfall tossed to the hogs. The family had given one corner of a meadow over to a collection of rusting trucks the kids played in; now the land must be worth a couple million.

There are no streetlights, it's like driving on Mars. The development's half-done, skeletal frames like giant birdcages mixed in with finished houses peaked and faceted like castles—and ugly: all fake brick and picture windows. The developers clear-cut the lots to open up the view and haven't sodded, so the yards are graded mud interrupted by boulders kept for that touch of New England. On concrete slabs by the curb, sarcophagus-like, sit locked electrical conduits wearing big CAUTION stickers. Brooks twists the handle of his spotlight to read the mailboxes, then, a couple of driveways down, sees a woman getting out of a Volvo wagon and opening an umbrella, giving him a little here-I-am wave.

It's the realtor, Tammy Something, a younger, more expensive version of Charity, her purse over her shoulder. "Thanks for coming out," she says, as if he's a potential buyer. "I didn't touch anything."

Everyone thinks they're on TV.

"Good," he says.

The house is dark, and done. Tammy explains that there's been no one living there since the original owners were transferred to Virginia. It was just bad timing, they were only in it three months. As always, Brooks tries to relate this to his situation, but the money makes that impossible. These are the people who've priced him out of his hometown.

He trains his flashlight on the front walk—no muddy

sneaker prints—and she falls in behind him. The front door's like his, a brass lockbox hanging from the knob. She twirls the combination and pulls out the key; he takes it from her and goes in first, stands aiming his flashlight into the front hall as the overheads flood on around them.

There's no furniture, only the polished hardwood floor, bare eggshell walls making their footsteps echo. The emptiness surprises him, seems a kind of failure—the brand-new dream home abandoned by its family. He wonders what the buyers saw when they looked at his place. What did Charity say about him, that the seller was motivated?

Two potato-sized rocks sit in the middle of the living room, and a scattering of wet glass. The two picture windows have holes in them radiating jagged cracks, letting in the cold.

"Great," Tammy says.

It's the same in the kitchen, glass in the sinks and on the counter, a muddy rock on the floor by the dishwasher.

They go through the rooms, no longer surprised.

"Every single one," she says bitterly, as if a couple would have been enough.

Upstairs, by the light of the downstairs windows, he can see footprints circling the house, criss-crossing the muddy lawn. It could have been one kid or a dozen of them.

(No one we know. This is like middle school shit.)

He's got to take her complaint for the insurance, and they tour the rooms again, counting the broken windows. He has her sign his clipboard, then tears off her copy of the form, which she folds into her purse. At the front door she resets the alarm, punching in numbers from a slip of paper.

"Why do people do things like this?" she asks outside, more mad than baffled.

Brooks knows, and knows why it's not obvious to her. He's even felt the urge himself. He wants to ask what her commission is on this one, and if it's her second time. He wants to ask her if she knows who this land used to belong to, or what it was. He wants to ask her where she's from, because she's not from Avon. He knows everyone from Avon.

"It's just kids," he says. "It's that time of year."

He waits for her to back out, then tails her downhill to Lovely Street, where she goes right. He goes left, north toward 44, hoping the radio stays quiet. He needs to check in on Tim.

Something about the house nags at him, he can't figure out what. Some personal connection beyond the obsolete farm, the unlucky family. Unimportant, he thinks, or else it would come to him while he's driving.

Orchard View Estates is the future of Avon, maybe that's it. Where he's the past. He could explain it to Melissa if she'd listen.

There have been times in the last year when he thought he could make things right if he could just make things right with her, as if she could forgive him everything. She can't. He can't. He's understood this longer than he cares to admit. Something— maybe the Marine in him—won't let him give up, even when he knows he's beaten. (Semper fi, do or die.)

He chews his lip as he rolls the Vic through the curves, thinks about his house without a thing in it, waiting for its new owners. Where will he be then? And Gram?

He'll be somewhere else; she'll be dead.

Both are inconceivable, and at the same time a relief, all of this gone, off his shoulders. For a moment, blasting down the long dark stretch before the lumber yard, the sparse streetlights whizzing like comets overhead, he feels free, the reality of the wheel in his hands and the car beneath him so much stronger than any questions. What is there to fear when the worst has already happened?

(Exactly!)

The mood vanishes when he has to slow for the light at 44 and wait beside Vincent's Funeral Home, and when he gets the Vic back to speed it feels forced. He's conveniently forgotten his obligation to Tim. (To us, really. But that's what we're here for.)

44, a straight shot, the road he's driven his whole life. He goes by the antique mall and the Acura dealer and the Cape Cod Fence Company, by La Trattoria and the Valley Car Wash, by the Dunkin' Donuts (Hey, Mr. Arnold!) and the Subway and the Staples and the McDonald's. He makes the light by the Mobil and the Shell, then takes the back way in to the Stop'n'Shop. He cruises slowly past the loading dock, where he's watched Tim and Kyle take their breaks, slides alongside the building, scanning the far row of parked cars for his jeep. Not there.

Out front, in the red glow of the sign, there's no one. He turns past the front doors and does one go-round to make sure, splashing through the back again. Tim said they'd be working.

Brooks stops and looks at the dock, holds there as the wipers rack back and forth (giving Toe a chance to pass a hand through his computer, the green glow surging for an instant), then turns the Vic in a tight circle around the one high light and heads for the front. He thinks he knows where Tim is—where they are. The time's right, if he remembers the report correctly, and he should, he's read the damn thing enough. He'd be surprised if he's wrong, but, as with so much in his life, hopes he is.

They come down out of the woods past the moldy compost heap and the shed and cross the yard half-blinded by the floodlight. If there was someone on the deck with a gun, they wouldn't see him until it was too late. The dogs are barking harder—a good sign. Travis thinks Greg might want to do something with them. Travis wants this to be quick, in and out, like *Mission: Impossible*, and besides, the dogs are innocent.

Greg reaches the porch and presses his back to it like a cop stalking a suspect. They don't talk. A glance and Travis takes the lead, sticking to the shadows as they round the house. The grass is wet and the rain through the trees covers their footsteps. The dogs have lost them for now, still at the back windows, but that won't last.

From the corner of the front porch he can see the road, just the opening for the driveway, the rest is screened by trees. With the light on, anyone passing could easily see them.

Travis listens. The cold and being lost have killed his buzz, and he's tired, soaked, his systems crashing, but they're here, they're going to do this for Toe. He sinks to one knee and slides his pack off, feels for the zipper and reaches in for the smooth steel of the can among the egg cartons. Greg has his out. He copies Travis as he lifts the plastic top off and tucks it away, slips his arms through the straps in slow motion, careful not to catch the nozzle on anything.

A streetlight out on the road suddenly cuts on, making black lace of the trees. Motion-activated, but there's no car, no last, straggling band of trick-or-treaters.

They wait until it goes out again. The dogs stop barking, then shout out single exploratory warnings.

Nothing but the wind pushing the bushes, the rain, tireless, dropping all around them.

The road's empty, and Travis decides it's time.

Greg nods that he's ready.

Travis holds up a fist, holds up three fingers, and Greg understands.

One. Two. Three!

They break for the stairs and pound up them, cans in hand. The footing's tricky going from the wet steps to the dry boards of the porch. The dogs have somehow beaten them there, raging behind the front door. Travis splits left, Greg right, careful of the lawnchairs. They set up where they're going to start, but Travis can't help but check behind them, paranoid, sure someone's coming.

Just the yard, the drops falling through the light.

He hears Greg rattling his can and does the same. The dogs are going nuts. He's afraid they'll come through the windows after him.

Now Greg's spraying, the aerosol hissing, and Travis remembers the letters he's responsible for, steps forward and starts tagging the vinyl siding, the paint looking strange, wrong, as he waves the can up and down, thickening the line. He wants it big, and has to stretch on tiptoe, then checks to see how tall Greg's doing his. It has to be readable.

There's just enough room. He has to slash across a window, and the line drips, but fuck it. He's on his second letter, but it seems to be taking forever. The dogs are roaring, going hoarse. He looks back to the road and the streetlight's on.

(Hurry up, Toe urges.)

Greg is almost done, squatting to finish the R. In a flash he's at Travis's side, grabbing at his pack, tearing him away. "That's good enough!"

Travis slips coming down the slick stairs and falls hard on his wrist, losing his can. He slaps the grass trying to find it, but it's Greg who scoops it up. They run for the shadows around the house, the dogs after them the whole time, and finally stop, breathing steam.

Neither of them says anything, as if they're hiding, being chased. There's no one coming. The light on the road is out.

His wrist feels okay, it just hurts to turn his hand.

Greg's shaking in the dark beside him, trying to catch himself from laughing. "We fucking did it," he whispers.

"We did."

"Part two, then we get the fuck out of here."

"Let's do it up," Travis says, made brave by their success.

They're not quiet this time, getting out of their packs. They've grown immune to the dogs. They could stay here all night if they wanted.

They each have two dozen eggs. This time they don't split up, they just stand in the front yard and bomb the shit out of the house. There's nothing wrong with his wrist, a little twinge. The eggs crack and splash, yolks bleeding over the windows and the lines of the siding. Travis throws his hard, remembering how he felt when his mom told him about the accident and Toe being dead. He was angry then but didn't know who to blame, and this feels good.

He misses the front door and hits a post, nails a window, and as he reloads and whips another, he wishes someone *would* come and catch them. Looking at what he and Greg have done to Brooks's house, he's proud. Even after he runs out of eggs, he stands there watching Greg, cheering him on. "Yeah!" he shouts over the dogs. "Fuck you! Fuck. You."

His hands are empty, and he needs something to fill them, something to throw, to keep this feeling going. It's not even a thought—automatically he bends down and starts searching the ground for rocks.

Inside, the rainbowed plumbing of the Playland is deserted; it's too late for little kids. There are people sitting in booths, people moving window to window through the yellow light like fish in an aquarium. Tim watches them talking, eating their fries and burgers, sucking on straws. Their mouths open and close without sound, just the radio turned low—Staind. He thinks he'd like to go in and join them, be brainless and free, escape like a kidnap victim from Kyle and Danielle and the rest of us in the jeep, except he's the one with the keys. (It's his plan, not ours.)

Across the lot, the line at the drive-thru moves up—business is light tonight—but the dash clock says it's not time yet. Beside him, Kyle doesn't understand why they're sitting here with the engine off, and Tim can't explain, distracts him instead by rooting through his lunchbox, gathering what he has to toss. His sandwich is squashed, the jelly bleeding through the bread like a wet bandage.

"Let's keep the Snickers," he says. "And the chips. How about these carrot sticks, you want them?" Because sometimes he does.

"I want a cheeseburger," Kyle says.

"You're getting a cheeseburger. You want the carrot sticks or not?"

"No."

"Thank you," Tim says, and takes the baggies and the napkin Kyle's mom folded in half and steps outside into the rain, goes to the curb and shoves everything in the mouth of a trash can. The bright lights throw shadows between the cars, the air smells warmly of cooking grease, and from 44 comes the wet rush of traffic. Looking at the silhouette of Kyle through the plastic back

window, he thinks of running, taking off for the darkness of the
woods, making it his hiding place, but only for a split second. He
knows what he has to do, and how the days have brought him
here, to the edge of what he's wanted for so long—the hours lying awake in the dark, the whole summer resenting the neat
houses and their perfect lawns, hating the trees for being alive,
the sun for shining. He's too close to fuck it up now.

Two minutes, a minute. He judges the line, trying to get it
right. He can be off by a little; it's the effort that matters. He
turns on the jeep—the radio skipping a beat—punches on his
lights and pulls under the striped clearance bar and into the lane.

"Tim," Kyle says.

"What?"

"What are you going to have to eat?"

"I'm going to have a number 4." It's a test; the Value Meal
menu stands right beside them, with pictures for each combination.

"What is that?" Kyle asks.

"Double quarterpounder with cheese."

"You had number 3 last time."

"That right?" Tim asks, but he knows it's true. Kyle remembers weird stuff like this and then forgets to zip his zipper.

The car in front of them pulls up to the board, and he thinks
they'll be right on time. Prices have gone up in the last year, but
otherwise the receipt will be the same.

"Get ready," he says. "You know what you want to drink?"

"Root beer."

The car's done, and Tim slides up next to the speaker. He has
to zip his window open.

"WelcometoMcDonald's, mayItakeyourorder?" a girl says

with a Dominican lilt—not from around here, probably Hartford or New Britain.

"Yeah," Tim says, "we'll have a number 4 with a Coke and a number 2 with a root beer—please."

"I want a cheeseburger," Kyle says, obliterating what the girl is saying to him—the end of the supersize question.

"No thanks," Tim says, and then to Kyle, "A number 2 *is* a cheeseburger." He should know this—he orders it every single time—but that's Kyle.

For a second there's nothing, radio silence, the scrape of a spatula on a grill.

"Will that be all?" the girl asks.

"Yes, thank you."

"Your order comes to seven eighty-seven. Please pull around to the first window."

He does, but stops short of the overhang. The other car's still there, giving him time to make sure he uses the right money. And then, when he gets his fistful of change, he realizes it doesn't matter which pocket he sticks it in.

The fries are hot inside the bag, filling the jeep with their greasy smell. The cups go in the cupholders.

"ThankyouforchoosingMcDonald's, haveagoodevening."

Brooks sits in the Staples lot across the road with his lights off, his eyes on them the whole time. He thinks he knows where Tim's going, and lets the jeep disappear around the side, its place at the pick-up window taken by a Blazer with tinted windows. There's only one exit; if he's wrong, he can catch up fast enough.

It's not easy letting him go. This is the first time Brooks has seen him since yesterday, and it's a relief, but only briefly. It feels like he's been trying to find him all night; now that he has, a queasy anxiety fills him, a father spying on his son, afraid of what he'll discover.

The jeep reappears on the far side of McDonald's, headed for the exit. At the stop sign Tim signals even though no one's there, and then again at the light to get back onto 44. Brooks pulls up so he can see over the groomed hump with its nude saplings. The Dunkin' Donuts is on his side but three stores down, and he's hidden by a line of Salvation Army drop boxes. He's written up people fishing in them for Avon's designer castoffs, some from right here.

Almost every car that passes is speeding. He doesn't need the gun to tell him.

Finally the light changes, and the jeep turns onto 44. It takes the left lane, slowly, only goes a hundred feet before its blinker flashes. So he's not wrong.

Brooks casts back, trying to remember his history. The car's different, the passengers, and Danielle won't be there (Mr. Arnold's gone home, leaving the keys with the night manager). And this is just the first time they're here. They come back later to pick her up, their last stop before he enters the scene. They're on their way to a party.

The jeep skirts the lot and curls through the drive-thru, as he knew it would. He follows it as it idles by the menu and then the pick-up window. The two of them talked then, Brooks knows; he only bought a donut so he could see her, a fact Brooks carries like a scar. Their conversation is a gap in his report, a blank spot.

(I don't remember, Danielle shrugs, uninterested. Probably trying to figure out which party to hit first.)

The jeep stops in the lot and kills its lights and wipers. He can't make out their faces but he knows they're eating. The wrappers are in some of his pictures, balled yellow wads on the floor, a brown bag under someone's sneaker, splashed with what looks like oil.

Brooks sits in the dark, watching like a hunter. He listens to himself breathe under the steady thrum of the Vic's engine, the defroster bothering his eyes. The cursor on his screen blinks, asking him if he needs anything. He wishes he could access his computer for the report. He's hungry and his back hurts, curved to fit the seat. He arches and makes chicken wings of his elbows, rubs his neck, then settles in again. Traffic bunches at the light. The line at McDonald's stops, just a girl in the window. They sit like this, a quiet stalemate that pleases him. If he could just keep him in sight like this, everything would be fine.

Of course there's a chance—he knows he's paranoid—that there's no one in the jeep, that they've seen him and crawled out the back window and hotfooted it across the lot, using the parked cars as cover. They could be crawling on the far side of the hump, circling around behind him to pound on the trunk, fucking with him.

The radio breaks the spell, it's always the way. A cough of static and then the electric emptiness of space, crispy blips.

"232. 232, do you copy?"

"Copy," he says, thumbing the mike button, just as the jeep's lights pop on. And like that, they're moving. Break time is over.

The bottle is just enough, half a glass for each of them as the waiter clears their entrees, then combs the crumbs from the table. She can feel the warmth of the wine in her face, a glow like the candle between them.

"Can I tempt either of you with our dessert menu?"

"I think so," Kyle's dad says, taking the initiative.

"I'll give you a minute to decide," the waiter says, and vanishes.

"Oh my," she says, noting a pumpkin crème brulée, a lemon zabaglione, a chocolate ricotta torte. "I think it's going to take me more than a minute."

"They have espresso," he says, because it's her favorite and she hardly ever gets it.

"What do you have your eye on?"

They strategize, plan on sharing. The place is hopping, conversation on all sides making the space between them seem intimate. Talking's not awkward as long as there's something to focus on. The town elections are coming up, with a hot referendum on condos; there's a new Mondrian exhibit at the Wadsworth. The wine fills any silences.

"Have you talked to Kelly about Thanksgiving?" he asks, because there's been some discussion of her spending it on the Vineyard with her boyfriend's family.

"Not yet."

"I hope she's doing okay."

"I'm sure she is." She thinks of bringing up Kyle's open house next week, then suppresses it. She knows he hates going to them, dreads sitting with the other parents while the teachers run through their syllabi. Kyle's artwork is on the walls like in kindergarten, signed with a neat, feminine hand.

"This is nice, just the two of us," he says, rescuing her. "We ought to do this more often."

She agrees, though she's not exactly sure what that implies, whether it's a concession on her part, a vindication of his way of not dealing with things. Again, she pushes the thought down, reaches across the table and takes his hand. She can't lose this connection with him. It seems, suddenly, that he's all she has left.

"I think I've had enough wine," she jokes.

"I see my plan's working."

"Not if I pass out first."

"Better make that espresso a double."

It's funny, but underneath their easy banter lies the fact that they haven't slept together in weeks. What else can they pretend never happened?

When the waiter returns for their order, they take their hands back as if he's a chaperone. He flits away, and she reaches out again. Kyle's dad's surprised but willing. She's not going to quit this time, give in to sorrow. There have been nights she was too tired, but today is too important. She thinks of her wreath on the tree, people seeing it. (Yeah, thanks a lot, Kyle's mom.) She doesn't know why the idea struck her. Maybe it's her way of putting that Before part of life behind her, setting it to rest, if that's possible (and here's the real Kyle, standing beside her, laying a hand on her shoulder). Maybe it isn't. Maybe it's not supposed to be.

They talk about his office, they talk about the weekend coming up. He doesn't ask if she went there today, and she understands. They need to be careful.

Finally their desserts arrive. They lean back to give the waiter room to lay the plates down, and new forks. Her espresso is thick as paint in its bone-white demitasse, a wedge of lemon and square of chocolate alongside. It seems simple to her, and complete, a pleasure separate from the rest of the world, as if she should be able to call time-out, stop what she's feeling to appre-

ciate it, yet even as she takes the first bitter sip, the taste mixes
with the day, the tree, the wreath, and she realizes things will
never change, that despite her best efforts she will always be this
way, this injured person she dislikes and pities.

"How is it?" he asks.

For a second, so caught up in thought, she doesn't understand, then smiles to make a joke of her ditziness, using the wine
as an excuse. She pushes the saucer toward him. "Try some."

There are moments we don't show you, things we leave out for
our own reasons. (Mercy, Spirit, show me no more!) Danielle's
sisters have called her all day, our parents and grandparents have
summoned us one by one. There's nothing we can do for them.
By now you've figured it out: We're visitors, our powers limited.
Like Tim, like the real Kyle—like Brooks, though he doesn't
know it—we're on a mission. We've chosen our heroes, hoping
they'll prevail (afraid they'll fail), and now we're stuck with them.

Toe's right, they're boring, some of them. Life is boring.
(Compared to what? Danielle says.) Right now Tim and Kyle are
stocking kleenex, building a wall of boxes. Brooks is driving to
his call, wondering if he left the dogs enough water. Kyle's dad is
figuring out the tip. The kitchen's closing, the dishwasher running its last load.

At the country club the costume party's in full swing, a
square band covering "Superfreak" for people who can't dance
while a pilgrim vomits on the golf course. Otherwise, Avon's
shutting down for the night, rolling up the non-existent sidewalks. The gas pumps at Mrs. M's are shadowed. A timer trips a
switch and the stoplight by the convenience store goes blinking
yellow. No one notices. In the hills, the streets are wet and empty,

the garage lights off, the pumpkins dark. The last trick-or-treaters have packed it in, their fingers numb from being outside all night.

Here, inside, under the bright light, is the best part of Halloween, the sugary heart of the season, tipping your bag and spreading your haul across the carpet, running a hand through it like treasure. This is never boring; even the adults are interested, sniffing around like hounds. Count how many pieces and compare that with last year—is it a record?—then sort it into piles, one for Reese's Cups, one for Kit Kats, Twizzlers, M&Ms, all the lollipops together. What did you get the most of? What happened to all those Mr. Goodbars from last year? Stop to marvel at the oddities and ridicule them. Who gave them out, the bagged popcorn ball and the full-sized Payday, the single white Crunch and the 100 Grand? The Mounds and Almond Joys are always a problem, immediately segregated from the rest. And then those in-between ones—Goobers and Jujubes and Black Jacks—that, weeks from now, will be the last ones left. Who likes Milk Duds? Does anyone like spanish peanuts? Trade or give away whatever you don't like, there's enough here so you won't miss it.

Besides, we've been scarfing constantly, starting with the party in homeroom. The chocolate gives everyone a buzz, a burst of energy that mixes with the exhaustion of too much fun and turns silly. Soon we're winging caramels at each other, roughhousing, wrestling on top of our loot like pirates. "You can have three things" becomes "That's it, last one."

And then, ridiculously, it's bedtime.

Pick up your candy, you can't leave it in the middle of the floor. Don't ask why, just pile it back in the bag in slippery handfuls. Come on, up you go. Don't forget your mask—and brush your teeth, please.

But you're not tired, and there's a cool movie on you've been half-watching all the time, a thriller that will give you nightmares, these kids in this small town being stalked by vampires— the kind of movie everyone's going to be talking about in school tomorrow. Beg to stay up and watch it, though you know it's useless.

Good night.

Please? Ten more minutes. It's almost over.

No. Don't argue. It's late, and tomorrow's a school day.

Their logic's impossible to refute. And then, when you surrender but don't go, they make a joke of it, chase you up the stairs so you can't see the good part, the music attacking and the screams.

What happened?

Nothing, they say.

I want to see.

Don't worry, they say. We'll tell you how it ends.

BROOKS CATCHES A BREAK. His suspicious activity's not far from his place, half a mile as the crow flies. He's sure it's kids, whatever it is. They can't stay away from the rails-to-trails, forget the weather. All fall he's been called to bust up keg parties and run down punks on minibikes. Brooks doesn't know what the parks department was thinking when they put the thing in. It's a perfect spot to case someone's house from, cutting through hundreds of backyards. There's no chance of being seen from the street. Hop a fence, pop a screen, and you're in.

He could take Old Farms but doesn't, choosing a shorter route, West Avon past the turkey farm, bearing left at the cemetery (it depresses Brooks and amazes us how many there are in town). Then left again, up Country Club, edging the 18th fairway. The clubhouse is ablaze, the bass of the P.A. thumping, carrying in the rain. People are already leaving the party, a steady stream of cars. A big Beamer pulls out, starts to take off and then

slows, realizing who's behind him. They float downhill in tan-
dem, turning through the curves, sticking to the limit. Brooks
feels like lighting him up just for being in front of him.

There's no hurry if he's right. Tim won't get off for another
hour or so. Brooks isn't sure what he's up to—a tribute to us, a
weird memorial—but he needs to be there. All of this may be for
him. (I told you, he's no fool.)

He lets the Beamer sweat, riding his bumper before veering
off, peeling a hard right into Winding Lane without signaling.
He follows the circle all the way around, gliding beneath the
streetlights, the rain falling in long needles. The houses back here
are like his, dumpy three-bedroom ranches from the fifties with
asbestos shingling and quarter-acre lots too small to build on. A
couple sport FOR SALE signs by their mailboxes—his competi-
tion. He wonders which ones Charity has shown the buyers. He
thinks, offhand—as if it doesn't matter—that he should accept
their offer and get out while he still can. (Too late, dude.)

He sighs, retracting the idea. It's not just Gram. This is his
town; he knows every dinky street. Stony Way to Stony Corners
Circle to Stony Corners Road. Most of the houses are asleep,
boxes in the darkness. He doublechecks the address and sees he's
right; it's going to be at the very end of the cul-de-sac, where
there's an opening for the rails-to-trails. He memorizes the name
of the complainant as he pulls in the driveway, an actor practicing his lines, squares himself before he reaches for the doorbell.
It's the Marine in him; if he keeps on top of his procedure maybe
the chief won't ask for his badge.

It's an older guy in a maroon jogging suit that has to be from
the seventies. The TV shouts through the house (a vision of his
future, the pooch gut, the lonely frozen dinners).

"Evening, sir," Brooks starts like a rookie—command posture, good eye contact, strictly by the book—then takes the guy's complaint as if he's fascinated.

About an hour ago the man saw a car go down the access road behind his yard. It hasn't come back yet, he'd've seen if it did. This isn't the first time he's called about this, he says, as if it's Brooks's fault. It's turned into a regular lover's lane back there. There's supposed to be a light but every time it's fixed the kids smash it again. He doesn't know what he has to do for someone to take care of this. He's called the town hall but they just give him the runaround.

Brooks nods along, his mind wandering to the Stop'n'Shop and Tim, then snapping back. That night, where was he, on some meaningless call like this? He probably wasn't even happy, just unaware. It seems years ago, another life.

Brooks lets the old guy finish, agreeing with him point by point, shaking his head at the unfairness of it, sharing his frustration, his taxpayer's outrage.

"I'll clear them out of there," Brooks promises, Officer Friendly. "And I'll put in a recommendation to the Parks people they cage the lights."

"There used to be a chain across the road, I don't know what happened to it."

"I'll have someone call them first thing tomorrow, that's the best I can do right now."

The nice guy routine doesn't quite satisfy the guy—not possible—but it's enough to get a half-hearted thanks out of him.

In the Vic, Brooks radios in, jots down the particulars on an incident report, tilting his clipboard under the fiber optic light-stem that grows from the console like a deep-sea fish's antenna. The car's probably long gone, slipped by the guy while he was watching TV, or maybe it's kids making out, steaming the windows, all notion of time forgotten. Brooks has no choice, he's going off-road.

He belts in before halving the cul-de-sac and easing the front wheels up over the low curb. The bumper mows down the high weeds like a scythe. He has to go a couple hundred feet—well out of the glow of the man's house—before the fence of the rails-to-trails looms in his lights like a prison movie, threaded with dead vines. He creeps toward it, at the last second bends right, rolling through two useless gateposts, letting the transmission pull the car along. The road is a pair of muddy ruts cut by power company four-by-fours and chewed even deeper by dirtbikes; the Vic dips and bucks in the chuckholes, jostling him against the armrest. The ground's sandy, and there's the real fear of getting stuck and having to call for a tow, another humiliation—and, worse, he realizes, possibly missing Tim.

He cranes over the wheel, picking his way between the puddles, sticking to the hump. The fence slides by on his side, a wall of pines pressing in on the other, boughs weighted by rain slithering across the top of the Vic like the brushes of a car wash. He passes the cut where the power lines swoop through, the sky open for a moment, then rocks down a gully, a stream running beneath him. By now he's pretty much convinced there's nothing back here. The road doesn't go much farther; it dead-ends at a turnaround and that's it. Ahead, Brooks can see the pile of leftover crossties that marks the spot, the bulldozed mounds of dirt. He reaches the clearing, trying to decide the easiest way to three-point it, when off to his right, at the edge of his headlights, tucked beneath the trees, a vague shape floats up out of the darkness like something underwater. A white car. A Volkswagen Cabriolet.

Brooks cuts the wheel and centers it so he can see, reverses and stops so he's blocking the road, levels the spot on it—a Golf, same difference. It's the same car as last night, the tag masked by a smoked plastic insert. No sign of its owner, just headrests, but they could be playing possum. He calls in a description and his twenty, taking no chances. He wants to do this right, especially if it's kids.

He throws on the takedown bar in case he hasn't gotten their attention yet, no siren. The blues and reds spin in the trees like a kaleidoscope. He opens his door and pokes his head out, uses his P.A. "Driver," he says, and his voice fills the clearing. "Put your hands where I can see them."

The only motion is the leaves tipping in the rain.

Brooks kills the overheads and takes his flashlight from its bracket, the machined steel cold on his palm. He gets it in his left hand, holding it up at eye level, his other hand cocked at his hip. Beyond the cover of the door he's a target. He keeps the beam steady on the driver's side as he crosses the clearing in long, purposeful strides (Semper fi!), then swings behind the car, using its own geometry as a screen. Even close up the license plate is hard to read. The rear window is translucent enough to see there's no one in the backseat. He ducks around the right side, cuts through the passenger's blindspot toward the front—peering in, reading the seats, ready to roll away from the muzzle flash (Yaaaah! Toe screams)—and sees at the door handle that it's empty.

And locked. In the backseat a baseball bat rests among a dozen crumpled beercans, and he wonders if these could be the punks that whacked his mailbox. (Jesus, Danielle says, wake up. No wonder you're going to die.)

He squats in the grass to read the tag and calls it in from his clip-on, asking them to run wants and warrants, registration,

everything. He could take care of things here himself—letting
the air out of the tires would do it—but he wants this car off the
road legally. He wants the owner to show up at the impound
yard tomorrow with a hefty check. He can't write him up for
last night, but he's already got him on trespassing, unlawful operation, disturbing the peace and a whole shitload of public nuisance charges.

It seems too easy. The longer he waits for dispatch to get
back, the surer he is the car's stolen, used and then dumped here,
the driver long gone. The plates are probably hot, another reason
to cover them.

Around him the wet woods smell of mulch, the liqueur of
pine needles, rotting logs and fermenting leaves, and standing in
the glare of his own headlights, in the chill night air, Brooks remembers jumping out of the Vic and running for the tree and
the Camry—unbelieving—and then stopping once he'd gotten
there, his training evaporating at the sight of us. (Because the car
was small and we weren't pretty.) His first instinct was to look
around for someone else who could help. In the backseat a boy's
voice was trying the same hurt vowel sound over and over, a cat
meowing. One door was torn off and lying in the weeds. Beyond
it, in the dark, he thought he saw a face flash, someone escaping
through the trees.

"232," his clip-on squawks. "No wants on that 10-44. Vehicle
is registered to a Travis Fowler, 383 Highgate Drive, no phone."

The name's unfamiliar, the address highpriced. "Copy,"
Brooks says, thinking. "Can I get a DOB on the registrant."

"Lemme check," then keyboard clicking, "6-22-86."

"86," he repeats, "copy," goes to the passenger side and peeks
in with the flashlight again. The CD player's there and the igni-

tion's not popped; it's not stolen, just kids out messing around. The bat and the beercans are almost enough for probable cause. He has a slim jim in the Vic but knows it's against procedure; the search wouldn't be admissible. He'd definitely get written up, then suspended. The best he can do is slap a sticker on the car and request a wrecker, let the guys down at the pound hold it overnight—a solution that has the added bonus of reeling in the parents.

Dispatch has to check with MacDonald's. They can't promise anything; it's been crazy with the rain, a lot of triple-A calls. They're looking at an hour minimum, is that all right?

"It'll have to be," Brooks says. "This car is not staying here."

He's wasted enough time. He pops his trunk and digs a blaze orange DO NOT REMOVE BY ORDER OF AVON P.D. sticker from the bin next to the first aid kit (that also made the trip to the tree with him, and was just as useless). In the front seat he magic-markers the Golf's tag in the blank, neatly adds the citation number. The finished product pleases him, a mini-revenge; the thing's a bitch to razor off.

If Brooks really was Officer Friendly, he'd put it on a side window in the rear, but no, he goes to the driver's side and leans across the hood, buffs a spot on the windshield with his sleeve. He bends the sticker in half, then has to fiddle with the backing a couple times before he slips his thumbnail between the layers and peels it away. It's a cheesy scene, the abandoned car in the dripping lover's lane, the unsuspecting cop taking too long. Here's where Jason or the Swamp Thing or some robot monster (or Kyle) should blitz from the shadows and attack him while his back is turned.

He rubs the spot again to get rid of a few stray raindrops,

then plasters the sticker right at eye level. One corner's wrinkled; when he tries to smooth it, it folds over, but so what. He knows it shouldn't feel good, but it does.

In the Vic, the paperwork takes longer than he wants. He hits the major points, tosses in a recommendation to cage the light and signs off on it as reporting officer, and that's it, mission accomplished. He calls it in and he's clear, 232 putting the roll in patrol.

"Tim."

"Tim," Kyle tries again, a little kid that needs attention.

"I hear you, and the answer is still no."

Now that he's had dinner, Kyle wants dessert. Tim puts him off with promises, saying it's too early. It is. They're breaking down the seasonal aisle in the middle of the store, gathering the plastic jack-o'-lanterns and the same old cardboard ghosts and black cats Mrs. McVeigh taped up in third grade, packing away Halloween for another year. It's that in-between time of night when Tim tries not to look at the clock, and he's glad to have something to do.

The flower shop's closed, and the salad bar, the pharmacy. The guy in seafood is dumping bloody ice into a trash can. Drunk people stumble in, bummed that the beer is covered up. Two guys play catch with a bag of chips, fake-tackle each other and laugh. (Idiots, Toe says.) A woman in a tuxedo and a white-painted face buys a gallon of milk. Otherwise it's quiet, the muzak constant—syrupy Beatles and U2 Kyle hums along with, out of tune. Darryl stops by and says he'll try to get them out a little early tonight; already he's letting the cashiers take off one by one, like hostages. Tim has to hide an inner flinch; he doesn't *want* to leave early.

"You don't have to get all the Thanksgiving stuff up," Darryl says. "Just the basics."

Meaning forget the brown and orange streamers around the poles for now. He wants them to hang the flat paper turkeys that accordion into full-breasted gobblers from the rails of the drop ceiling, and bring in any gourds or pumpkins from outside that haven't sold. The shedding corn shocks can stay, and the dusty Indian corn. Let Karen deal with the displays of boxed stuffing and canned cranberry sauce tomorrow; no one's going to buy that stuff for another week.

"But first I need you to get the bread done, so stop this and start that." (Oh crap, Danielle says. Bread. You know what that means.) Because it's the last of the month, the expiration date coming due. Before dawn a whole fleet of trucks will be backed up to the loading dock: Pepperidge Farm, Thomas's, Hostess, Nissen, Entenmann's. Tim doesn't want to know where the old bread goes, but he'll have it ready for them.

Having two things to do is even better. They grab a cart and start on the doughnuts, reading the dates off the boxes. Beneath the cellophane windows, the doughnuts sit in rows like tires, and like every month this year, Tim slows and contemplates them as if they're a great mystery—circles of fried dough. The shape seems so random; why not squares, since they'd fit better for shipping? They seem strange in themselves, odd, not just because they were the last thing we ate.

The combination stops Tim, unable to fit his thoughts together. He freezes with a box in his hands, as if he might have a seizure. He's in the car with us again. He can smell the dough-

nuts we've just eaten, taste the lard and sugar coating his own
tongue. Outside, the night flies by. She's on his lap, his arms
around her. And the road only goes one way. It's like his dreams;
nothing's different, he's belted in, helpless to change a single
thing. As he stands there, the rest of it moves through him like
blood.

(I hate this fucking place, Danielle says.)

They climb in single file, keeping the dogs behind them, off their
right shoulder. Travis leads. The flashlight's done, and he holds
both hands out in front of him like someone blinded, his feet
stirring the leaves. Branches graze his face, wet cobwebs. He trips
on a rock and almost falls, catches himself and laughs, and Greg
laughs with him.

"I thought they'd at least chase us."

"Nah," Greg says, "they're fucking chickens. All they do is
bark."

The hill's longer than Travis remembers, probably because
they're going up. He tries to walk in a straight line. He wishes
he'd brought a compass, though he's never used one in his whole
life. He lifts his knees, striding over invisible rocks. They've got to
be almost to the top, but the slope goes on and on, becomes even
steeper, clogged with pricker bushes that grab at his poncho.
More rocks, logs, it's an obstacle course. His breath burns in his
throat, and he can hear Greg huffing behind him. The dogs have
stopped—or not; he can't tell and doesn't care.

And then, in a dozen steps, the rise rounds off and they're on
level ground. Yes, the dogs have stopped, too far off to hear.

"Hold up," he says, and scouts around, hoping they might be
high enough to see a light from a nearby house.

Nothing but trees. (Sorry we can't help. Danielle wouldn't even if she could; she thinks they're being mean, but she's got a soft spot for Brooks.

I do not, she says. They're just being assholes.

Whatever, Toe says.)

In the dark, Greg unzips his backpack. "Here," he says, and presses a solid object into his hands—a beer. Travis takes it, shaking off the feeling that someone's following them. They're far enough away, and they need a break. He slips a fingernail under the tab and pulls.

"To Toe," Greg says, holding his up.

"To Toe," and they touch cans.

The beer tastes warm, but only because it's so cold out. Travis gulps his like a soda, a fizzy rush, and thinks they've earned this celebration. They did it, the two of them, everything they've planned so far, from the mailbox on. The toughest part of the job is finished, but instead of feeling relieved, he's even more nervous, as if they messed up and someone's coming for them. There's no one. What they did was right even if it did get out of control. He thinks it will take a while to really appreciate what they've done, that gradually his fear will fade and he'll be proud. For now he's dizzy with success, his mind in a flat spin, disconnected. This is what it must feel like to win something big. They should be drinking champagne.

Brooks is racing the radio, racing Avon. He thinks he's going to swing by his place, grab the report, water the dogs and get back on the road before the next call. All he needs is five minutes. He takes Scoville through the woods (not far from us), way over the limit, braced for the glow of oncoming lights as he cuts the curves. He drives like the professional he is, threading the narrow stone bridges, shouldering low into turns, concentrating, shaving seconds off his personal best; any private citizen watching him would think he's insane, but he knows what the Vic can do in this weather. It helps to know the roads.

That was our problem, he thinks—and his, for thinking we did. A smaller car is supposed to hold the road better. If he let up, he'd lose us. Already we were disappearing with every bend, every blind rise. Now he finds us too easily. He sees the Camry out in front of him, his lights bleaching our heads in the window (Tim's and Danielle's a double, Kyle's to the side), and slows, the vision confusing.

He used to tell Melissa that he dreamed of us, when it was just his memory, factual and undramatic, the normal torture. "You can't keep doing this," she begged him, catching him in the basement, going over the photos again. She said it as if he had a choice, as if a month of counseling would let him forget.

He's on autopilot, distracted by the past, and tries to catch up. It's not far. A right, a left, and he's on his street. He doesn't know his driveway anymore without the mailbox, and overshoots, standing on the brakes, cutting the wheel hard for the empty post. The tires grab for traction, slide as the nose dips, and he has to back up.

Behind the screen of pine trees the yard is lit, and the house, a white cake melting down the windshield. His mind's on the report—sitting on the desk next to his computer—and the section he needs: Tim's voluntary statement (we didn't give anything voluntarily, and Kyle was too far gone). It's only when he pulls in and the wiper clears the glass that he realizes something's wrong.

His heart tingles like a struck funny bone; goosepimples pop on his arms. Someone's been there. Graffiti mixes with the black shadows on the porch, huge floor-to-ceiling letters in thick spray paint, a single word interrupted by the front door. He can read it from across the yard, and accepts, with what feels like an admission, that it's for him: **LIAR**.

His first thought is that it can't be Tim—who'd be justified.

His second is for Ginger and Skip. The windows are broken. Whoever did this might have done something to them.

It's probably hit-and-run, a commando raid like Orchard View Estates. Kids who knew us. He pictures the Golf, maybe a half mile away through the woods.

"Motherfuckers," Brooks says. He rolls the Vic up to the garage and throws it in park, automatically reaches for his mike, then stops himself, deliberately withdraws his hand. He's not going to call this one in.

As he steps out, the dogs are barking. He's relieved but can't allow himself to relax. Our friends could be in the woods, waiting for him to make a mistake. He hustles across the walk and up the steps like a SWAT team leader, swiveling his head for any movement. Rocks and eggshells dot the floor of the porch, smears of yolk dripping down the siding. The door's locked. "It's okay," he calls to the dogs, "it's just me," but they don't believe him (and they're right; like always, we're right beside him). He has to dig for his keys, feeling watched, and then—like the guy trying to start his car as the monster reaches in the window—he fumbles them, drops them with a clank and has to pick them up again.

Nothing happens. No werewolf appears. No hand punches through the door and grabs him by the throat. He opens it and Ginger and Skip are there, standing back, wary.

"It's all right," Brooks says, and they pad over to welcome

him. Ginger bows her head and nudges his knee, her version of a hug. Brooks kneels and gathers them to him, their noses wet, their breath hot on his face. "I know," he says.

There's glass everywhere, rocks on the carpet. The TV's still there. He checks their paws, then lets them out the back. They scrabble down the steps of the deck, barking, reclaiming the yard, and then when they're done, walk around sniffing the perimeter. Skip's interested in the shed; Brooks goes out in the rain to investigate, but it's locked.

He gives them treats when they come back in, sweet talks them into the downstairs bath, the one room whose windows aren't broken. He's taken this call a hundred times; now he understands how it feels, the rage and helplessness after the fact. "Motherfuckers," he keeps saying, as if he's continually surprised at what they've done.

The cop in him says it's the Golf. He'll circle back and trash it, he doesn't care. Honestly, what's he got to lose?

He brings the dogs their water bowls. "You be good," he says, then shuts the door.

He's going down the basement stairs when his clip-on emits its two-tone chime like a cell phone. "232."

Brooks answers without stopping.

The report's where he left it, and his beer can, evidence from another crime. LIAR.

"232, 577 requests back-up on traffic stop, vicinity 1189 Country Club Road. Can you confirm?"

It's Saintangelo with drunks from the club. His luck—it's too close to blow off. "Confirm." He tucks the report under his arm and heads for the stairs, chopping the light switches.

"Can you give me an ETA?"

He commits to five minutes, then is pissed that he has to go at all.

The only reason he's here is Tim. Everything else is fucked.

And it's true, he is a liar. It's not a secret. The papers called it from the beginning but couldn't make the allegations stick. He has the proof in his hands, the truth, and the longer he carries it, the heavier it gets.

He doesn't bother to lock the front door. Why? The place is destroyed. That shit's not going to come off vinyl. He should call Charity right now and accept the buyers' offer, get the hell out of town, but there's nowhere to go, there never was. Brooks knows it's pointless to run. He's felt our claim on him all along, the weight of an unpaid debt that only grows with time. Like us, he's stuck here.

She wants him to undress her slowly in the dancing glow of a candle, to kiss her long and soulfully (I don't know, Toe says, this could get pretty gross), but when she comes out of the bathroom, he's already in bed with the lights off. So much for her sexy underwear. She has to find the hamper in the dark, lift its creaking wicker lid. Her dress needs to be drycleaned, and she lays it over a chair, strips off her pantyhose, crooking one foot, then the other. From habit she scratches the pinched skin at her waist as she makes her way to bed. (Like I said, Toe says.)

He holds the comforter open so she can slide in beside him, his legs cold against hers. She jumps at his touch. "Your hands are freezing."

"I know. Warm them up."

She does, rubbing them between hers like a child's—and remembers going sledding one Sunday afternoon at the hill by the middle school, Kyle wiping out and splitting his lip—then tenses as he lays them on her again. He rolls so he's half on top of her. His first kiss is tentative, as if she might turn him down, and she pulls him in, shows him the passion she needs. He tastes like Listerine.

(How much of this do we need to see? The worst thing about being a ghost is having no control. It's like Mr. Magoo— show me no more, o Spirit!—except it's backward. The dead are at the mercy of the living. Maybe that's why we're so pissed off. I mean, we like Kyle's mom, but come on. It's bad enough having to watch our own parents.

And of course the real Kyle's here, standing by the drapes beside the dresser like he's trying to hide, our own Michael Myers.)

Kyle's mom tries to lose herself in the dark, in his kisses, his fingertips. She wishes they'd ordered more wine. She does love him, but love isn't enough; she needs this togetherness to forget how alone she's been. His lips are on her neck, and her body responds, gives in, but in her head it's an effort. Even as she's rising inside, balanced on the hot, promising swell, she keeps slipping off into guilt, seeing the wreath on the tree, remembering. She strokes his head, directing him, and his thin hair and smooth scalp beneath her fingers trigger a vision of Kyle, the tube sticking out of his shaved skull, the faint remains of the purple marker the surgeon drew on for the craniotomy. He'd talked to them afterward in the closed waiting room, still in his scrubs, sitting on the table ranked with magazines so he'd be right at eye level. It had been an endless night, and he smelled ripe, as if he'd just come from a gym. "I'm not going to sugarcoat it," he said. "Your son has sustained a very serious injury." She wanted to laugh at him. Did she look stupid? Of course it was a serious injury; his face was smashed in. The doctor talked calmly, laying out the possible complications. The probability of permanent memory loss in a case like this was high. He didn't want to speculate about Kyle's motor skills until he regained consciousness. There was a slight chance he might not—slight, but a chance, he wanted to make that clear. Through it all, Mark held her hand, their four hands clutched between them, squeezing in response to each other, a kind of doubled prayer.

Beneath him, she returns, guilty and disappointed with herself. Stop, she wants to say, but doesn't. The darkness covers her, and from years of experience she knows she can please him without really being there. There's no reason they should both feel this way.

"I love you," he says after, and she repeats it with feeling. She means it, but it's beside the point. They lie there quietly, trying not to read each other's minds. A jet goes over, scouring the clouds, its engines whistling as it descends. He holds her a long time before she goes to wipe herself. As she navigates the room she can hear him ripping tissues from the box.

Alone on the pot, she listens to the rain tapping at the window and thinks Kyle's shift is almost over, that he'll be home soon. She'll make herself a cup of coffee and wait up for him, try to pretend tonight isn't special, their anniversary. Kyle won't know.

Kyle's dad lifts the comforter for her. She's not angry with him; he's just as helpless as she is, and yet she detects a resentment in herself, as if he's escaped, somehow gotten out of carrying his share of their marriage. He grieves; he's not heartless. She understands he's afraid, that the prospect of Kyle always being this way terrifies him, that he'd rather not deal with it. But someone has to.

He wants a goodnight kiss, a ritual older than Kyle or Kelly, and she gives him one. In the dark he can't tell that she's distracted, and it's too late to get into it, it's the wrong night. They used to talk in bed, argue and then reconcile. They made their big decisions here together while the children slept. Now they compare their schedules over breakfast and they're lucky to make love once a month.

She lies there, dead tired and trying to stay awake, a familiar exhaustion. It's been a long day. Her watch on the bureau mixes with the rain. Another plane scrapes the air—FedEx or UPS; it's too late for passengers to be coming in to Bradley. Beside her, he sleeps. She envies how easily he drops off, as unnatural—as unfeeling—as that talent seems. She doesn't have the luxury, but closes her eyes, just for a minute. The bed's warm around her, the covers snug as a cocoon. It's dangerous, lounging like this. She has to get up and let Kyle in. Tomorrow's the first of the month; she needs to write a check for his milk. She sees Peggy pulling up and the van filled with kids, a sunny day, the grass a summery green.

(And here Kyle walks out of the darkness and kneels by her side, raises a hand over her face as if he might smother her. He covers her forehead as if testing for fever, then lets it rest there, his own head bent knightlike, in devotion or apology. They stay like that until she's asleep, and we have to leave.)

The creek they finally come to is high and running backwards. It can't be right, Travis thinks. Everything drains into the river.

"Which way?" Greg asks.

The water's loud and too wide to jump. Against his instincts Travis goes left, following it downstream, figuring it has to connect with something. They can't get any more lost than they already are.

Walking's easier here, no tangle or prickers to pick through, hardly any rocks. The ground slopes down, grows softer as they trace the creek into an open flat carpeted with skunk cabbage. Their feet sink in the mud, deeper and deeper until they reach an arm of standing water. It's a swamp, that's why there aren't any bushes.

"This is fucked," Greg says.

"We're probably on the other side of the beaver pond," Travis says. "We've got to hit something soon. There's not that much woods out here."

They have to curl around the swamp and then find the outlet on the other side. It's not the beaver pond, it's smaller, at least from what he can see. He's tempted to squirt his lighter fluid on the water and set the slick on fire, just to see where they are. A plane flies right over them, invisible, no help. In its wake he can hear the slop and trickle of running water somewhere ahead of them. He stops and tilts his head to locate it, and does. He's afraid it might be a storm drain but doesn't tell Greg.

It's not—a victory. The new creek's bigger, which means they're headed in the right direction.

"This is like fucking *Survivor*," Greg says. "Except without the chicks."

"You don't want those chicks," Travis says, celebrating. "Those chicks'll fuck you and then eat you."

(Please, Danielle begs, somebody just kill me.

What? Toe protests.)

The creek twists through the brush, cuts through a small hollow, knolls rising on both sides. The footing's good, and as they round the base of a hill they see a light swooping behind the treetrunks to their right—a UFO that morphs into a car crossing a low stone bridge directly ahead of them. Its lights reach up into the trees as it passes. Travis recognizes the curve it takes, the old-fashioned guardrails and the rise it climbs and then disappears over. Scoville Road.

On Country Club, Saintangelo has a big Lincoln pulled off to the side, the driver performing in his headlights. It's someone's grandmother in a flapper outfit complete with a tiara, and Brooks thinks he doesn't need back-up, but calls it in, leaves the Vic sticking out a foot to screen them from traffic. Before getting out, he slides the report under his seat.

The woman's trying to walk an invisible tightrope and not having much luck. She gets three steps and staggers backwards. Sandy has to catch her wrists and haul her upright.

"Can I just try one more time?" she asks.

"What's up?" Brooks interrupts.

"I got three others in the car, all worse than her." He tips his head at the back window (and for a second it looks like us). "I'm going to need you to transport them. Either that or book her, your choice."

It's no choice. He hopes they're local.

They are, but from the far corner of town, retirees from Farmington Woods.

First he has to get them out of the car. They're confused. Why can't Ellie drive them? She's not drunk. Why's she being arrested? Are they being arrested? Then why can't one of them drive? They can't leave the car here.

Helping a man in a tux out of the passenger seat, Brooks flashes on Tim—ducking in the hole left by the missing door, unbuckling his belt and pulling him free. He didn't save his life, as the papers claimed; the car wasn't going to explode. He never felt like a hero, never tricked himself into believing it. Brooks thinks that's worse, his sin one of omission, his silence the real lie.

"Watch your head," he tells the old guy, and sits him in the Vic.

Saintangelo helps him with the other two. A line of cars from the party creeps by, staring at their bad luck. The driver has refused to take a breathalyzer, an automatic suspension. The instant punishment's strangely satisfying to Brooks. His mind is still on the Golf, on Ginger and Skip cowering while the windows exploded all around the house. It's been less than an hour, he thinks. No way the wrecker's there yet.

They tuck the Lincoln up onto the grass and flag it with a sticker, more work for MacDonald's.

"Can you handle her by yourself?" Brooks asks.

"Yeah," Sandy says. "Thanks." He acts like he has more to say. Brooks should tell him he doesn't completely blame him for the review board, but in truth he does. One day he'll need a break, then he'll see how it feels.

"Just doing my job," Brooks says.

"Attention shoppers," Darryl announces from the ceiling. "The store will be closing in ten minutes. At this time, please bring any items you wish to purchase to the front registers."

Tim and Kyle stop building Thanksgiving. He wants them to do the carts, so they throw on their vinyl ponchos that smell like model airplane glue and their reflective vests and go out into the cold. It's not that early, but after waiting all night—all summer, his entire life—Tim feels rushed. Any minute he expects Brooks to come splashing across the lot. At the far edge, the jeep waits, his pictures of Danielle in the glove compartment. His mind is like the store, packed and vacant at the same time. He wonders if he's crazy. People will think it anyway.

Kyle wanders toward a stray cart (the real Kyle right behind him, sticking close), gazing up at the rain falling through the high lights, and Tim thinks people won't understand.

It's too late to explain, even to himself. If he's unsure it's be-cause he's afraid, and there's no reason to be. He won't have to wake up and pretend anymore. He won't have to smile and make up things to say.

Behind him, Darryl lets a customer out—the last one, from looking at the cars. Someone's father in a wood-paneled mini-van. The man blows through the stop sign next to the green-house, brakes at the blinking red a second before heading for 44, and like a channel being switched, the lights go out, a purple after-image fading on top of the night.

Kyle comes walking back as fast as he can, leaving the cart in the darkness beyond the glow of the windows.

"Someone turned off the light," he explains, agitated, and Tim has to talk him down. Together they retrieve the stragglers and bull the train toward the door—not many; it's been a quiet night.

The cashiers are punching out, but they still have to do the floors. Darryl tells them to mop just the front. "I should really make you do the aisles," he says, as if they should be grateful. Tim almost is. They're going to end up getting out right on time.

What else is open this time of night?

Not much. The Mobil and its minimart, but not the Shell

across from it. The McDonald's is closing, the Staples is long gone. Dunkin' Donuts, and then a half mile down the strip, the Friendly's and the Blockbuster right beside it, both of those go till midnight. In town center there's the Double Down Grill, that's it, the rest of the olde shopping village is sleeping. Traffic passing through sees the floodlit steeple with its stopped clock and the shiny rows of O'Neill Chevrolet, but no motion. The dry cleaning carousel in Battiston's window is frozen, the mannequins in Victoria's Secret unloved.

Back in the hills Halloween's over except on TV, the blue glow leaking into the yards like something toxic. Most of the homes are dark. People who have to work tomorrow are already in bed, their alarms set. Streetlights cast shadows of branches on empty intersections; mailboxes and stone walls guard miles of silent roads.

The rain has taken care of those in-between places where we used to hang out—the railroad trestle behind the car wash, the farthest set of bleachers at Sperry Park. Even the picnic pavilion at Fisher Meadows is deserted, and the little shelter on the golf course. No one's doing anything except Travis and Greg. It's what we always hated about Avon. The place is a fucking ghost town.

She can't be sleeping is her first thought, struggling to wake up. The comforter lies on her like a weight. She snakes an arm free and twists to read the clock. Thank God—it's only a little past eleven. She can see him standing on the stoop indefinitely, waiting for her to open the door.

She slips out of bed and fits her arms into her robe, quiet as a spy. The outside light is enough to guide her, a pale square on the ceiling. Carefully she palms the doorknob, pulls it closed behind her so the hall is in total darkness, then blindly swipes at the switch at the top of the stairs.

She only puts on what she needs, the hallway and a table lamp in the TV room. (And there's the real Kyle right beside her, faithful as a shadow.) The news is on, today's disasters waiting to be forgotten. Three killed, two critically injured in Meriden, an SUV that rolled over, tying up traffic. Sometimes she thinks it's more than a coincidence, that the world is designed to remind her of her life. She's used to the one minute coverage, the cars broken in the middle of the road and the state trooper being interviewed. The way they gloss over the hard parts shouldn't bother her, knowing how intimate the rest of the story is, the creeping weeks and months by his side, reading aloud, leaning across the bedrail and whispering in his ear, hoping her voice might break the spell. She can't imagine having the cameras on her like in those TV shows, their suffering turned into entertainment.

The audience would have loved Kyle, the drama of his comeback. When he finally resurfaced he didn't recognize her. The doctor said it was common. They'd have to begin from scratch. The teacher in her immediately thought of flashcards, names and labels for everything, Richard Scarry picture books, the two of them reclaiming the world word by word, except he couldn't read. He'd never have that kind of language acquisition. The key was repetition, the therapist said, and gave her a list of phrases to work on between visits. "My name is Kyle Sorenson," he recited like a child. "I live at 53 Indian Pipe Drive." Day after day until he could repeat their phone number, and then her name.

She called him Kyle—his name, yet it felt strange. She'd

taken for granted that he would be the same person once he recovered. He wasn't. His new face was a mask of scars, his body hollowed out; even his voice had changed, his tastes, the way he walked and held himself. She didn't know him either.

A year later, she thinks she's come to love him, if she ever stopped. She's his mother, that's how people know her now; they're a pair. But she misses the other Kyle, the sullen kid who listened to death metal and hid drugs in his room. Her Kyle. She's quit looking for signs of him in his eyes, and she can admit the possibility—here, the merciless TV her only witness—that he's gone.

She changes the channel to escape, a mindless reflex, her finger on the clicker. (The real Kyle takes his hand away and stands. He curls around the coffee table, already fading, turns at the door for a last look.) She hears the creak of a step in the hall and mutes the TV, waits for it again. Nothing. Her imagination. It's late and she's jumpy, itchy in her skin. Her eyes catch a flash of motion, but it's just her reflection in the window, a woman in a robe on a couch. Kyle's mom.

The last passenger gives him the wrong address, and Brooks has to call the guard booth to find the right one. The old guy's looped and can't see well, and all the streets in here sound the same—Millwood, Millbrook, Woodbridge. The place is make-believe, row on row of identical townhouses stepping down gentle curves. He lives by himself, so Brooks waits to make sure he gets inside safely. He flicks on his console light and fishes the report from under the seat, flips to the section in question, passing highlights on the way.

Sgt. Sylvester was the third officer to arrive at the scene and stated he assisted officers already at the scene and later assisted in the identification of the deceased.

Neg 01 Westerly view of collision scene illustrating right wheel tire tracks off north shoulder.

Neg 02 Westerly view of collision scene illustrating vehicle at rest and contact marks on tree.

Neg 03 Northwesterly view of vehicle at rest. Chalk marks indicate ejected passenger's position at rest. (That would be you, Toe tells Danielle.)

All he wants is the timeline, and when he finds it, he studies it like the combination to a safe. There's the McDonald's and the lot of the Dunkin' Donuts, just as he remembered them. The numbers from last year match exactly, the movements. It could be innocent, a tribute, but the precision of it worries him. He wonders, if he's late, will Tim wait for him? And what if he doesn't show up?

The walkway lights of the condo flicker, and Brooks drops the report on the empty seat. He takes the back way out, but doesn't call in, maintains radio silence as he rolls through a whole development he'll never afford, slowing only for the gatehouse, tossing the rent-a-cop a wave.

There's time, he knows, but finds himself rushing. His destination is a mile away, five minutes at most, yet he's pushing the Vic, taking a chance at the blinking yellow by the fire station (a light on inside, as if the trucks are for sale). He has gas—that's good; he doesn't want to stop—and then he worries that he'll get stuck back there in the sand.

"359," the radio calls for Eisenmann. An alarm at the high

school, probably false. They've been having problems with their new system. Brooks is almost to Stony Corners Road when he hears the kid verify it, a whiff.

Back in the cul-de-sac, the guy who complained is still awake, the only sign of life. Brooks noses the Vic over the curb and follows his own path, a swath of bent vegetation. He gives it a touch too much gas and gets a little sideways, the tires spinning in the wet grass. The fence rises in his lights, and the bend, the posts with nothing between them. He rocks over the road, too fast, smashing puddles, the front end shuddering, and unconsciously apologizes to the Vic. The truck would be better for this—wrong tool for the job.

Pine branches scratch at the roof. He keeps on, reining himself in, by the clearcut and down the gully. The radio's quiet, only the slapping of the wipers. He replays the time he wasted at the house and backing up Sandy, taking the old guy home. He won't be surprised if the Golf isn't there, then crushes the thought. It can't be more than forty minutes; McDonald's is never that fast, even on their best night.

Ahead, the trees give way to open space paved with dead leaves. As he nears, the dirt mounds and the pile of crossties take shape, then loom out of the darkness, sharply defined. If his kids are there, Brooks thinks, he's given them fair warning, so no finesse is necessary. He swings the Vic into the clearing and throws on his highbeams—and instantly finds the car under the trees at the far edge, right where he left it.

From habit, he has the urge to call it in—a kind of phantom pain—but parks the Vic instead, goes around to the trunk and gets his slim jim.

It would be easier to just cut through the cloth top, he realizes as he digs in the window well (we watch him from inside, a silent movie, his face pinched with concentration). And then a quick fisherman's tease of the wrist and he's in.

He's not interested in their beer cans or the contents of the ashtray. This isn't a probable cause hearing. He reaches between the seats and grabs the bat.

(Don't, Danielle says.)

He doesn't kid himself that he's acting as a private citizen, that tonight of all nights there are mitigating circumstances, his loved ones in peril. He doesn't hesitate, knowing that this will end his career, forget the chief's review board. He closes the door, takes his stance by the right headlight and swings, then turns around for the left one, switchhitting. The bat makes an unsatisfying clonk in the socket; the glass breaks but doesn't shatter, not like the old sealed beams with their thin, silvered shells. He walks around to the rear and smashes the taillights, one measured stroke for each set. And it's not like Brooks is going Mad Max on it; he's more like the guy at the fire department carnival paying a dollar a pop for a good cause, taking his time, making each swing count. Even bashing the windshield in, he's calm, bringing the bat down like an axe in the middle of the sticker until the glass sags. He leaves the windows alone, and the body, puts the bat back where he found it and locks the door again, then kneels by the front tire, unscrews the valve cap and lets the musty-smelling air out with a thumbnail. That's enough, it's disabled (as if that's all he wanted). Walking away, he discovers the valve cap in his hand—a sleepwalker snapping awake—looks at it a second, then pitches it in the weeds.

Two minutes and they'll be perfect. He stalls, helping Kyle take off his apron. The aisles are dark, just the red of the exit signs caught in the dull floor. Darryl's upstairs, locking the offices and switching on the surveillance video. Tim has seen the checker-board of screens and pictures himself and Kyle moving from one to the other like rats in a maze all the way to the lot. The tape will be evidence, like their timecards, a useless history.

There's something solid in the pocket of Kyle's apron—a Snickers bar.

"What's this?" Tim asks.

Kyle looks away, and Tim realizes he's being too hard on him.

"It's okay," he says. "It's Halloween." He stashes it in his jacket, thinking he'll have to remember to give it to him later, then worries again that he's wrong to include him. It was always the five of us, but helping Kyle's the one thing he's done right since the accident. He could ask Darryl to drive him home, though he's never offered before, probably doesn't even know where Kyle lives.

The timeclock clunks, the numbers turning, perfect, and Tim fits his card in the slot, the punch banging it like a stapler. He does Kyle's and sets it in the rack next to his. They're a team. How could Kyle get to work without him? What would he do? (Don't be selfish, Danielle says, giving him the Vulcan neck pinch. It does nothing. You'd think we'd be getting stronger as midnight closes in, but no.)

They make their way to the front under the infrared eye of the camera, Kyle sticking close to him.

"Gentlemen," Darryl says like every night, and releases them. Tim's played by the rules for so long he wants to tell him they won't be in tomorrow, make up some lame excuse.

"Goodnight, Darryl," Kyle says—the right answer—and they split, walk away to their cars. Tim looks around for Brooks but there's no one, just the floodlight guarding the greenhouse.

It's cold in the jeep, and he gets the heater going first thing. As they start across the lot, he cues up the mix CD, starting with Toe's Black Crowes and Jimmy Page, "Since I've Been Loving You," a lowdown, end-of-the-night blues Toe used to sing along with. Kyle has no reaction, as if he's never heard it before. (Kyle hated any kind of dinosaur rock, and especially Zeppelin.) Tim ignores him, falls to the murky bottom of the song, a place he's traveled in his room too many nights, stoned and dreaming of this moment, the headphones connecting him to another world. *Working seven seven seven . . . to eleven leven leven, makes . . . life-a-drag . . . drag, drag, DRAAAAG.* Brump, brump TSSHHH!—dead John Bonham blasts a cymbal in the original—and the road and the streetlights seem to belong to the music, the bright drive-thru of the Walgreen's, the toxic bronze haze above the Staples. *But si-ince I been loving you . . .* dunt dunt dah . . . *I'm about to lose, whymaboutalose, WHYMABOUTALOO-WHOSE, my worried mind.* Tim nods along to the plodding bassline as it descends, in deep agreement, the connection physical and religious (because it's true, this feeling; it amazes him that someone *does* understand), and then (it figures, this town), they have to stop and wait for the one red light left in Avon to change.

The whole time they were going the wrong way. They must have cut behind Old Farms because they're on the far side of the tree, the curvy part above the soccer fields where people fish in the stream. Driving, it's like nothing, but it's a hella long way to walk.

"You got another beer in there?" he asks Greg.

"What do you think?"

"Then bust it loose, Bruce."

"I'm saving them." He's serious, and Travis respects that. This part of the mission is just as important.

"Hey," Greg says, "you believe in any of that stuff—weegee boards and shit?"

"No, once you're gone you're gone."

"I guess." But he says it like he doesn't know. "I wonder where Toe is right now."

(Still in fucking Avon, Toe says. And we're all gonna be if you guys don't hurry up.)

"Didn't we just visit him this morning?"

"That's not him," Greg says. "There's got to be a part of you that goes somewhere, like a spirit or a soul or something."

"You show me one and I'll believe it."

(And we'd love to materialize right in front of them like an-gels, backlit and hovering, bearing glad tidings. The best we can do is spook a raccoon in their general direction, a thrashing of leaves and then a dark shot across the road.)

"What the fuck was that?" Greg asks.

"Maybe it was your spirit."

"Don't joke, man."

"Okay," Travis says, because tonight's about Toe. He wishes they could cut the fucking thing down, chop it into kindling and burn it all winter—or chip the bitch, turn it into sawdust and piss on it.

Around them a faint glow floats through the trees like the moon rising. Travis looks behind them to find the source and sees light gathering behind a far-off rise.

"Car," he calls, and they ditch it into the woods, charging up the bank and across the mushy leaves, his backpack rattling. He dives for the nearest tree and catches the rough bark, presses himself against it. Greg hugs the one next to him. They're both soaked and shivering. They look at each other like this is fun.

One headlight breaks the plane before the other, as if the car's lopsided. It dips and slides down the rise, and between the trunks he can see the spread of light in front and behind—from all four corners. The swish of tires grows, and then the engine. They've just slogged that same set of curves down the hill to the bridge and up again, busting their humps; the car gobbles the distance in a minute. Shadows shift and double, chase each other past them through the trees, making them pivot to stay hidden. As it passes below, loud as a jet, Travis can see from the darkened light bar and the stripe of reflective decal on the door that it's a cop car. He can't read the license plate (AV 36, our lucky number), but he knows who it is.

"Dude," he says when they're alone again, "we are so fucking lucky."

The Dunkin' Donuts is closed. No reason, it just is. (Mr. Arnold's not there, Danielle says, that's why. Those bozos took off early.) Inside, in the dimness, a see-through machine pours an eternal waterfall of orange drink. Tim checks the clock on the dash as if he might have lost fifteen minutes sitting at the light. It's the right time, it's not supposed to close for another ten. The plan rushes through his head, unintelligible, no help. He's come so far. Is this it? It feels like someone's playing a trick on him. He's got Kyle beside him and doesn't know what to do. (By now he's got all of us in the car, Danielle behind him, the real Kyle inside Kyle, making us nervous.)

He feels exposed, the only car in the lot, but thinks he'd draw even more attention if he tried to hide in the back of the drive-thru. All Brooks would have to do is block him in and it would be over. He worries that part of him wants this, to be rescued again, saved from the way he feels. They'd try to fix him with drugs like Kyle's mom, turn him into a zombie.

As always when he's in doubt, he turns to us. He undoes his seatbelt and leans across both Kyles, opens the glove compartment and pulls out his stack of pictures, Danielle right on top. He leaves the door open for the light, tips the pictures to kill the glare. Kyle watches him, empty-handed, and Tim remembers the Snickers.

"Thank you, Tim," Kyle says.

There she is in the bus in her red sweater.

There they are on the chairlift, giving a thumbs-up with their gloves. (Mr. Kulwicki took that one.)

Here's a shot of all of us at Six Flags for Rocktoberfest, stoned, arms over each other's shoulders, the real Kyle in the middle. Danielle has a pink ball of cotton candy and he remembers kissing her on the Skyride, making fun of the people walking beneath them.

Beside him, the live Kyle breathes chocolate, looking straight ahead as if they're driving. Tim shows him the picture—no sign of recognition.

"Do you know who this is?"

Kyle chews, ruminating, then places a finger on it. "Tim."

"Right. Who else do you see?"

He pops the last bite in his mouth. My song's on now, Everclear: *I don't believe you when you say, everything will be wonderful someday.* Tim isn't listening—he's heard it a million times. He's waiting for Kyle to name just one of us, as if that might save them.

"Who's this?" Tim asks, pointing to Kyle with his half-assed goatee and his big silver chain. "Look." He holds the picture closer and Kyle shies back, frightened.

"I don't know."

Tim flips to one of me and Toe at the shooting gallery. "This is Marco," he says. "This is Toe." Flip. "This is Danielle."

Kyle sits there with the Snickers wrapper in his hand, staring at them like this is too hard. (And what's the real Kyle's deal, not helping him? Is this supposed to make it easier for Tim?)

Here's one of Kyle in line at the Demon Drop giving him crossed fingers, a corndog stuck in his mouth like a cigar. Later he tossed the stick from the top just as we went weightless to see if it would beat us down. It floated even with us a second, and then we were plummeting. We never saw it hit.

"Who's this?"

Kyle doesn't know.

"It's Kyle," Tim says, then thinks he's gone too far. "It's another friend of mine named Kyle. You two have the same name."

Why should Kyle know what to say to this? He licks his fingers. Tim fits the picture of Danielle in the bus into the pocket over his heart, rewraps the stack and puts it back in the glove compartment. He takes the wrapper from Kyle and shoves it in the ashtray on top of the burnt butts.

Please don't tell me everything is wonderful now. Please don't tell me everything is wonderful now.

He still can't believe the Dunkin' Donuts is closed. He remembers when we picked up Danielle he gave up shotgun so she could sit on his lap in back—meaning he would have been sitting where I was, and I would have lived. If.

He wishes they were open so he could get a doughnut; that's all he wanted. It doesn't seem like much.

They joked with Mr. Arnold, busted on Danielle for her uniform—"nice costume." Then they got in the car.

The CD is like a countdown, Zero Tolerance's "Negative Influence" for Kyle, who doesn't notice. He doesn't know why they're here. Tim looks around for Brooks again and thinks he's given him too many chances already. He can't wait any longer. It's time to go. If Kyle's getting out, it has to be now.

(This is where the real Kyle finally makes his move. He turns and reaches over and plants his hand in the middle of Tim's chest and closes his eyes, concentrating, as if he's draining the life out of him.

Stop it, Danielle says, grabbing at his wrist, but her hand passes through him.

We all try together—1, 2, 3—but he's just too strong. For a minute he's all Tim can think about, and we're nowhere.)

Brooks doesn't have to check the report again. He positions the Vic in the far exit of Battiston's lot, angled toward 44 with his parking lights on, but doesn't let himself settle in. He leaves the Stalker off, watches a silver Eclipse whip by doing around sixty, too fast for conditions. It's a car he'd usually stop. He's officially derelict in his duties, but what can they do to him? He's decided this is his last shift.

A year ago he was here, parked over the same oil spots. He can't recall what he thought when he saw us—kids speeding, a possible seatbelt violation. It was the end of the month, the beginning of the month, it didn't matter, his numbers were good. That time of night, he could have popped every driver that went by, but for some unknown reason he chose us. The car was non-

descript, inoffensive, not a low-slung roadster or gold-chromed
sedan. Maybe it was the way it accelerated, an invitation to the
chase. There was no hesitation, just a simple split-second decision
he'd made a million times. He marked the car and he rolled. A
minute later he was riding in our blind spot, close enough to call
the tags in. He thought it would be an easy stop—local kids—
but when he hit the lights the little idiot took off on him. (Fuck
you, Toe says.)

It's too late to go back and correct his mistake, change history. Maybe he's here to apologize or pay tribute like Tim. If he's
responsible—Melissa would say he isn't, but she's gone—then he
needs to make amends. (He's crazy.)

"232," dispatch summons him—Ravitch, working graveyard.
A Buick wagon passes with that fake wood paneling.

"232, please copy," Ravitch requests, the letters automatically
marching across his screen.

Brooks slowly folds his computer closed, the glow trapped
inside its plastic shell.

"232, do you copy please?"

In the dark, the instruments give his skin a greenish tinge.
Brooks looks to the road, but the radio wants his attention again,
calling his name like an SOS. He reaches a green hand to the
knob and clicks it off.

She tells herself to wait another five minutes before calling, but
isn't convinced. It's too easy; the number's on the list right by the
phone. They know her there, Kyle's overprotective mother, but
he should be home by now. Tim wouldn't take him anywhere,
not tonight.

The news has her spooked, the usual trick-or-treat horror

stories from around the country, urban legends come true: razor blades in apples, pins in candy bars, children in black cat suits hit crossing the street. They showed video of an x-ray tech scanning someone's haul, the parents standing by. How careful do you have to be? From experience she knows you can't control everything. Right now her imagination wants to take off, like every night, and show her the worst that could happen, the trees and telephone poles lining the slippery roads, his stitched skin pulled apart again, the policeman already on his way to notify her.

She throws the afghan aside and stands. (Kyle's gone, she's all by herself.) It's cold in the house, and she uses this as an excuse to go to the living room and turn up the thermostat. She moves to the front door and peers through the window at the stepping stones and the driveway and the darkness beyond and thinks it must be five minutes by now.

Maybe they're working late, maybe it's that simple. They could be unloading a shipment of something in back.

She doesn't need the list; she knows the number by heart. The kitchen floor is chilly, and she stands on the rag rug at the sink, listening to the ring on the other end (all of us except Kyle gathered around the phone in the dark office). Two, three. Sometimes they don't pick up right away.

A new ring suddenly interrupts, meaning she's been switched over to a machine. It clicks in, telling her that she's reached the Super Stop'n'Shop, reciting the store's hours and asking her to please leave a message at the tone. If she would like to hear more options—but she knows those are dead ends.

The beep beeps. She isn't sure if she should leave a message, worried that she could lose whatever credibility she has there. She doesn't want to come off as hysterical—her great fear. She fixes on the clock above the fridge and thinks she's justified.

"Hi," she says, hurrying, trying not to sound desperate, "this is Mrs. Sorenson. I know you guys are closed, but if Kyle's still there, I'd appreciate it if someone could give me a call. Thanks."

Oh, and then wishes she'd said Happy Halloween.

(Looking out over the aisles from behind the one-way glass, we hear her hang up. The tape stops and resets with a click. The red number on top of the machine blinks. Back by the pet food, one screen shows a bright blip zip across the floor like a missile: a mouse.

Run, dude, Toe says, and we both laugh.

This isn't right, Danielle says; I should be with Tim. And disappears.

Toe looks at me and I look at him, half impressed and half like: we're all we've got. It's nothing new. That's just what happens to guys like us.)

They come up on the tree from behind. They're so tired they almost walk by it in the dark. Travis is looking down and happens to catch a white bow out of the side of his eye, and then the bouquet of roses it holds together—yellow, to remember us (from Mr. Stone, for Danielle). The base of the tree is heaped like a shrine, just the side we hit; everyone knows which way we were going. Travis flicks his lighter to see what new offerings people have left, the mylar heart balloons and scented candles and laminated sheet music. The trunk is shingled with soggy cards, Kyle's mom's wreath prominent above them, a permanent fixture, our shellacked faces smiling into eternity. They lean in and read it like something in a museum.

"Jesus," Greg says, "that is creepy."

"No shit."

"What time is it?"

Travis peers up doubtfully into the rain. "I don't know. It's close enough."

He sheds his backpack and kneels to unzip it, reaches in and finds the solid bulk of the charcoal starter, the metal of the can flexing as he grips it.

Greg kicks the nasty, waterlogged teddy bears and shit into a pile Travis squirts with fluid. He lets Greg douse the trunk, then drenches the pile again. It smells like a cookout.

They think they hear a car coming and freeze, but it's just the wind.

"Okay," Travis says, "stand back," and touches his lighter to a soaked troll doll.

The fire spreads in lapping blue waves, unspectacular. Only the surface burns, the stuffed animals' fur crisping. Travis squeezes the can and with a whoosh a satisfying ball of flame boils up, warming his cheeks.

"*Nice,*" Greg says.

The trunk catches, and the wreath; the pictures blister and curl. The fire flares bright for a second, lighting up the crooked branches overhead, then dies in wavering lines. Travis applies the starter again but only manages to drown the last flickering remnants.

"It's too wet," Greg says.

"We just need to put enough on," Travis insists, and shakes the can to show they've got a lot. "Hey," he says, "no one's leaving till I have my other beer."

There he is, there he is. Brooks can barely believe it, the red jeep, the one he's been tailing all year in his dreams, but there it is, splashing past not a dozen feet from where he's sitting, the tan hardtop, the Wrangler tire cover, the memorized license plate. It's him. He feels delivered—not forgiven but reprieved for now, in this case (not us, we're fucked). To have his mission set in front of him after a year of wrestling phantoms is a relief. He wrenches the Vic into drive, makes sure the lane's clear and takes off, flicking on his headlights as he powers out.

Ahead, the jeep accelerates away as he tries to reach speed. It's wet, he reminds himself, his foot gently riding the pedal as he angles for the left lane. They're the only cars on the road. Brooks steers straight and the transmission kicks through the gears, the big V-8 presses him back in his seat. The Friendly's and the Blockbuster whip past, shades of human figures frozen in their windows. He's got the car; if it were just a race it would be no contest.

They fly down the hill by the Wal-Mart, past the Fleet Bank and onto the flat with the D'Angelo and the Boston Chicken. He's gaining—maybe too fast. Tim is only doing around seventy. Brooks can't make the same mistakes as last time, and eases off. And then when he does, the jeep pulls away again.

That night, he ran right up behind us and chopped on his takedown lights. Procedure, but the kid freaked. (Right, Toe says. Who had to go to driving school?) Now he leaves them off and shadows him at a safe distance, measuring his reaction time in seconds from a phone pole, keeping a cushion. Tim speeds down the straightaway by Stub Pond and Brooks sticks with him. The night's black around them, and he feels the tunnel vision of pursuit kicking in, his focus narrowing to the two points in front of him, locked on like a fighter pilot. He realizes he's holding his breath, his lips clenched, and consciously opens his mouth and sucks in a gulp.

He's going to stop the boy and talk to him, apologize, admit everything the department lawyers said they couldn't make public—as if that matters to him. Brooks could tell him anything and it wouldn't make a difference. His friends are dead, his girlfriend. He's what, seventeen?

Brake lights fire ahead, swerving into the ess. The jeep's top heavy and poor in corners. It's all Brooks can do not to shoulder low into the chute and push his advantage. He thinks of cutting him off, pulling even on his right and blocking him so he can't make the turn onto Old Farms, but he might try to stop short and roll over. Brooks wonders if he's frightened or, like him, ready to fulfill their shared destiny. (I told you, the guy's cooked. He fried a chip that night; everyone says.)

They survive the curves and rip past the station, where Ravitch is probably still calling his name. They flash by the office park and the bandstand on the town green, racing for the orange glow of Avon center, the white steeple and the gleaming rows of O'Neill's. Brooks could have him here but backs off, brakes as he brakes to let him set up for the turn. He's going too fast to take it that tight, and the rear of the jeep swings wide, threatening to send it into a spin. Brooks grips his wheel in sympathy. The kid brakes—"No," Brooks says—and the jeep skids sideways, tips up on two wheels and veers wildly across the oncoming lane before slamming down on all four and correcting and jetting off again.

"Jesus Christ," Brooks says, shaking his head, and slides smoothly through the turn after him. He guns the Vic, trying to catch up, then has to yank it hard left to avoid someone lunging out of the back of O'Neill's.

He slips—by inches—around the hood of the other car, leaning away from the collision, and sees, behind him now, turning to pursue, an Avon Police Tahoe. It throws on its lights, and like a teenager Brooks flattens the gas.

Tim's so close and still rushing from almost rolling it, his head throbbing. He doesn't understand what Brooks is doing laying back, and no longer wants him there. He's the only one following the plan, but it's like something happening to him, someone else's bad dream he's just a part of. He wants it to stop, to make himself wake up and find us alive.

Arch Road goes by, the railroad overpass. He's trying not to look back, but can't miss the red and blue lights, the strobing glow like a fire, the siren coming for him. He's got the jeep redlined and it feels like he's going nowhere. Rotondo Concrete stretches on forever beside him, precast septic tanks and sewer pipes for all of Avon to shit in stacked under silver floods. He'll be fine once he passes the last streetlight, he thinks, and then when he does, the night doesn't seem dark enough. He wants to ditch it, slip into the woods and down the rails-to-trails to the hiding places only we know. He wants to go home.

He can feel Brooks closing on him and straightens out the blind curve by the Towpath condos, slicing all the way across the oncoming lane.

He's on Danielle's song, Natalie Merchant: *I may know the word, but not say it. I may know the truth, but not fay-hayce it.* (Danielle's right beside him in the empty passenger seat, telling him not to be stupid. We were worried about the real Kyle but he's vanished, gone like the live Kyle, his mission accomplished.)

Tim burns through his options, when it's too late anyway. The forces around him are greater than he can understand. He can't think of any reasons not to. If they catch him, they'll send him away; his parents will visit and sit with him. They'll have to talk with the doctors. He's answered enough questions in his life already. How are you doing? his mom asked over and over this whole year. Are you okay?

If I'm on my knees I'm, begging now. If I'm on my knees, groping in the dark.

How easy it is to let the jeep speak for him, how impossibly complex an answer.

He remembers how it was with us. It seems so long ago, those last moments, his nose in Danielle's hair, telling Toe to slow down. Our biggest fear was that we'd get in trouble, our parents called to take us home. This is different.

Country Club Road, last chance to bail. He looks in his mirror and sees Brooks coming on strong, and someone behind him, another cop, the guy with the lights. He doesn't slow for the intersection, heads straight past the gatehouse for the pillars.

Natalie's finished. The track switches, and on comes Billy and the Smashing Pumpkins, the plinking jack-in-the-box beginning and then the crushing power chords, the soaring carnival guitars parting so he can sing: *To-day is the greatest, day I've ever known. Can't live for tomorrow, tomorrow's much too long.* At least something from the plan is working. The victory gives him strength, lets him take the curves faster. It's 11:57 and this is his song.

There's a drive-up pay phone in the front corner of the Dunkin' Donuts lot. Kyle takes the quarter Tim gave him (a talisman that, unlike us, survived the crash) and thumbs it into the right slot on his first try. He bends down to read the numbers, then punches just three, and quickly, unKylelike. He straightens up with the receiver, a finger in his ear, and calmly watches a car descend the hill by the car wash, then turns away as someone answers.

"Hey," he says, "yeah," and the voice sounds like the Kyle we used to know. "I'd like to report an accident?"

When he's done, he crosses 44 and cuts through the landscaped apron of the McDonald's, goes directly to the drivethru window and scrounges around on the pavement for more change.

On, on, paring the curves, pulling g's to keep his lights in sight. Brooks has to catch him; he's going too fast. He wants the Tahoe gone, as if it's the problem, its lights and siren distracting, burrowing into his brain. He can't risk the radio; he needs his hands free to drive. The road dips between the banks, swaths of fog flying up out of the night to blind him.

Brooks has a faster car, is a better driver. With every twist of the road he draws closer to the jeep, grows more convinced he can overtake him—dangerous at this speed. It's exactly what happened last time, as if he's fallen into the same trap. The report on the seat beside him tells a different story, his speed and following distance reasonable, but this is how it went down. He was right on Toe's ass as we came into that last rise. ("Slow *down!*" Tim shouted from the back.) Brooks was so surprised to see our taillights flare that he panicked, pushed his foot harder on the gas when he meant the brake, bumping us.

He remembers the Camry yawing nauseatingly in front of him, flying sideways over the rise and off the road, going airborne. That's accurate in the report, the raw velocity at which we collided with the tree, the precise angle of impact, but it's too late to erase the lies. Avon's a small town, and rumors become the truth. (Another reason we love the guy: not for a minute did he try to deny it to himself. This entire year he's been gouging his heart out, haunting himself, and don't think we don't appreciate it. Brooks, dude, you are the shit, we don't care what anyone says.)

But what no one knows—not the chief, not Melissa, not Tim—is that he saw us hit. He nudged us and then corrected, overshot as we spun around the tree, a weird carousel shedding pieces. He saw Danielle come out as he was braking. He'd never seen anyone ejected, only read about it; he knew people survived or died depending on their luck. She flew and struck another tree, limply cartwheeled off and landed. He stopped and backed up and ran. She was lying face up and the top of her head was off; she wasn't alive. *He* did this, he kept thinking. He caused this. Someone was screaming in the backseat, and when he ducked in, the car smelled of blood. (O Spirit!)

Brooks has to leave that in the past. He has Tim within reach, he needs to get between him and the tree. He's got the car, he knows the road; it's as if he's been preparing for this his whole life, our very own Flying Dutchman.

He lets the Vic wind out as they tear down a long flat and gets within a few lengths, then tucks in behind him on the curve, his lights finding the Wrangler logo on the tire. He doesn't want to nudge him like us and send him sideways, so he swings wide and noses forward, races—not to overtake him but to see if he'll slide outside to block him off, a sucker move. He does, and Brooks lets up a split-second and crosses hard right and stands on the gas, trying him on the inside. He's got position, inching even with the rear fender and then the door, the front wheel. He thinks he's almost there when the jeep leans in and bangs him.

The Vic slaloms, the back end breaking loose. He manhandles the wheel left and then right as the weight shifts, gassing it to straighten the nose, struggling to keep it out of the leaves. He's afraid the jeep is fishtailing worse than he is, swerving out of control, then sees it ahead of him in the middle of the road, pulling away.

The phone shocks her heart, chiming by the refrigerator. She's on it before the second ring, and then there's no one there—a joke or an obscene caller.

"Hello?" she says. "Hello?"

"Hello," Kyle echoes.

"Where are you? Is Tim there with you?" He must be; Kyle doesn't know how to use the phone by himself. "Kyle, answer me."

She thinks she hears traffic in the background.

"Kyle," she says. "Kyle, tell me where you are."

Has he hung up on her?

"Kyle."

She hears the receiver clunking against something, as if he set it down and is just now picking it up.

"McDonald's," he says.

"Where's Tim?"

"Tim."

"He's supposed to be there with you."

Kyle doesn't answer.

"Just stay there," she orders. "Don't move, do you hear me?"

Her ratty gardening sneakers are in the closet. She pulls a jacket on over her robe. Grabbing her keys, she swears she's going to kill Tim.

He keeps looking back, expecting Brooks to stop following him, but he doesn't. If he would just leave him alone, Tim thinks. He's so tired he wants to close his eyes. Somewhere back in there is the old Scoville mansion. He imagines himself sliding into one of its canopied beds, its heavy white sheets welcoming him, a clock in the hall striking midnight.

I tried so hard, Billy sings, *to cleanse these regrets . . .*

No one will forgive him, he knows that. He's grown adept at reading the silence of other people. He's sorry for his mom and dad, that's it. (Danielle sits beside him with her arms folded, pissed off. The real Kyle's with us in the backseat again. It's like a reunion; there's even music.)

Today is, today is . . .

He should be there by now; the song is ending. It can't be much farther.

Behind him, Brooks is relentless. If he would stop, but he keeps on coming. What does he want? He's taken everything already. He can't take this one last thing from him, the only thing he has left.

"No," Tim says finally, his mind made up. He's not afraid. (Come, out into the night.)

The jeep leaps a rise, and there, across a shallow flat, a fire shines—the tree, like a beacon in the night, a sign. The flames call him on, all he can see. He aims straight for it.

(Let's go, Toe says, and we all put our hands on Tim, even the real Kyle, even Danielle.)

Brooks doesn't have room to catch him clean from behind at the last second, and doesn't try. His only chance is to run up beside him and give him a push and hope they both clear the tree. He punches it and makes up enough space across the flat to turn into him, just clips his rear.

Tim overcorrects and catches a tire, the jeep heeling precariously, capsizing. Brooks tries to go right but slides into him and thinks: Oh *shit.* They both vault off the road sideways, somersaulting through the leaves, the Vic chasing the jeep into the tree.

There's no slow motion. Travis and Greg drop their beers and run like fuck but only get a few steps, diving as the cars roar toward them. The jeep rolls and catches air, smashing the tree dead-center, the hardtop buckling, spraying a shower of glass. Before it can land, the cop car right behind it spears its midsection, T-boning it squarely, the rear flipping straight up and tipping over so the undercarriage scrapes the tree high up, shearing off branches, then topples and pancakes on its roof.

Everything settles, leaving a wide-empty silence. The tree's still burning weakly, little flickers worming across the charred bark.

"Holy shit," Greg says. "Ho-ly shit."

Travis can't stand. Greg has to lift him by the arm.

A cop in a Tahoe pulls up with his rack flashing. He runs

at them, waving a gun. "Get down!" he screams. "Get on the ground *now*!"

The asshole kneels on them like something from *Cops*, shoves their faces into the leaves. They can't explain what they're doing there, and he makes them stand with their hands on the hood of his truck.

The cop goes to the jeep first. It's on its side, and he has to stand on tiptoes to see in.

(We can see in. A dust hangs in the air, the dry lubricant from the airbag, popped and hanging limp from the steering wheel. Tim's lying still in the bottom, one arm caught underneath him. The cop shines his light on his face. There's no question.

I can't believe you, Danielle says. You are such an asshole.

He's better, Toe says, like he'd been sick.

We tried, I say.

Bullshit, Danielle says.)

The Vic sits on its roof, its wheels in the air. The cop runs over and goes to his knees to look in. He has to use the butt of his flashlight to smash the window.

(Of course we go over. This is why we're here.

Brooks's airbag has gone off too, filling the interior with shimmering fairy dust, a shaken paperweight. He's hanging out of his belt, his neck bent back at an angle so his face is pressed against the ceiling, blood from his ears wetting the headliner. One hand is stretched toward the door, as if he was trying to escape at the last minute.

Eat shit and die, Toe says, gloating.

Shut up, Danielle says, and runs off toward the jeep.

Brooks drips, kissing the ceiling, and I wish everything had been different from the beginning, that we didn't require this sacrifice. But we did. You would too, believe me. Didn't you ever see *The Wicker Man?*

The cop reaches in to take his pulse, a formality more than anything. Just as he's about to press his fingers to his wrist, Brooks's watch goes off, that cheap double beep. It's midnight, and we have to leave you.)

BUT WAIT, DON'T GO YET. Come back with us, before all this begins. Stick the leaves back on the trees, glue the acorns back in place. Use your magic tape to reconstruct us like Brooks never could. Come on, it won't take long. It'll be easy.

Start at the cemetery, the sod parting for the gravediggers to empty the squared hole shovel- by shovelful. The undertaker replaces the hydraulic frame to raise our caskets as the priest speaks backwards. Flowers leap into mourners' hands like souvenirs before they disperse, scattering to their limousines. The mortician at Vincent's drains us of embalming fluid and fills us with blood, drives the hearse in reverse to the hospital loading dock. The pathologist fits the heart back in the empty chest cavity. The scalpel heals the incision.

In the ER, doctors tug on bloody gloves, lift the sheets and work for hours taking our stitches out, cleaning their instruments on our guts. Nurses pull IVs from our arms and tubes from our throats, sew our clothes up with scissors. Trauma teams lift us from the operating tables onto stretchers and orderlies jockey them through the halls to the waiting ambulance.

The EMTs take us from there, tearing across Avon to the scene. They throw open the rear doors and roll the stretchers out, fold the metal legs and unbuckle us, set the backboards on the ground and check our vital signs. Firemen use tools to delicately fit us into the crushed car so Brooks can take his pictures. He uncovers Danielle and packs his yellow slicker away in the trunk.

The rescue squad turns off their portable floods. People start to leave. The ambulance, the police with their lights flashing. For a while there's only Brooks and Tim, a single pair of headlights trained on the broken Camry, and then Brooks escorts Tim to his seat and returns to the cruiser. He pulls forward, then backs off fast, leaving rubber. Kyle stumbles bleeding out of the woods and gets in the other door, holding his face.

The Camry levitates (I told you you were magic), circling the tree. Danielle lifts, pinwheeling, from her resting place in the leaves, clips a different tree and sails like Peter Pan straight through the open door into Tim's arms. The tree slaps the door shut and Kyle bangs the dent out of the window's center post with his head. Me and Toe slide from under the dashboard, mending the knees of our jeans, and then we're clear, flying free, inhaling screams.

We shoot through the weeds. Toe gives Brooks a nudge in the bumper, regains control, and the chase is on, racing through the roller coaster curves until he loses us, ducking into his tricky little hiding place as we flash by.

We're alone on the road then, all of Avon closed and rewinding outside. (Okay, Magoo, you can stop it right there.) Now breathe. Ride with us awhile—this'll be the last time, I promise. It's still Halloween and Toe has the radio going. Kyle's stoking up this big spliff, telling us how he's going to get Rage tickets over the internet. Behind me, Tim is trying to feel up Danielle. We've just gotten out of work and we're tired because all you can find around here are shit jobs. Kyle hands me the spliff and I pass it across the headrest to Danielle. An old Nirvana tune comes on and Toe turns it up, sings along with Kurt so badly that we all laugh, even him. "Fuck you," he says, and Kyle slaps him in the back of the head.

And it's all right, right here. We're happy in this present past, just driving, all of us in the car together like a tribe, a band of outlaws on the lam. There's no future, only now, this minute. It doesn't matter what time it is; we don't want to go home. We're young and fucked up in the dark heart of the country, safe inside our expensive innocence, stuck behind enemy lines. It's late and there's nowhere to go because this town sucks so much, but we don't care. We're just a bunch of dumb kids having fun. We want the night to last forever.